The Man Who N

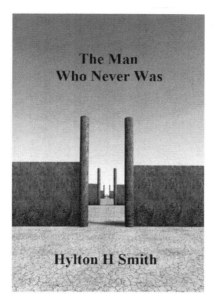

Hylton H Smith

This book is dedicated to:

Bella 1890-1972
Jack 1910-1979
Hilda 1914-1989

Chapter 1
Winlaton Mill 1987

As he stood on the Butterfly Bridge, Philip Greenwood was all but overcome by a rush of negative thoughts. He'd let his dog off the leash several minutes ago and lost sight of him. The River Derwent was unusually swollen and the forecast intimated that worse was to come. The old footbridge creaked and moaned incessantly as if it knew it couldn't survive much longer. It was Philip's favourite route and yet he had underestimated how many times Rocky needed to traverse the bridge before it would become second nature to him. He cursed himself for such naivety, especially in this freak weather. Deciding which side of the river the Golden Labrador was on had become critical, as the rain was now so relentless it was affecting his range of vision.

Philip was already pretty downbeat before he'd lost Rocky. He had been made redundant from Derwenthaugh Coke Works less than a year ago. At sixty-one he was resigned to perpetual unemployment, and he was still angry at the way the NCB had handled the closure of the works. It had been painful to watch the demolition begin in 1986 and although some considered the complex to be a blot on the landscape, it was now a massive spoil heap, and in his view that was even worse. The grandiose plans to turn the area into a recreational park with a small lake and ambitious landscaping would take years. The de-contamination process itself was expected to take a very long time. His father had worked in the coking plant from its inception in 1928, and in its predecessor, Crowley Ironworks, which had been the largest iron producer in Europe at one time. 'What a bloody mess', he thought, 'I'll be dead before me village recovers from this sodding abandonment'.

He gathered breath in the middle of the bridge while he whistled for Rocky. Every few moments he had to pause his intake of fresh air in order to listen for any response. It was difficult enough with the raging river, the pounding rain, and the rapidly rising winds. And winter was just around the corner. Since the demolition kicked into gear, a perimeter fence had been erected around the site for safety purposes, but also to prevent thieves from purloining all manner of scrap metals. There were also pockets of coke which had been unintentionally buried in shallow seams by the earthmoving plant, and they attracted scavengers. He heard a faint bark and was pretty sure it was Rocky; his heart skipped a beat because it came from the direction of the perimeter fence. 'Shit, I hope he hasn't bumped into them security guards, they might injure him or bloody worse'.

He put up his hood and zipped it tight again as he headed for the fence. Philip had become a little overweight since he lost his job, and he couldn't run more than a few yards at a time, due to having been told he had angina, so he kept calling out Rocky's name. As he got closer to the fence the barking changed to a whimper and he feared the worst. Then, as he conceded to putting his distance spectacles on again, he saw the breach in the wire containment. Dispensing with his glasses because of the almost immediate distortion conferred by the rain, he forced himself to run through the treacly mud toward the aperture. "Rocky, come on boy, here Rocky."

He almost blacked out, gasping for air. 'I've got to get through this damned hole, but I'm far too big'. He frantically looked around for something to make the hole bigger. It seemed like an eternity had passed, all the while he rebuked himself continually for coming out in this weather, then he saw it in the patch of grass, about thirty yards away. A forgotten scaffolding pole. He charged through the deep mud again and was on his knees as he grabbed the flattened end. Several times he alternately lifted then pulled it horizontally before it was released from the compacted earth. He was rapidly running out of energy and his shoes were beginning to disintegrate, but he began flailing the wire with the pole. After two frustrating failures and a third session of pummelling, he squeezed through the fence. "Rocky, Rocky, here boy." The whimpering seemed to have stopped, his feet were now very painful, gripped by icy, squelching mud. Philip had to crest a mound of earth to get his bearings again. As he scrambled to the top he heard the dog once more, and this drove him on, with at least some idea of direction. He thought he saw the outline of Rocky through the blinding rain, but the landscape was no longer familiar. He pressed on and within a minute the explanation was revealed. Two days of torrential weather had caused a landslip where he estimated one of the engineering offices had been. The demolition people had not yet removed or decided not to remove a huge concrete foundation slab, which had lurched then crept down the slope toward the river. It had created a precipice, layered just like an archaeology dig. One of the layers seemed to have extruded part of the skeleton of a human arm. Rocky was sniffing and then whimpering, cautiously followed by careful pawing at the bones, as if they belonged to a living person. He was obviously waiting for some reaction before engaging again.

Philip was utterly exhausted but relieved that Rocky was unharmed. He quickly put the confused dog on the leash and headed for the security post. He didn't receive a particularly warm welcome, but he silenced the intended admonition with his declaration. "You buggers have got human skeletal remains on ya site. Me dog got through a hole in ya 'keep oot' fence and followed his nose to a mudslide. There's a flippin' arm sticking oot the vertical section, aboot twelve inches from the bottom." Only then was he offered a seat and a mug of strong tea while one of the security guards called the police.

Superintendent Oswald Moss lit his pipe for the umpteenth time as darkness began to descend on the city. He let the phone ring several times before picking up the receiver; it was part of his routine, ensuring as much order and tranquillity as possible. He hated false urgency. Moss was a big man, over six feet six inches tall with a shock of black unkempt hair which rested on his dark-rimmed spectacles and obscured most of his forehead. Tweed suits were his stock-in-trade and nobody had ever seen him without a waistcoat.

"Moss."

"Sorry to bother you Sir," said Detective Inspector Black, "we've just been made aware of a skeleton amongst some earthworks at Derwenthaugh. Uniform are already there and they want us to take a look."

"You'd better do so then, can it wait until tomorrow?"

"Apparently the foul weather is washing soil away from the bones and WPC Reichert thinks the medical people would want to recover the skeletal remains as soon as they can. They've got floodlights and have already put a tarpaulin over the area but the weather is worsening. I think I should go now and ask Carr to come with me."

"Fine, call me at home when you're done at… remind me where is Derwenthaugh again?"

"It's the coke works which was demolished last year, between Swalwell and Rowlands Gill. It's supposed to be a secure site for all sorts of reasons. Apparently, a ruddy great slab of concrete has lurched down a slope and exposed this skeleton. I'll need to trace any managers who were familiar with the site layout, because the security men are just contractors. I'll get back to you."

Richard Black was considered to be a very promising recruit for the Newcastle force. His promotion from D.C. to his current rank had been meteoric, and largely based on his performance in his native Manchester. In his early thirties, he exuded confidence, was extremely thorough, and was gifted with an almost photographic memory. He was living proof that the man makes the clothes, rather than the reverse. He tended to speak too quickly for most of his colleagues, particularly Superintendent Moss, and was often reminded to slow down. He was universally liked despite being highly results-driven, simply because his disarming self-critical approach was contagious, and thus promoted real team ethic. Every subordinate was encouraged to issue challenge as long as it was directed at overall progress. Even Oswald Moss had been sceptical at first, but results had validated Black's methodology, and offered the attendant benefit of making his own job easier. Impeccably groomed, sharply dressed, perennially brimming with energy, Richard J Black had soon been inflicted with the respectful nickname of 'Jet' Black.

He picked up Constance Carr, the senior medical examiner, and they fought their way from the Market Street HQ through the evening city traffic exodus. "I think we should avoid the western bypass tonight Connie, there are serious road works in progress. I'll try Scotswood Bridge."

"It's probably going to be jammed whichever way we go; it always seems to be worse when we have such driving rain."

She was right and they pulled up at the security cabin an hour and a quarter later, when normally it would take no more than twelve minutes. Despite the blue light and klaxon, there was simply gridlock everywhere and they had to wriggle through stationary traffic most of the way. Black was, as expected, over-prepared with industrial grade waterproofs and footwear, while Constance had pink wellington boots and a designer Gore-Tex luminous jacket. WPC Reichert had already insisted that the security people erect three converging floodlights around the scene. This unwelcome chore had prevented them from enjoying a sausage roll around the warm gas fire, dispelling the prospect of a cushy shift.

Maggie Reichert had taken a statement from Philip Greenwood and asked him to stay until C.I.D. arrived, and he was happy to oblige.

Constance took a close-up flash photo of the arm, which had already been padded about by the dog, and now the rivulets of storm water were forcing it to point downhill. The security men stressed that they all needed to vacate the area as soon as their examination was complete; the precipice was gradually being carved apart by the downpour, and another slide could be imminent. Black and Maggie replaced the tarpaulin in the hope that it would minimise further disruption to the skeleton. A forlorn hope was judged to be better than no hope.

Black scurried back to the cabin to speak to Philip Greenwood and rang HQ to ask D.C. Freda Collins to search for an experienced local archaeologist who may be willing to help tease out the skeleton as soon as the rain permitted. "Ok Mr Greenwood, I have your statement, can you just run through it again for my benefit? I want to make sure you haven't forgotten anything."

During Philip's recap, Black intervened to ask about how he knew that the concrete slab was part of the engineering office. "Because I've worked here for years man, and I knew the place like the back o' me hand. I cannot remember exactly when they poured the concrete for the office building but that's definitely where the foundation was."

Black's brain whirred and registered a link between concrete being poured and a hidden body being underneath, or next to it, as part of what was thought to be miscellaneous hard-core base. "Great, well thanks again Philip, WPC Reichert has your address if we need to speak with you again, and thank you Rocky, without your sniffing about we'd be none the wiser."

8

As the two security men were puzzling as to how their delayed lunch had disappeared, Black asked them for the telephone number of anyone who was involved in the management of the closure operation. They could only offer one such contact. He rang the number.

"Hello, Jeffrey Stark."

"Hello Sir, this is D.I. Black from Newcastle C.I.D. and I'd like to speak to you about the demolition of Derwenthaugh coke works."

"What is it you need to know? I'm simply the financial winding down officer, reconciling all closure costs against the budget, and taking care of legal procedures. I know virtually nothing about the plant itself, in fact it was partly demolished before I was despatched there from London. I'm only at the site when there are contractors working there."

"I see. Well, we've found human remains on the site, so I need you to put me in touch with any ex-managers or directors who had responsibilities for running the plant."

"Of course, but I'll have to call you back when I can retrieve such personnel records. Give me ten minutes."

"Thanks. I'm at the site cabin with the security people."

The phone rang as promised and it was picked up by an irate security guard who was still cursing about the missing sausage rolls. He handed the receiver to Black.

"I have two names for you and if they aren't able to help you, they can at least point you to someone who can."

"Ok shoot."

"Eric Paisley was the operations director and Neville Travers was the engineering manager. I've asked them to ring you as soon as possible at the police station."

"Thanks Mr Stark. I'll need to speak with you when you're here next, when will that be?"

"The day after tomorrow, I can call at the station and if we need another site visit then so be it."

"If you don't mind me saying so, you don't seem to be overly concerned at the discovery of these bones."

"Not at all, but as I said I'm currently in London. Will another couple of days make any difference?"

"I suppose not. See you then."

Black rubbed his chin as he filed another note in his brain registry. "Come on Maggie, let's get back to the station." Turning to the security boys he couldn't suppress a smile. "I don't think you guys would make it as detectives, the packet's empty and there isn't a single crumb in sight from the sausage rolls. My money's on the dog. By the way, you might get on to your head office and get that breach in the perimeter fence sealed, I'll be back tomorrow to check that it's done."

Chapter 2

For once the weather forecast was accurate. The best had to be made of a bad situation and steel girders were carefully driven into the rapidly softening soil, in a horseshoe shape, around the projected area of the skeleton. This was intended to prevent damage or break up of the remains. The hand had already become detached once the fingers had been lowered into the mud by random erosion of the precipice face.

The 'archaeological' phase took on the complexity of a potential Caesarian section. Allowing more time for the rain to abate could endanger the find. The expert Black had recruited advised that they should wait no longer than another four hours regardless of the weather. "The more shear stress which builds up as the water table rises, the more the bones will be disjointed or fractured. I'm prepared to use a water lance with minimum pressure to carefully loosen the soil around the target in a controlled way. You have to make a decision before it is made for you."

"Right, what the hell, go for it now," said Black, "we don't want to be pissing about in the dark."

Several additional personnel had been brought in to ensure that any emergency rescue requirement of operatives could be employed quickly and expertly; a second landslip seemed more likely with the wind now approaching gale force. Two hours into the water lance phase they found that the right leg had been detached from the hip, and it became the first new section to join the hand, which was already marked up and residing in one of many sealable plastic boxes. There was worse news when the clumps of clinging mud were gently encouraged to desert the torso; the rib cage was collapsed and several bones were broken. Miraculously, there was no more serious damage, and there was considerable relief that the skull seemed to have survived in good condition. The better news, or so it was thought, came in the form of isolated pieces of semi-rotted fibres, which were assumed to originate from what the unknown person had been wearing. However, the most intriguing revelation was an oval metallic disc with holes punched opposite each other, and in between these holes there was some kind of numeric or alpha-numeric pattern. The disc was so badly pitted that it was impossible to make sense of the legend, but it was a starting point. Constance had managed to arrange the connected parts in the pre-labelled boxes and sketch in the recovery location of any individual bones, giving each one a reference number.

Black immediately called the station and spoke with Moss. "We're going to try to identify the person by two methods. I've arranged a conversation with two ex-managers of the plant, and I want to decipher the funny symbols on this disc independently, in case I get a whiff of bullshit from them."

"What did you have in mind, by independently?"

Black knew it would cost money and suspected Moss would want it accurately itemised before approving any speculative foray, prior to having evidence to support it. "The University has all manner of equipment and people who can do this. I seem to recall that you still have friends who lecture there. They must be able to help, and they're people you can trust. Can you set this up? It would allow me to get Constance straight on to the boxes of bones we have recovered so far."

Black anticipated a pause. It was longer than expected but he wasn't going to speak again before Moss did. "Very well, I'll make discreet enquiries as to what can be done in this field and get back to you. I think you should dispense with the archaeologist chap, we don't need to join any more dots for outsiders."

"I agree," replied Black, "I'm sticking my neck out but I can't believe these remains are recent. Just a second Sir, I'm hearing that we've pulled out more stuff from the same area as the bones." Moss puffed on his pipe, and looked briefly at the crossword; he was infuriated by being stuck on three across, and he entertained the notion that the compiler was in error. "Sorry about that Super, it looks like broken remains of a barrel and bits of hessian. I'll speak to you as soon as I know more."

As they travelled back to the station, the skies showed no promise of the rain easing off and the late afternoon gloom thickened by the minute.

"There's something familiar about the markings on that disc Sir," said Maggie, "I just can't think where I might have seen them before."

Black didn't offer any curiosity, he was more concerned to hear what Constance would make of the remains. He expected her to dampen his impatience by telling him to call her in the next couple of days. He was still confident he'd be able to winkle first impressions out of her. "Sorry Maggie, what'd you say?"

"Nothing, it will come back to me, I'm sure."

Once more the journey seemed to take forever and Black was annoyed that he'd missed Moss, who'd apparently gone off to the University of Newcastle.

Detective Inspector Richard Black didn't like being controlled by events, and his displeasure on this occasion was approaching danger level. He was having difficulty in persuading Eric Paisley, the ex-operations director of Derwenthaugh coke works to take him seriously. During this verbal exchange he was informed that Neville Travers, the ex-engineering manager was on another line. He was just about to deal with this when he was given a message from Moss – to get along to the University as soon as possible. He put Paisley on hold and turned to D.C. Freda Collins. "Take the damned call from Travers and tell him

13

he can either come here to assist us or we'll land on his doorstep, well, at least you bloody will."

When he picked up again with Paisley the line was dead. "Shit, this guy is trouble, I just know he is." Black waited impatiently for Freda to finish speaking with Travers, but once he heard her giving directions to the station he rushed out of the office to the car park. "Bollocks, that's all I need." Kicking the flat passenger side front tyre, he ran back to tell Freda he needed her to drive him to the University.

"It's not too far to walk Sir, and anyway I'll have to stay here to see Mr Travers, won't I? He's on his way."

"I'm not walking anywhere in this bloody weather, I've had more than enough of it already at Winlaton Mill. Give me your keys."

"I can't do that Sir, you aren't insured to drive my Beetle. I can take whatever you need to the University if you would like to stay to see Mr Travers."

"No way, I'll get someone from uniform to take me." He found that wasn't an option as all cars were out dealing with traffic restrictions and accidents. He capitulated to calling a taxi, and was promptly informed that it would be a minimum of fifteen minutes before a cab could be there. "Forget it!" he said, conceding that he would have to walk. At least the all-weather clothing was still in his car. The short journey restored his even-tempered professional persona, and upon arrival he was directed by the receptionist to a meeting room on the second floor.

"Is there somewhere I can leave this cape and hat?" She giggled as two passing students whistled the theme tune to Batman. "Of course, just leave it there on the floor Sir, and I'll get one of our janitors to dry it off for you."

Moss was in his element, holding court with three university staff. "Ah, here he is, gentlemen, can I introduce you to Detective Inspector Black. He has a puzzle to solve and thinks you may be able to help us. Do you have the object with you Black?"

"Yes of course Sir." The disc was laid on the glass table and the explanation of its retrieval given. "I think this must be related in some way to the coke works or the individual, or both. It was revealed by a large foundation slab sliding down a slope. Apart from the disc itself, I'd be grateful for any ideas with respect to the mechanics of the landslip, because I need to know if the body was buried by the concrete or just happened to be alongside the excavation prior to the foundation being poured. We'll have more evidence shortly as to the bones, but I'd like to know if we're dealing with an accident, an old grave, or something suspicious. Well, what do you think?"

Two of the 'dignitaries' politely excused themselves, citing impending lectures as the reason. The third, an expert in mechanical engineering and fluid dynamics expressed quite a strong interest. He was introduced as Dr Joseph Leven. "I'm sure we can use imaging technology to clean up your disc, but I'm intrigued by this landslip. From what you've said I should take a look at the site before any further erosion takes place. Can we go first thing in the morning? I have a lecture at 9.30, but if you can meet me at the site, around say 6.00 am, we would miss the rush hour and it would give me time to take photographs and measurements."

Black mused to himself, 'Up at sparrow-fart to slosh about in the mud again, no thanks Professor.' He smiled through the prospect of a third day at the coke works, expressing utter delight that Dr Leven was so keen. "Certainly Sir, I'll be there on the dot. Can I leave the disc with you now?"

"Yes, I'll get one of my people on to it right away."

As Black was about to bundle his caped crusader kit into the back of Moss's car he was brought up short by his boss. "There are some old newspapers in the boot, put some in

15

the passenger side before you get in with those filthy shoes. It was very embarrassing to see you so dishevelled in such a revered seat of learning Black, a bit scruffy to say the least."

"Yes Sir, it won't happen again," apologised a downtrodden 'Jet' Black, thinking only of the flat tyre awaiting him at the station.

Chapter 3

Everyone seemed to be preparing to go home, and Black just managed to catch Freda as she was coming out of the ladies locker room.

"Well, what did Neville Travers have to say?"

"He wasn't much help, but he seemed really upset that we'd found human remains on the site. All he could say for certain was that the metal disc wasn't used at the works for personnel identification. Apparently they used fabric badges which were stitched on to the work-suits. He did agree with the man who found the remains about the engineering office being set on a large concrete slab, but said he would need to go to the site to check the position before he could be sure of the exact location. I asked him to do that and called the security people to tell them he'd be arriving. That's about it really."

"No it isn't Freda, did you recover Paisley's number? I asked you to do it when I rushed off to the university."

"Yes, it's on your desk. And don't say thanks SIR!"

"Oh right, thanks for merely doing your job D.C. Collins, it would be nice if we were all congratulated on answering the phones or taking a statement. What's wrong? Why the long face?"

"You obviously haven't looked at your car since you got back. I asked WPC Reichert to take your wheel to a garage and get the puncture fixed. You owe me one, and don't think that I'll forget."

Freda Collins was a rare breed of police officer. Never having 'lived' with or been married to anyone, she didn't have to deal with bitching from a partner about late, unsocial or irregular working demands. She cohabited with her mother who offered continual praise for her dedication to society. One consequence of this was her ability to compartmentalise her life. Her desk was always neat, she seldom got bad-tempered, and never took the job home.

She wasn't interested in promotion and yet was fiercely proud of her ability to spot details which others missed, which occurred fairly frequently. So, Black was quite sorry about mistaking her reaction for petulance.

"You're wonderful Freda, of course I noticed the tyre had miraculously recovered, I just didn't know who'd sorted it. You must admit it's not like you to go the extra mile when it's almost time to go home. Anyway, I'm really grateful." He blew her a kiss and flashed a contrived smile.

"Don't think that makes us even, and for your information, I just felt really sorry for you being drenched all day and then having to walk to the Uni. I'll let you know when I need a favour."

"Right, I see. Well, as heart-warming as it is to hear you felt sorry for me, you didn't actually have to lift a finger to sort out my tyre, in fact you just lifted the phone and got someone else to do the legwork. You never got off your arse at all did you?"

"I would have done Sir, but then I thought that WPC Reichert wouldn't want to miss a chance to suck up to you. She'd do almost anything to get your attention. Almost… why did I say almost? Are you blind or what?"

"Yeah right, get off home or you'll miss kids' TV. See you tomorrow, although I have to be at Winlaton Mill at 6 am, so I may not get back until lunch time."

Fortunately, Freda was out of the car park before Maggie Reichert returned. She went straight to Black's office and seemed to be bursting to tell him something. "Hey thanks Maggie for sorting my tyre, it's really appreciated, I've really had one of those days."

"Yes Sir, no problem. That's not what I came to see you about though. I finally remembered where I'd seen some inscriptions similar to those on the disc we found."

"Really," muttered Black distractedly, "I've given it to a professor or some boffin at the university."

"Oh, ok then, let's wait and see what he comes up with. Goodnight Sir."

"Wait a minute Maggie, I'm seeing him tomorrow at the coke works, and he's going to take a look at the landslip for me. Can you get your boss to let you come along as well?"

"I'll see, what time?"

"Six o'clock I'm afraid, there's no room for negotiation on that, but if he needs say, an hour for the slide, how about you get there for seven?"

"Ok, I'll see if I can swap with someone who is on traffic for the western bypass road works, and I can shoot along for five minutes, it's only a couple of miles. See you tomorrow unless something comes up."

*

Relief came with small patches of blue sky, moderate winds, and dry spells. Dr Leven was already at Derwenthaugh when Black arrived. He was scrambling around the precipice like an ice skater who knew he was going to fall sometime soon. "Good morning," was all it took. The professor seemed to be totally unconcerned about his wetsuit being completely coated with pungent mud. He happily rolled down the slope, stood up and shook himself like a dog coming out of the sea, breathing heavily but with a boyish smile on his face. The unbroken dawn and floodlights conjured up a surreal movie-like backdrop. "Hello Inspector, I have some interesting observations to report. Shall we start at the high end of the precipice?"

Richard Black was having difficulty keeping a straight face and simply nodded enthusiastically. "Firstly, look at the difference in the stretching of the layering here and the lower end, over there to your right."

"I can't see any at the lower end."

"Precisely," enthused Leven, "this indicates that the shearing process began at the high end."

"Oh, right."

"Now, this becomes rather academic but nevertheless important. The precipice is not vertical as you reported, in fact far from it. In fluid dynamic terms we must adhere to the facts. Although the angle at which the shear stress caused sub strata cleavage is apparently almost vertical, to the naked eye, it will undoubtedly prove to be an unreliable observation."

Black was standing there being lectured to by a chocolate-coated cartoon character, whose remit was one of educating our progeny, moulding scientists of the future. And yet he was rapidly losing the battle to be taken seriously. Black chose to say nothing, steeling his stomach muscles, merely nodding as if he understood every word. Leven continued. "I've taken all the pictures I need in order to make more precise calculations, but I can already see that the erosion caused by the incessant rain at the base of the precipice has significantly altered even the visual perception of verticality. Ergo your initial error of judgement. Suffice it to say that the layering strongly suggests the area where the skeleton emerged is inconsistent with it being buried adjacent to the edge of the landslip. It was encased by earth at a depth significantly below the bottom surface of the slab, and directly underneath it. I will be able to be more precise once I have scanned the photographs into the imaging programme with the various dimensional data. The variables involved are extremely complex in terms of pinpointing the exact origination location of the skeletal remains, but I am confident in the qualitative prediction I've given you. Is this preliminary conclusion useful to you?"

"Ab..Absolutely Dr Leven. It rules out certain possibilities and that's very important. However, although I'm looking forward to hearing whatever refinements your imaging process comes up with, can you just summarise your conclusion in plain English, so that I can add it accurately to my report?"

"Certainly. When the slab began to slide there were many forces involved, but the two major ones were the purely downward compressing effect of gravity, and the lateral shearing action, also controlled by gravity but related to the steepness of the slope. So, we have compression and pulling apart occurring together. This leads me to believe that the remains were deep enough to resist sliding with the slab, but shallow enough to emerge in the lower residual precipice. I must mention once more that this is because the precipice is leaning backwards rather than producing an overhang."

"Ah, I've got it now," lied Black, "I'll just note that the skeleton was originally under the slab, until you have your final imaging results. Well thank you for your help Dr Leven, it's an important starting point for us."

For the first time since he arrived Leven seemed to be highly conscious of his appearance. Black had to look away, pretending to be examining the precipice again. Leven tapped him on the shoulder. "I wonder if those security chaps have any spare tarpaulins to put in my car. I'm going to need a shower when I get home; one can't go to a lecture smelling like this."

"I'm sure they can help, maybe they have some spare overalls too, let me go and ask them while you load your samples into the car. Alternatively, I have some waterproof clothing in my car which you can use to drape over the driving seat and into the foot-well. It's the least I can do Dr Leven. Oh by the way, do you have any idea when your people will have anything on the metal disc?"

"I'll check when my morning lecture is over and call you Inspector. It will be fairly straightforward."

Black accepted a cup of scalding hot tea from the security men as the professor left. "This doesn't get you off the hook with the gap in your security fence, it's still there and you need to fix it. Come on, make a temporary repair until your bosses get a new section installed." The men pulled long faces but agreed.

Two cars pulled into the makeshift parking lot. Black recognised Maggie Reichert's vehicle immediately, but the driver of the Mercedes took a long while to emerge. The security men checked the number plate against their list and informed the two police officers that it was Neville Travers, so he hadn't come yesterday evening as he'd promised. "Good morning Sir," said Black, extending his hand. The firm handshake from the former engineering manager was encouraging. "I'm D.I. Black and this is WPC Reichert, thank you for coming so soon."

"No problem. I spent most of my working life here and there are lots of memories, mostly good, but I understand you have found a body, well, rather a human skeleton. It all sounds rather sinister, but anyway, how can I help?"

The answer was put on hold as the telephone rang. "It's for you Inspector." said one of the security men. Constance Carr had responded to his request to offer initial, if speculative information on the remains. He asked Maggie to escort Travers to the landslip while he took the call. She wasn't happy that she'd missed Dr Leven, her only interest in coming had been to discuss the metal disc.

Constance spoke slowly. "I can tell you that we have the remains of a male who died pretty young, perhaps 20-30 years old. In my opinion this isn't a recent death, hopefully I'll have more on that later. That's all I'm prepared to say right now, and as you agreed you won't pester me again until the full post-mortem is complete."

"Thank you Connie, I'll wait to hear from you then, when will that be?"

"Sod off, you'll hear more when my report is typed."

Travers was able to reconcile the landslip location with a site plan he'd brought with him. "The slab can only be from the engineering office; that is certain. I remember the very day we laid the foundation. God, I could never have imagined it would come to this. Sorry, but this is a very sad situation for me, you see this is a small village, and much of the workforce was indigenous to Winlaton Mill. The closure dealt a crushing blow to the community, and I was part of the management which administered the redundancies. The villagers refused to be broken by the edict of closure and the accompanying hardship, vowing to fight on to preserve their communal identity. However, this won't help their cause. Someone, either resident in the village, or an ex-employee must know whose remains these are. I would be happy to assist in any way I can."

"Well then," Black said cautiously, "you can start by telling me the date of this ceremonial pouring of the concrete you remember so well."

"Yes, when I said I remember the day, I meant the picture was still in my mind. It happened in 1945, I will have to check with my diaries for the exact date, but I seem to recall it was late spring or early summer."

"Christ," gasped Black, as the eyes of Maggie Reichert and the security men widened, "you mean this concrete has been....." He just managed to stop himself in time.

Chapter 4

Black suggested that WPC Reichert should escort Travers back to the station while he retrieved the disc from the university. She whispered, "Sir, what the hell is going on? You asked me to meet you here and all I do is walk Mr Travers around a pile of mud. He seemed as if he wanted to say something more about the time of the foundations of the engineering block being laid."

"Yes I know, do I have to draw you a picture? We can discuss this at the station, we need to record the interview. Let's just get on with it, I'll explain later."

Maggie Reichert had always wanted to be in C.I.D. and so she complied. She had a promotion board coming up and she wasn't going to foul up over such an issue, but she was annoyed. She'd done a lot of negotiation to get to Winlaton Mill and felt she had been used. She would take this up with Black whichever way the promotion interview went.

*

Meanwhile Black detoured to the university and Dr Leven was confused by the DI's insistence that he must take back the metal disc, but it became pretty academic once he'd asked his subordinate to hand it over. The preliminary imaging had already been done and nobody was any the wiser with what was revealed. Compensating for the pitting did indeed display a clearer picture of the symbols, but they didn't make a lot of sense. "I can't thank you enough gentlemen, this is all I need from you right now, but don't relax, and I may be back."

Dr Leven and his assistant were even more perplexed but shrugged their shoulders and went their separate ways. Back at the station Black joined Maggie and Travers in interview room number two. He got straight to the point, switching on the recorder, then explaining his strange behaviour.

"Mr Travers, you hit a couple of nerves back at the coke works site, and I didn't want to continue the discussion in front of those security people. Firstly, I need to confirm that I do want to take up your offer of helping out on this inquiry, and this interview is simply to get started on that path. I want to record everything, to make sure absolutely nothing is missed or forgotten. You weren't there when the professor hinted that the skeleton was actually buried under the slab, and not alongside. The inference then, is that if it had indeed been alongside, it could have been put there at any time, whereas if it was placed directly underneath, it was almost certainly put there just before the concrete was poured. You said this occurred in 1945, and you also felt that someone who worked at the plant or lived in the village, or both, should know something about who may have been responsible. Now, there is something else. I believe you told D.C. Freda Collins that the metal disc which we found with the remains was not issued by Derwenthaugh Management. Any ideas where it could have come from?"

"Sir," said Maggie Reichert, seemingly not wanting to pursue this line of questioning, "I think we need..." She was cut off by Black.

"Can we just proceed Mr Travers? It could be very important." He flashed a facial reprimand at Maggie, who was becoming increasingly agitated.

Travers sat in silence for a considerable period of time, which added to the mounting tension between the two police officers. Finally he spoke. "The only possibility which I can think of is an individual rail wagon tag for a distillery in Scotland. They were one of our biggest customers. The weighbridge labels had to be very robust to survive the journey, with its data – you know, batch numbers, date, consignment details and the like. You would need to check this out with the production management, as you know I was in engineering."

"Great, can you think about who would be the most appropriate person and direct them to me?"

"Yes of course. Is there anything else?"

"Not right now, but I want to keep in touch with you. I was impacted by your description of the emotional trauma this closure inflicted on the people in the village."

"I'll do anything I can Inspector, and that is a promise."

"Thanks, and can I just take your number again and give you my card?"

Travers nodded enthusiastically, wrote down his home number, picked up the rather pretentious card of D.I. Black, and walked out of the room. Black's face betrayed self-congratulation, whereas Maggie could no longer stay silent.

"Sir, can you please sit down for a minute? There's...."

"I think that went rather well, don't you Maggie? Progress on all fronts, even the bloody weather has been kinder to us. Make it quick, I need to update Moss."

"Right, well in that case you can decide whether or not to tell him that I know where the disc came from."

"How the hell can you possibly know that? It's a wind-up, right?"

"I've tried at least three times to tell you this but you always cut me off. We have probably allowed more information to become public than we needed to, so I'd think carefully about what you tell Moss. Do you want to hear it or not?"

"Well, come on then, spit it out."

"I told you I'd seen something similar to this disc before but I couldn't remember where. It was years ago, when I was a little girl, that's why it took me a while to nail it down. It's a military service identity disc."

Black's eyes rolled back and forth from the disc to Maggie's face. "Go on, how do you know that?"

"Because my father has one exactly like it."

"Your father? He hasn't done any military service has he?"

"No, he inherited the disc from his father."

"Are you going to get to the point? *Is* there a point to all this?"

"I believe there could be. My grandfather was in the Luftwaffe."

It hit Black like a sledgehammer. "And the remains were buried under the concrete in 1945, immediately after the war. Shit and corruption! I'm sorry Maggie, I'm stupid, this is vital information and I wasn't listening. You're right, I, we have to know more before I mention this to Moss. Now that we have a cleaned up image from the university, we can try to connect the code to a person. But how would a German airman end up here in the Northeast?"

"You should talk with my father, his name is Reichert too; a bit of a giveaway don't you think? Apparently, there were some bombing raids over this region, targeting shipyards, power stations, and other fuel sources. My Dad says that almost all power stations at that time were coal or coke-fired. Ring any bells?"

"When can we speak with… what's your dad's name?"

"Frank Aaron Reichert, my grandfather was a pilot in the Luftwaffe, serving over the eastern front against the Russians. His aircraft was shot down, but he parachuted safely to the surface. My Dad has never talked about this before, but granddad was one of many German youths who were pressed into the ideology of the Third Reich. He had to choose that path or one which would ultimately define him as a traitor to the cause. The S.S. apparently didn't agonise over such protestations. Somehow he survived, thanks to having learned English at college. He had come down near to the Polish border and was welcomed back by the occupying German forces for rehabilitation. He was almost ready to be discharged back to the Luftwaffe, but he went AWOL and sought out the Polish underground resistance. He was treated with extreme suspicion at first and then he was handed over to the British. They took a long time to check out his story and eventually set him a test, which was designed to turn him into a spy against the Fatherland. He apparently refused to cooperate at first and he was taken to a P.O.W. camp in the south of England. Finally, he accepted what most ordinary German servicemen did not want to believe – that civilians were being systematically exterminated. His pride in his country had to take second place. That's how my granddad came to live in England, under a new name, courtesy of British Intelligence. When the war was over he insisted on taking back his German identity, believing he'd served the right cause in helping the allies. That's not how it was perceived by the powers that be or the community he lived in. It was just as difficult for grandma, even though she was English by birth. After granddad passed away my father persuaded his mother to return to her native northeast and start a new life. She was reluctant but accepted that there were still people who despised Germans long after the war ended. She reverted to her maiden name of Hewitt, while my Dad at least had the cover of an English sounding name - Frank. Although I've never had a problem with Reichert, my Dad says it wasn't easy for him in the south of England. He said the northerners seemed to be more prepared to accept that many German people hated Hitler. Possibly that was because the intensity of bombing was much higher in the south. Shall I ask my father to come and see you?"

"I think we should do him the service of talking in the privacy of his own home Maggie. I get the feeling there is a lot of personal stuff which he may find difficult to speak about. Let's make this an unofficial chat, after all, we only want to find the name of our man at the coke works."

"Ok. I'll set it up and let you know when we can meet with him. In the meantime, if you give me the cleaned up image I can ask him to look at it. It may save us time if he compares it to the one belonging to my granddad. What do you think?"

"Leave it until we go together Maggie. We would have to log out evidence just as we did for the university. Let's keep this between us until we've spoken with your father."

WPC Reichert left the room in a strangely subdued mood. She couldn't help connecting the skeleton at Winlaton Mill, with possible skeletons in cupboards within her own family. Why had it taken a discovery like this to get her father to open up about Ernst Johan Reichert, her grandfather, for the very first time?

By contrast, 'Jet' Black's mind was ablaze with all kinds of conspiracy theories. Someone from the Luftwaffe involved in a suspicious death forty years ago! In downtown Winlaton Mill! All because an untrained puppy had escaped its owner on a filthy day, ignored 'Keep Out' signs, and sniffed out something irregular. 'Give a dog a bone, would you believe it?' It had turned the investigation from being a chore to one of nascent notoriety, or so he thought.

Chapter 5
High Spen 1945

"How many times have I told you that you're not to climb on that air-raid shelter," screamed Isabella Henderson at her grandson, "you'll fall off the damned thing and break your neck. And who do you think will be blamed?"

Little Harry Smyth was almost five years old, but had yet to clap eyes on his father. He'd seen his mother on a few occasions but he didn't understand why she didn't come home more often. Jack Smyth had been away for most of the war, and after miraculously surviving the desert campaign against Rommel, he was shipped to Italy, advancing steadily toward of the horrors of taking Monte Cassino. Finally, his unit of the Durham Light Infantry was involved in sweeping up through the low countries of Belgium and Holland. Here he avoided capture by the Germans, but only by hiding in the cellar of a Dutch family in Venlo for several weeks. The array of medals which he was about to be awarded, including the Africa Star, didn't seem to compensate for five years of cheating death in roughly dugout trenches, and eating hard-tack biscuits with powdered egg. He hoped time would soften the awful guilt of surviving, when so many comrades did not. His demobilisation would at least let him try to come to terms with a new start, his somewhat estranged wife Hilda, and the rest of his family, including a son whose photograph he'd seen, but to whom he had never spoken. His brother Jim had fallen near Ypres, during the First World War, at the ripe old age of eighteen, and Jack was not yet a teenager at the time. The concoction of it being all over, coming home, leaving friendships on the battlefield, and the prospect of civilian life weighed heavily in his thoughts when he desperately wanted to feel unrestrained joy.

For the first two years of the war, Hilda had worked in an Italian-owned ice cream parlour to help make ends meet. Harry had been conceived before Jack and Hilda were married, primarily because of the slim odds set against him returning home. Figliolini's parlour was in the neighbouring village of Chopwell, and she had to walk the one and a half miles each way along the railway line every day. That the Italian nation had aligned with the Axis doctrine would normally have threatened 'Figgy's' business, but the family had built up a strong social standing in the locality over several generations, with door-to-door delivery of all manner of goods by a fleet of vans, which were truly mobile shops. Hilda had waited patiently for her chance to fulfil her dream of becoming a teacher. When the letter of acceptance for training college at the imposing architectural retreat of Wynyard Hall arrived, she wept without restraint. She would have walked the fifty miles of countryside paths to deliver the completed forms by hand. It was a three year course and she had to reside on site. Isabella, known only as Bella, agreed that she and her husband, also named Jack, but nicknamed 'Cappy'' would take care of Harry until the family could be re-united. Hilda's aspirations were firmly on the rise, whereas Jack Smyth had issues to confront.

"Harry, this is your last warning, will you get down?"

"Ok Grandma, can we go and see the men?"

She knew he meant the men in the P.O.W. camp. Even in those days, political correctness made cameo appearances. The camps were officially named 'Units for Displaced Persons'. There was however no fooling the plebs, and the occupants were exclusively those men who had fallen from their flying machines. Luftwaffe boys, young lads who also had mothers back in Germany. The surrounding villages contained extremely polarised views on these intruders from the skies. Male leanings were skewed toward immediate retribution in various forms, whereas the women, many of whom had suffered the agony of sons in a reciprocal predicament at the hands of the

31

Reich, exercised a more tolerant attitude, almost seeing their own progeny through this parochial looking-glass of the war. It shouldn't have divided families which had been cohesively behind the principle of stopping the Fuhrer in his increasingly evil tracks. Especially now that the war was over, wasn't it? Bella was fifty-five and well known for her feisty demeanour, stout in build as well as character. She had to work, because her husband, Cappy Henderson, had fallen victim to what was referred to as 'Consumption' at the time, in addition to being on a collision course with members of the National Union of Miners. The distillate of this was referral and regular treatment at the 'Spa Baths' of Harrogate. It had to be paid for and there was no other means available to Bella. She worked for the Cooperative Wholesale Society – locally known simply as 'The Store'. She was the caretaker of the library, reading room and concert hall, a massive undertaking, as all of these facilities were on the upper floors of the Co-op 'Empire' in High Spen. The stairs were over ten feet wide and there were many of them. They were, together with the actual rooms, expected to be cleaned every day. And clean meant both floors and tables should be fit to eat from. One tangible benefit of this burden was the continual interaction with virtually everyone in the village. They all knew the tyrant who implemented the wishes of 'The Store' and nobody wanted their quarterly dividend openly discussed. The consequent respect Bella had garnered over the years helped her to get some of the women to exercise their own decision over whether or not to visit the Luftwaffe Boys.

"Very well Harry, go and get a few biscuits from the barrel in the kitchen, but we can't stay long today."

Harry slid down the corrugated metal sheeting of the shelter and landed at her feet. He hugged his grandma and disappeared into the terraced house.

The camp nestled in the hollow between High Spen and Greenside, villages which had similar populations, peering at one another over the valley. The allocated meadow was dotted with army issue tents and ringed with high, wired fencing. A stream ran through one edge of the containment and served as a latrine. When Bella and Harry arrived, there weren't many other residents around, because a couple of young men were shouting abuse at what they called Nazi sympathisers.

Bella Henderson had been through many hard years, and evidence of this was sculptured into her face, a ruthlessly honest face, and one which was always ready to confront bullies. "If your lot practised what they preach, you'd have been over there fighting the Germans instead of spouting off at women. The miners and shipyards in this area are doing their bit, and lots of women joined the land army. You aren't even conscientious objectors, you've never got off your backsides to do a day's work in your life. Now bugger off or I'll smack you around the ears and report you to the village constable. I know who you are, Jimmy Jackson, I'll be talking to your father as well." Bella approached them with a raised hand and a fierce scowl, at which point they retreated, chanting more obscenities, nevertheless conceding temporary defeat. The few scattered women and children regrouped and waved at some of the prisoners who had observed the spat. One or two of them came to the fence and smiled, amazed at the bravery of one lady in particular. There wasn't much exchange of words, primarily because there was an edict of no fraternisation, but in any event none of the villagers could understand a word of German, other than Hitler, yet a couple of the airmen knew a few English phrases. Harry threw some ginger snap biscuits toward one blond-haired young captive in particular, and three made it over the fence. There was no scuffling amongst the recipients, they just divided the biscuits by breaking them into fractions.

Harry was determined to get the remaining ginger snap over at the second attempt. The young blond pilot caught it and asked, "How much years you are?"

Harry was startled and Bella grabbed his hand as she held up all the fingers of the other and mouthed, "Five."

In Harry's developing young mind, his fascination was related to dangerous caged animals. Pictures of lions, tigers, crocodiles and snakes filled him with a foreboding shiver, and if these airmen had to be fenced in, they must by deduction be dangerous. Throwing biscuits to them was exciting, but they could actually say things, and this disturbed him. "I Karl, who you are?"

Bella responded, "His name is Harry, he is very shy but he likes to come and see you and your friends."

Karl couldn't make out much more than the boy's name, and brought another pilot into the conversation. "Hello, Karl was wanting to thank you and Harry for your being kind to us. We all say this. Some have little boy like Harry as brother at Germany, if they are not killed now. We don't know."

Bella felt a rush of sadness. These men, under normal circumstances would have been considered polite. Perhaps they themselves couldn't really understand what they were doing in a remote village, living like stone-age primates, and with no immediate prospect of ever seeing their families again. After all, the blitz of London and other urban manufacturing centres had been reciprocated one hundred times over in places like Berlin, Dresden, Essen and many more. It was the true beginning of impersonal warfare, in which infrastructure and people could be obliterated from the distance of the skies. The days of seeing the whites of the eyes of the adversary as a bayonet skewered them were receding very quickly. Mass destruction, soon to be accurately delivered upon Japan would become a perfect example.

"Is there anything else we can give you other than a few biscuits? I don't mean food, we haven't much of that ourselves, but what about something to keep your mind off what is happening in Germany?"

"Oh, I can understand only a little bit please. I am Gunther let me say. Just one minute." He conferred in his own tongue and it produced rare smiles. After more than five minutes there was consensus and Gunther spoke again. "We could all ask the same for a ball, for making fussball game. Is Harry having a ball like this? We give back after we play. This would be, how must I say, very lovely for us. Will it be allowed by the commandant? I am not knowing how he will say about it."

"Well, there's only one way to find out. But first I have to talk to Harry about lending his football to you."

"Sorry, what is lending?"

"Lending is taking something for a little while, not keeping it forever."

"Aha, yes this is it, for a while, a small time."

Harry wasn't impressed with this at all. His football was his most precious possession and these strange people might burst it. How would it be replaced? Bella reasoned with him that his own dad, who he'd only heard about, could be in a similar camp to these men. She knew he desperately wanted to find his father, and it was becoming quite an acute longing, exacerbated by his mother only being there once in a while, and other children all seemed to have fathers in the pits or factories.

"Well, they might have something for you to borrow in return for the ball, should we ask? They could have secret things which nobody else knows about."

This seemed to do the trick, mystery was right up Harry's street. Bella explained the situation as best she could and Gunther eventually got the message. There was quite a long discussion before he spoke to Bella again. "We are not having things for a little boys, but Karl has asked if his plate would be ok."

"Plate? We have plenty of plates, we are short of things to put on them to eat, and Harry doesn't often ask for a plate."

"Oh yes, I mean I say the wrong word, look – it is this."

Karl took off his identity disc and swung it from its cord. Gunther explained that this was a risk for Karl because it would be needed if they ever were to be repatriated. "So Harry must be keeping this safely, and a big secret."

The lock-jam was brushed aside when Harry could make out strange numbers on the metal disc as it reflected the sunlight. He was more than happy to go and retrieve his ball. Bella indicated to Gunther that the hardest part of the deal was done, but she had to speak to the 'commandant'.

Chapter 6

Maggie's father and mother lived in a modest bungalow in Hexham. Frank was looking forward to retirement from his daily grind as an auto-electrician. Cars were becoming ever more complicated in design and he was having difficulty in absorbing every new-fangled system. Unfortunately, he still had a few years to go. When he was introduced, Black noticed a distinct nervousness in Frank. He fussed about where they should sit, and didn't seem to want his wife Ellen to be present. Maggie went into the tiny kitchen with her mother to make tea. It gave Ellen a chance to ask Maggie what the visit was all about.

"Your Dad has been on tenterhooks ever since you arranged for this policeman to come here, but he won't tell me why. What's it that's got him on edge?"

"Mum, I'm in the police force too, or had you forgotten? If there was anything to worry about I'd have told Dad. It's just a chat to see if he can point us in the right direction to find out more information about an artefact we discovered in one of our case investigations. I remembered Dad showing me Granddad's dog tag from the war when I was about eight, and this one is very similar. If Dad can tell us anything which helps us identify the soldier who it belonged to, it will save us a hell of a lot of time. And it won't do any harm to my chances of passing my interview exam. Just give us ten minutes and stop worrying."

Ellen brought in the tray with antique china crockery and biscuits, Maggie followed with the teapot. "There now, help yourself to biscuits, these chocolate digestives are very nice. So, if you'll excuse me, I have to get on with the washing."

Black nodded his appreciation and turned to Frank. "Maggie tells me you may be able to throw some light on this disc we found next to human remains in the old coke works at Winlaton Mill. The disc itself is badly pitted, but we do have an enhanced image from the university which helps a little in trying to decipher the symbols." He laid the two items on the table. Frank ignored the image and picked up the disc. He walked to the window as the cramped living room was quite dark even with the lights on. He then searched several drawers impatiently, whispering something under his breath. "Your mother moves stuff around from one place to another for no good reason and never tells me what she has done or why.... I'll have to...oh, here it is." He produced a hand-focussing lens gadget and promptly examined the disc with it. The minutes ticked away and Black was becoming less hopeful that he'd get anything useful from Frank, when there was a rush of relief from Maggie's father.

"I was worried that I'd find some connection to the unit my own father served in, but that isn't the case."

"Can you be more explicit Sir," said Black, his interest reviving somewhat, "anything, all manner of knowledge may be important, no matter how insignificant it may appear."

Maggie was beginning to get restless. "Well Dad, say something."

Frank asked them to sit and retrieved a small box from the sideboard. Maggie knew what it was. "Inspector, this is my father's disc, or dog tag, as this country refers to such objects. Look at them together. Yours has a zinc coating and mine is pressed from aluminium, as most of the earlier discs were during the war. My father's was issued right at the start of hostilities, but yours was not produced until the beginning of 1943. Apart from this I can tell you of another difference; yours is from a Luftwaffe training unit, whereas mine refers to a unit already in action."

"Fascinating," mumbled Black, smiling at Maggie, "and what else is there? The numbers and letters must mean something to you."

"They do mean something but I'm no expert. I can see from your disc and the image that there could be several interpretations of the legend. First of all, the two halves of the disc have exactly the same meaning, just the bottom half is a mirror image of the top, but is upside down. This enables anyone to read the duplicated information whichever way it hangs on its cord. It would normally be hung from the single hole, and the cord passes though the two holes at the bottom to keep it flat, I suppose."

Black was beginning to regret being so unspecific in his questioning. "Aha, and this surely means if a letter is pitted on one half we may possibly get it from the other half."

"Exactly," exclaimed Frank, seeming to relax, "you can therefore work out the wording. It is '3/FL. AUSB. REGT. 43'. This means it was issued to a man who was part of a regiment which was undergoing training at that time. Mine is totally different and has additional information, including a blood group letter."

"Right, great, so what else does ours tell you about the person to whom it belonged?"

"I'm afraid that I won't be able to tell you anything about that. There is another irregularity though. You see the number which refers to the person − it is above the serving unit description, and that is wrong. Look here again, my father's is correct, the number is below his unit reference."

"Wow," chuckled Black, "does that mean it could be bogus?"

"Not necessarily, you see, as the war progressed many units had the capability of pressing new discs as the need arose. There are many instances of pragmatism, the rules were bent, in this case it could be because the unit description is so long it couldn't be placed higher up on the oval disc, and it all had to go on one line. So they may have put the number 277 in the wrong place just for convenience."

A deflated Black shrugged his shoulders. "Oh well, that's that then. Still, it has been helpful Mr Reichert. Thank you for your time."

"Wait Inspector, that isn't the end of the line, just my capability. As you can imagine, even after the war was over, there were many reasons for not allowing the definite identification of the individual to become public knowledge. Imagine the feelings of the parents of a dead soldier if they were contacted by someone other than the proper authority, and that's where we must inquire now. The Abwehr was the German Military Intelligence organisation from the 1920's until after the war. The information still exists and the keepers of this archive will respond to an official police request, especially if it will help fill in a blank in their records. It could be of great service to any remaining relatives of this man."

"Brilliant," said Maggie and Black in unison. Then Maggie queried one of her father's words.

"Dad, you said we could go to the Abwehr, did you mean we the police?"

"No, I meant 'we' including myself. I think we may get a quicker response if they know I'm half German."

"But what if they check back on Granddad's cooperation with Britain?"

"I've always thought about that Maggie, and I have changed my mind a thousand times on what it all meant. These days the new breed of West German citizens want to confront these issues head-on instead of burying them. Their guilt over one Austrian megalomaniac is being assuaged by more understanding of the motives of soldiers like my father. They wanted to end ethnic and social cleansing. They may have been in the minority but they were amongst the bravest. But it wasn't healthy to mess with the Gestapo back then."

His hand was shaken vigorously by Black but Maggie shed a little tear of pride. She asked D.I. Black to give her a couple of minutes with her father.

"Dad, are you sure it's a good idea for you to get involved with the Abwehr? It could lead to a lot of unpleasantness."

"Do you think I don't know that? However, it's about time I put all this stuff behind me. It isn't just the uninformed in Britain who still treat German people with suspicion. There are still those in Germany who hold preservation of the 'Fatherland' and Aryan bloodlines in particular, as a holy grail to be restored. They treat people like my father, but who were repatriated, as treasonous outcasts. I want to flush these bigots out into the open, and this person, whoever it is, presents an opportunity such as your grandfather never had. He seriously considered going back there, and had it not been for your Grandma, and the fact that I came along, he would surely have done so. It won't be easy but it isn't so dangerous these days."

Maggie could sense Frank had experienced some kind of watershed moment and it was as if he'd shed a great burden. They hugged and she felt him shaking, and he bade her to go. "I need to speak with your Mum."

*

There was a note on Black's desk from Constance Carr which simply said, 'Ring me'. Just as she answered he scalded his tongue with the coffee Freda had left for him. She'd warned him about it, saying the new machine was having teething problems, but as often happened his mind was elsewhere. It seemed to be a function of his photographic memory, a prioritisation of registry when there were many factors competing for attention. "Bloody Norah!"

"No, it's Constance, sorry to disappoint you." Now that the glitch in the coffee machine had worked its way up the ladder of importance in the most dramatic fashion, the

41

exact moment would be embedded into his cerebral hard disk.

"Hello Connie, there is no Norah, you're still the only one for me. Do you have something for me?"

"Nothing of that kind I'm afraid. I have revised my initial estimates a little following the full series of tests on the bones. I believe the person was in his early twenties at most, and when I said it wasn't a recent death I didn't expect it to have been so long ago."

"You mean about 1945?"

"Well, I can't be that precise, but…"

"Sorry Connie, you did tell me to back off until you'd finished your examination, so you wouldn't have heard that the professor from the university is pretty certain that our man was buried underneath the concrete slab, which was installed in 1945. You see, if I'd been a pest, you'd have known this already."

"Mmm, well at least my findings don't contradict your theories and circumstantial hearsay evidence. Anyway, to the facts, there is clear indication of severe trauma to the cervical vertebrae. The most obvious cause could have been the crushing weight of concrete, but on closer examination I found definite evidence of blows from some kind of sharp implement. An axe, a heavy bladed tool. There are multiple strike patterns which produced many fractures. I'd say this was a violent death."

"So we're looking at murder then. I had a feeling that this might be the case. I tried to think of why or how a corpse just happened to end up neatly tucked away under a presumed impregnable foundation slab, and I couldn't come up with anything. I was partly drawn to this conclusion by the proximity of a barrel and hessian, possibly from a sack. It all added up to hiding a body in a place where it would never be found."

"In that case Inspector you'll be interested in my report on the remnants of those very pieces of hessian and fragments from the barrel. I took the liberty of passing these to our budding forensics department and they discovered something unusual. The various parts were clumped together with compacted mud and they are still working on what the victim may have been wearing. By washing the mud away very carefully, some of the fabrics have been isolated, apparently not pure wool, but one patch fell away and yielded a gold ring. It obviously wasn't being worn, probably tucked away in a pocket. It has an engraving – the letters M.V. are inscribed on the inside face."

"I owe you one Constance Carr. I have to let Moss know that this really is a suspicious death, in my opinion a murder."

"Well you're the detective, I just deal in facts and educated hypotheses, so I'll leave the speculation in your capable hands. I'll let you know what I consider to be appropriate if you really feel you 'owe me one'."

Chapter 7
High Spen 1945

Even if the rest of his classmates all had mums and dads, Harry was the only one in the entire village who had a Luftwaffe dog tag. High Spen, at that time, was a thriving community despite having a small population, many of whom were pitmen. Amongst the facilities there were no fewer than three working men's social clubs – the Field, the Road-End, and the Central which was curiously known by the locals as 'Headsy's. The Palace cinema stood proudly in a prime location, surrounded by Suzy Best's sweet shop and temperance bar, the Venture bus garage, and the Corner confectionary emporium. Scattered along this main street were many other businesses, giving the illusion of complete self-sufficiency. Two hairdressing salons, a milliners, a hardware store, two greengrocers, a butcher, a newsagent, an elegant ladies dress store, and Cumberledge's, an immaculate example of one of the first one-stop food outlets to rival the Co-operative. Not content with the three clubs, there were plenty of supporters of the Miner's Arms and the Bute Arms pubs. Three delineations of religious worship were on offer, and bestriding the whole community was indeed the Co-operative Wholesale Society. It was a classic portrait of competitiveness arising out of complacency. Despite the quarterly dividend of the Co-op offering a seductive rainy day fund, the villagers unconsciously or otherwise spent enough in the peripheral businesses to forge a parasitic or symbiotic relationship within the economic community. The bustling nature of High Spen thrived for decades, and it could only be brought down by the unthinkable – closure of the coal mine.

In Harry's little world there was also evidence of a seemingly disproportionate investment in local education. He attended the Infant and Junior Mixed School, and would have a choice at the age of eleven, depending upon his ability. He would attend either the Secondary Modern Senior or Hookergate Grammar school establishments, the latter drawing pupils from surrounding villages within a five mile radius. For Harry there was an abundance of school children who would eagerly divest him of the dog tag. Its currency increased by the day. Bella advised him that it had to be kept in a safe place, because it was so important to Karl, its German owner, and anyway it had to be returned at some point. There was no bank in the village, people were paid in cash, spent cash, and were hardly able to save, except for the Co-op dividend. They certainly couldn't afford to borrow money at that time, even though the war was supposed to be at an end. Bella, for that very same reason didn't want to incur costs of depositing such a controversial item with a solicitor in Blaydon, the nearest small town. Harry cried when she told him they would have to give the disc back to Karl as soon as possible. It was his only grasp on street credibility, even at such a young age. Boys and girls alike wanted to glimpse such a symbol of rebellion against the decree of authority.

"Grandma, you said I should lend the men my ball, why are you saying I have to stop lending it now?"

"It's too hard to explain Harry, you'll understand when you grow up."

"But that will be a long time. Why can the men not stay here instead of going away?"

"Because they have families in Germany and anyway the tents they live in here are cold and damp, they aren't fit to live in for a long time."

Harry thought about this for a while and reasoned that Germany must be even further away than Newcastle, also in his opinion, it would be quite exciting to live in a tent. In addition, the men were his friends even if they had a family. So why would they leave? He couldn't go to his family, and they didn't come to see him very much, whereas his friends were there every day. "Listen Harry, if you give the disc back to Karl, I'll buy you a new football and some proper boots to play in, then the men will become even better friends if you let them keep the old ball. You can then expect them to give you something else as a present, something even more exciting than a silly disc."

The prospect of something unknown but more exciting than the dog tag worked its magic. Harry couldn't sleep because he was imagining a new football *and* a mystery present. It felt like Christmas.

Bella suddenly recalled that she had intended to talk to the 'commandant' about the initial swap, but she'd forgotten. Her juggling of keeping the various Co-op halls pristine, the house tidy, cooking meals, attending to her husband's deteriorating health, including taking him to Harrogate Spa, was taking its toll. On top of this it was a challenge in its own right looking after a little boy with somewhat special needs. It was a sort of blessing that the commandant was merely some delegated underling from the Home Guard. "Mr Proudfoot, I suppose I have enough on my plate without having to get involved in red tape. My grandson accidently kicked his ball over the fence where you keep these airmen locked up. Now, I know the rules say there should be no fraternisation, but we don't want the ball back, it won't last much longer anyway before it bursts. I just wanted you to know they can keep it. They offered it back, but Harry is getting a new one. I sincerely hope your people won't look on this as some kind of Quisling situation."

Proudfoot's brow furrowed. 'Good.' thought Bella, 'he doesn't know what to do'.

"Good God man, what use would the Home Guard be if we had been invaded, when you can't deal with a simple decision like this? It's a football I'm talking about, not spying and secret agents. I only told you out of courtesy, but you'll have to tell me if there's a problem or I'll go higher up the Home Guard Command."

"No, er no, no it should be ok, in fact it's better that we don't bother anyone else with this."

"Yes, but I have told you about it, and my friend Polly here is a witness, so you can't deny it."

"Well, as you said, it was accidently kicked over the fence and you don't want it back, so that's the end of it."

Bella looked at Polly and rolled her eyes. "God help us if we ever do have to depend on these geriatric paper pushers for anything important."

A couple of days later she took Harry to see the men again. They were all engaged in what she thought to be a friendly football match, but to Bella's amazement, the continual shouting and ferocity of each tackle conveyed a weird kind of fear, emotionally almost on a par with being free again. When one of them spotted Harry, he called to the others and all of this tension evaporated, the game was paused. They came to the fence, every one of them had a beaming smile for the little English boy who'd given them a kind of cohesive activity for the first time in this wretched camp. Gunther came to the fore. "Yes, hello, we are pleasing to see you, we are hoping that we will keep the ball some days more. Do you not want this?"

Bella smiled and lifted Harry up into her arms. "It's yours now, my Grandson Harry says it's a present to you all."

"Oh, wunderbar! I am sorry, I mean this is very kind in him. As you see, it helps us to pass the time. We all love him, is this ok to say?"

Bella replied after clearing the frog in her throat. "Of course, he thinks of you as his friends. He has also come to give back the disc to Karl, where is he?"

"We don't know," said Gunther, "he has, how to say it, left us."

47

"You mean he has been sent home?"

"No, not home. He is not now in the camp, but the commandant will be looking for him. Ah, now I have the word - he escapes."

"My God," muttered Bella, "well, we brought the disc with us and it's now even more important that we give it back, will you take it?"

Gunther nodded and she threw it over the fence. As it made its way through the air, Harry's vision clicked into slow motion, each turn of the disc seemed to flash the sun's reflection, like Morse code, with the potential of revealing secret stories. He wondered if the present he was about to receive could possibly be more exciting than the dog tag of the missing man named Karl. Harry was having second thoughts about the swap. He wandered along the fence looking for Karl. Gunther picked up the disc and Bella decided not to ask for a replacement gift.

Harry was crestfallen. That is until his grandma told a little fib. "The men wanted to buy you something because they have nothing anywhere near as exciting as the disc. They asked me to take you to Newcastle and look in all of the toy shops to see if there's anything you would like. Isn't that nice of them?"

Harry had only heard of Newcastle, he'd never been there, but he had seen pictures and it fascinated him. All those people, the riverboats, bridges and trains. His little facial expression turned from morose to one of nascent anticipation. "When are we going Grandma? Today? Are we going on the bus? I need to have a Wee-Wee now."

The day was saved even though Bella could hardly spare the time. Still, the break would do her good, and she couldn't get the news about Karl's disappearance out of her mind. She decided to pretend she didn't know about it, surely the news would break soon and she would look suitably horrified.

The trip to the city proved to be more expensive than anticipated, the new football and boots took all she could spare and Harry was so impatient to try them out that he temporarily forgot about anything else. He dragged Bella to the bus station. She put it down to visiting the riverside for an hour, and it not having lived up to his expectations. She was relieved that the present from the men could wait for another day.

When the escape report broke it gathered pace like a prairie fire. The little village was locked in indecision. The Home Guard wanted volunteers to conduct a search, but feared it could turn into a lynch mob. Some of the women extrapolated the gossip, to liken it to a hunt for a murderer. A curfew was suggested and rejected. The local constable was finally asked to request reinforcements to assist the Home Guard. It didn't however stop a growing band of vigilantes conducting their own search. Families began to take sides over the issue. But at least nobody had yet asked about the disc. Bella felt it was only a matter of time before one of Harry's classmates spilled the beans, and then their parents would take serious interest in his temporary guardianship of a German identity badge. The waiting was unsettling.

Chapter 8

Frank Reichert had prepared the letter for the appropriately ranked police officer to sign. Maggie read it through and queried his decision one last time. "Dad, are you absolutely certain that you want to do this? We all understand how difficult it must be."

"Yes, we've been through this already, that's why I've drafted this for the police to sign and send to the Abwehr archive. For now at least, I've decided to listen to your advice and keep my name out of it, but if your boss allows me to help in drafting any further correspondence I'll be able to judge if I stand any chance of extracting information about my father's unit."

"Ok, I'd better get this to D.I. Black, as he wants to justify additional resourcing for this case. Thanks for this Dad."

*

Black eventually succeeded in running Eric Paisley to ground, and showed up at his house in the northeast coastal village of Alnmouth. He was patently annoyed at the police arriving unannounced, something which Black had gambled upon, hence justifying his decision to be accompanied by Freda Collins. She wasn't often out of her personal, ergonomically-designed office chair, never mind being out of the station. "If we may come in Mr Paisley, we can get this over quickly, this is D.C. Collins, and we just need to ask a few routine questions. I must say your ex-colleague Neville Travers has been very helpful, I hope that you can do the same."

Paisley, the ex-operations director of the coke works was far braver on the telephone than he was face-to-face. He looked distinctly flustered at the mention of Travers' cooperation with the police. "Very well, come in. I have a dental appointment so I must leave in good time."

"Excellent," bluffed Black, "Freda will take notes, as we appreciate you giving up your time to help us, and we don't want to have to trouble you again. There is some general stuff we would like verification of and one specific item we hope you may be able to shed light on."

Collins took out her notepad and maintained an extremely severe facial expression, contrasting well with Black's affable demeanour. Every word, no matter by whom it was spoken, was recorded, beginning with Paisley's invitation to sit. Both police officers were struck by the space and décor of the house. High, corniced ceilings complemented an eclectic mix of antique and modern designer furnishings. They were apparently seated at present in the family room, at least twenty feet square, and it seemed odd because he had no family – they'd checked him out before confronting him. These observations were in stark contrast to his appearance. Black had imagined from his telephone voice that he would be a towering heavyweight – not so, more akin to a whiskered rodent. Being so diminutive made the abundance of space seem even more bizarre.

Black spread the plan of the old site next to that of the post-demolition phase, and then arranged the recently taken photographs of the landslip. "We have two people who have independently stated that the landslip occurred on the original site of the engineering office. Does this make sense to you?"

Paisley studied the display and saw Collins write something down before he'd uttered a single word. "Yes, as near as I can tell without seeing the site itself."

"And would you be willing to do so Mr Paisley?"

"Of course." It was working.

"That's very kind of you Sir, tomorrow would be a good time for us, unless you'd like to come after your dental appointment?"

"That's completely out of the…. Well, perhaps I can rearrange things for tomorrow."

"Good," whispered Black, nodding to Collins, before moving on to the next question. "Do you remember exactly when the concrete for the foundation of this office block was started and how long it took to complete?"

"Oh, well I wasn't actually working at the plant then, I was brought in to manage Winlaton Mill after a series of mine closures in Yorkshire, all small, uneconomic seams. That was in the late seventies. However, there will be records of the foundations being laid. Maybe I can lay my hands on them by asking someone at NCB records to retrieve this information, I still have friends there. I'll make the call when I return from the dentist, and either ring you or bring the exact date tomorrow."

"Wonderful," enthused Black, as he smiled at Collins, who'd been instructed not to show any emotion whatsoever, "that really would help, and we don't need to bring up the other points at this stage if you can furnish that date."

This about-face perturbed Paisley somewhat, but before he could relax in the belief that the interview was over, Black threw the dog tag on to the site plan and startled his quarry. "What do you make of this?"

Paisley couldn't recall whether or not Black had mentioned this when they had their abortive telephone call, just after the skeleton was discovered. His brow furrowed, he started to say something and then shook his head. "No, I'm afraid I can't help you. Where precisely did you find it?"

"That's not important if you don't know what it is. We thought it might have something to do with your production at the plant."

"Well I can definitely rule that out, because the rail trucks, or wagons as we called them had open tops and travelled in all weathers, so we used a system of permanent marking of each truck. Then the shipment paperwork itemised what was in each of them. One for the customer and one for our records and invoicing department. I can't even begin to imagine what that object could be."

"Fine, well that's us done for now. See you tomorrow."

*

On the way back they stopped at a roadside coffee shop and mulled over what they'd each made of Paisley's body language and the opulence of his mansion, which didn't have the slightest hint of anyone else living there. Maybe he had a cleaner or a maid or both. The place was scrupulously clean and tidy, perhaps indicating obsessive compulsive tendency. Freda Collins thought he was even slimier than he was on the phone, and was sure he had something to hide. Black was more intrigued by his reaction when the Luftwaffe disc was suddenly and demandingly thrown on to the table. "He was lying when he said he had no idea what it was. I'd like to know what he was going to say before he changed his mind. We'll have another go at him tomorrow Freda."

"Not out of the office two days running!"

"Don't worry, this isn't the favour you think you are going to collect for getting my tyre repaired. Now I'm going to the gents, there's a phone box over there, can you contact the office to see if Moss has signed off the letter to this German secret service organisation."

"Yes Sir! Then do I get a pee break too?"

"As long as it isn't more than ten times longer than mine."

When he exited the men's room Freda had one of those looks on her face. "Moss has not signed the letter and apparently wants to discuss it with you. The switchboard also said you were called by a Sophie Redwood, some journalist who wants to talk about the skeleton. Somebody must have blabbed."

"It was bound to happen, it could have been many people, the whole village must know by now. The security guys will have seen to that. You're using up your comfort break talking to me, come on, and get a move on."

Black pondered why Moss had specifically left a message - that he *hadn't* signed Frank Reichert's draft letter. It was out of character, he would normally have sat on it, milking the frustration of the applicant, and only then asking for more justification. A thought flashed into his mind. This journalist, who had tried to contact him, could have been referred to Moss. If that was true, it would probably mean there would be problems ahead. He sensed some kind of interference, the kind which Moss would not dispute. Finally Freda emerged from the restroom with the good news that she'd decided what favour she would be happy to call on for getting his tyre fixed.

"Don't go there just yet D.C. Collins, I want to keep that surprise for a really good day. I need to clear my head before I see Moss. Let's go."

As the return journey was resumed, the sky became threatening once more, adding to his pensive mood. He broke the silence by telling Freda to ask forensics about the ring which Constance had rescued from the mud-cemented fabrics. "Ask them when they can release it, so you can check around the local jewellers to see if there are any marks which can tell us where it was made. It could have been purchased in Germany if it has been under the concrete with the bones since 1945."

"Another line of investigation out of the office, wow."

Her cynicism reminded him he'd also promised Connie some 'reward' for such diligence in finding the ring. He had to stop such gestures, or he could expect his soaring reputation to suffer.

*

Black's apprehension was justified. He could see Moss having a heated discussion in his office with two people he didn't recognise. He glanced at Freda, who shrugged her shoulders and said she would make some strong coffee. One of the junior C.I.D. trainees nervously thrust a note into Black's left hand, as his other was still grasping his case file. It was disturbing in its brevity.

'Can't sign off on this letter. Instructions from above.'

He tapped on the door and was beckoned to enter. "This is D.I. Black, take a seat. Can I introduce Charles Stone and Marion Wentworth?" said Moss, overtly uncomfortable with their presence. "I'll let them brief you on what happens next." He left the office.

It was Stone who delivered the speech while Wentworth watched every aspect of Black's reaction. "It's more a case of what doesn't happen next Inspector. We don't like this any more than you do, but that isn't going to change much with respect to how we must proceed. First, we need the complete case file on this skeleton you found. We aren't at liberty to discuss the content until both Marion and I have read the entire file. The reason for this is somewhat obscure at present and is likely to become convoluted at best. My remit is with MI5, and Marion represents MI6. I'm sure you will therefore realise I report to the Home Secretary, whereas Miss Wentworth functions under the guidance of the Foreign Secretary. As I explained to your superior, there's to be no concessions, we won't interfere in the detail, but we must oversee the case. Presumably he's gone to make phone calls which will confirm what I've just said. I'm sorry about the abruptness of all this, and I'm sure we'll get along just fine once we've established the next step."

Marion Wentworth had still not spoken or smiled. Her poker face was lined with years of experience, she was impeccably dressed and looked anorexic. Black estimated that she looked about fifty, but was probably five to ten years younger. The severe containment of her ash-coloured hair in such a tight bun reminded him of an old school mistress. Charles Stone, in contrast, seemed to like hearing the sound of his own voice. He was a little overweight, prematurely bald, possibly in his early thirties, and had overdone the antiperspirant. Black decided to say nothing at all until Moss returned. As he glanced through the window at his own office, he noticed the case file was gone from his desk top, presumably taken by his boss.

Chapter 9
High Spen 1945

The hunt for Karl, the German airman, was in full swing, and by disparate groups with different objectives. The news that Harry had possession of the dog tag, even for a few days, had spouted from his school friends, despite him swearing them to keep his secret. The official search by the police-bolstered Home Guard was purely and simply to return Karl to the camp. Whether or not he had been able to hear about the commencement of repatriation procedures, was a moot point. There were cliques of young men who were keen on claiming the modest reward being offered from the police for information leading to Karl's recapture. Other militant bands of anti-Nazi persuasion wanted him to answer for many fallen relatives from the village. The women seemed to be much more homogeneous as a group. They did want him returned to the camp and onward to Germany, but were intent on preventing what they considered to be a pointless death. The German surrender had been officially accepted and these women wanted the killing to stop. Unknown to any of these protagonists was a stranger whose purpose was to interrogate Karl, and all of the other airmen in the camp, before they were to be deported.

The terrain between High Spen and Greenside was conducive to a fugitive remaining undetected. Apart from the main road between High Spen and Greenside bordering the front of the camp, rolling hills, two meandering rivers which would ultimately unite, and expanses of open woodland, were kind to Karl. Added to this was the swathe of dense forest named Chopwell Woods. If he'd already made it to this refuge, even air searches would have trouble spotting him. His greatest difficulty could however come in the form of not being found. He needed sustenance. Water wasn't a concern as there was always access to rivers within a few miles, but food was difficult to come by even if you weren't on the run. Cultivated supplies in allotments were jealously guarded against local thieves, including unsavoury neighbours. There had been instances of shooting at such looters. Also, there was the risk that successful stealing could give away his approximate location. Wild berries were scarce and protein was in short supply. He had to wait out the initial, highly-fuelled search, counting on apathy creeping into the equation. He knew that there had been little interest in the surrounding villages toward the camp and its inhabitants, and he made this the cornerstone of his strategy. He got by with wild mushrooms and tubers. When he felt the intensity of the search was on the wane, he would cross open land to another village at night, hoping to appropriate supplies from a farm or allotment complex, and then make a run for it until daylight became bedtime. He was however, about to find another unexpected and somewhat serendipitous solution. There was also another group of people which nobody had considered, who were intensely interested in his recapture – the airmen back at the camp.

*

"Mrs Henderson, tell us everything you can remember about this disc your grandson took from the fugitive. Please take your time, because you may be facing a charge of fraternisation." The police sergeant from Blaydon had a reputation as a stickler in adherence to procedure.

"I beg your pardon," shouted Bella, "I haven't come here willingly to be lectured by the likes of you. This has already been explained to the Home Guard. Mr Proudfoot was informed that Harry kicked his ball accidently over the fence and the 'displaced persons' as you stupidly refer to them, thought he'd given it to them. They just loaned him the disc as a way of saying thanks, and it was given back two days later. I told Mr Proudfoot that they could keep the ball, as it was very old, and I bought him a new one. I threw the disc back to one of the airmen, and that was after the other one went missing. So, how can you say this is fraternisation? You people should have better things to do with your time. Would you like to hear how much free time I have? None. Now I want Proudfoot to come here at once, to see what he has to say about this."

He was summoned while Bella waited outside the tent. He arrived, a little out of breath. As he was about to pass her, not knowing why he had been called back from the search, she whispered, "I haven't told this over-officious sergeant that you told me it was best if nobody else knew about our previous conversation. And, my friend Polly can verify this. I expect nothing has changed, it wouldn't seem right to get you into trouble over a storm in a tea cup."

Proudfoot walked slowly into the tent and re-emerged less than two minutes later, nodding toward the tent, but saying nothing. She went in and was asked to sit. "I apologise Madam, there has been a misunderstanding, which Mr Proudfoot has cleared up. I'm inclined to dismiss the incident, as I'm satisfied there was no real contact. Are you able to remember any details from the disc while your grandson had it in his possession? Anything at all?"

"Well, it's Madam now is it? I can't be sure, but I think he made a drawing of it. If it's accurate, I can let you see it and make your own copy. It was a galvanised metal finish with numbers and letters pressed into it. I feel sure that Harry would have copied these carefully because he was fascinated with it."

"That would be very helpful Mrs Henderson, as soon as it is convenient please."

Bella wanted to strike while she had them on the defensive and she trudged back home to collect Harry from his friend's house. When she told him why he had to leave there was the anticipated refusal. "I gave them the disc and it's not fair if they want my drawings. Anyway, I never got my present from the men."

She jumped at the chance to leverage the bit about drawings – plural. "Now Harry, it's the police who want the drawing, not the men. Did you say there's more than one sketch?"

"Yes, but Grandma, what about my present?"

"The men have to go home soon and because of this Karl running away, we aren't allowed to talk to the other men any more. If we don't do what the police say, we might go to prison."

"You mean like the camp which the men are in? Oh, can we do that? Please Grandma."

"No, it won't be the camp darling, it will be a nasty, dirty dark room with nobody else in it but the two of us. There are rats in there as well. If we give one of your drawings to the police and keep the rest we might get the reward for helping to find Karl. What do you think?"

"Ok," groaned Harry wearily, still angling for a present, which he thought would be much better than a reward, "can we help to find Karl? He would be pleased if we were friends again, and he would buy me a present."

"All right, we will help for an hour tomorrow morning, now can we get the drawing, it will soon be dark."

They hurried back to the tent and Bella breathlessly handed the drawing to the sergeant, who was now sitting next to the unknown stranger assisting with the search. His accreditation had been verified by a high-ranking politician from London. When he'd studied the sketch he put a question directly to Harry. Bella tried to intervene but was silenced. "Hello Harry, this is a super drawing, and it is very helpful that we can keep it. Tell me, are you absolutely sure about the number at the top and the upside-down one at the bottom? Think carefully, because it is very important."

"Yes Sir, it's two hundred and seventy-seven. I asked my Granddad why it was a big number and he told me."

"Really, what did he say?"

"That it might be when he was born, his number was like mine. Granddad said I was born on the eighteenth of August so that is 188, and Karl would have been born a long time ago, on the 27th of July. So his number was 277."

The interrogator's face lit up. "I see, and his name was Karl was it? Well that is helpful, the other men wouldn't tell us that, and of course that means we can't shout out his name when we're looking for him if we don't know it, so how would he know we are trying to find him? Anyway, even if your granddad was wrong in thinking that it represents Karl's birthday, you are really, really sure about the number two-seven-seven?"

"Yes Sir, I'm not a stupid boy. I traced it from the disc with greaseproof paper, and my Granddad helped me."

The discussion was ended amicably and the stranger was about to leave the tent, when Harry stopped him in his tracks, by revealing something Bella had kept to herself. "Anyway Mister, you can get the disc from the other man."

Bella's eyes rolled and the stranger turned around. "Which other man Harry?"

"I can't say his name properly, you say it Grandma."

"I can't remember which of the airmen said he would keep it for Karl. We didn't know all the names, by any means, just a minute…. it could have been Gunther, yes that sounds familiar, Gunther. Haven't you asked them about it?"

"Of course, but they said it was missing. Thank you for your assistance, you may go."

Bella was unhappy that this had been forced out of her but she couldn't implicate the family any further, and anyway, what did Gunther have to hide, especially as he said they were worried about Karl.

*

It could have been a freeze-frame when they spotted one another at the same time. Karl's instinct was to run, but it was the fishing rod which checked his impulse. Michael,

61

on the other hand, instantly recognised the uniform, and had heard all the circulating rumours. Being a target of abuse and persecution himself, he felt some empathy with the fox rather than the hounds. This section of the twisting river Derwent, was at the bottom of a steep gorge in the forest and was not easily accessed, which was why both men had chosen it. Michael wanted to fish for his lunch but couldn't afford a permit, and Karl simply wanted to be near drinking water but out of sight. He'd found a recess in the side of the gorge which was surrounded by a thicket.

Michael was the vagabond of three villages, and like Karl, slept rough in multiple locations. He beckoned the young German officer to advance, holding up a trout he'd landed earlier. Despite the prospect of sharing a hot lunch, Karl was cautious. Michael put down the rod and walked slowly toward him, smiling and pointing upstream. They finally came close enough to speak, yet the gestures continued. Michael mimed sitting around a camp fire, rubbing his hands together and then holding them out to take in the warmth of the imaginary burning logs, then pulling something from the fire, and finally blowing on it before eating it and discarding the bone. At last Karl smiled. They wandered through several dense thickets before they were confronted with a vertical fissure in the solid rock wall of the gorge. At first it seemed impossibly narrow for either of them to enter, but Michael pulled up a cleverly camouflaged trap door. He got on to his knees and crawled under the split in the rock, through an excavated tunnel. Karl handed the rod though the aperture and then followed. Michael pulled the trapdoor back into place with the attached rope and secured the coil by rolling a mighty boulder over it. The cavern was much bigger than Karl could have imagined, roughly conical in shape, and as it thinned toward the top, daylight poured in from somewhere. Wondering exactly where the light was coming from, Karl's eyes gradually adjusted to the poor illumination as he scanned the roof again, and he saw the spiralling cavity worming its way to the left hand side near the top of the gorge. Some of the angled sunshine reflected the colours of an array of exposed minerals. He'd temporarily forgotten just how cold he was. The little primus stove was already throwing out a little warmth, a little which felt like a lot to Karl. A crusty smile on Michael's old face was accompanied by the smell of burning fish.

Chapter 10

When Moss returned to his office all was quiet. Only Charles Stone had spoken in his absence and even his verbosity had stalled. Moss rudely dropped the case file into Stone's lap. "It's all yours, now if you can excuse us, we have other cases to progress. I'm sure you'll have questions when you have read the file, but I'd be grateful if you respect our hierarchical command in the same way you have stated we acknowledge yours. You will address all queries through me, no one else. If you don't, it will be reported. For the time being, we can offer you an empty office on the top floor, with a nice view of the city traffic. By the way, if you don't mind slumming it for a few days, we have a decent canteen on the ground floor." In other words, 'get your own drinks, we may have to cooperate but we aren't your servants'.

Stone and Wentworth stood up, the latter feigning politeness, while Stone was about to protest. She finally spoke. "Come along Charles, let's acquaint ourselves with the facts in the file before making judgements. You'll hear from us once we've compiled a list of questions pertaining to the case Superintendent Moss. I'd like to begin in the canteen Charles, it's not a good idea to analyse the evidence on an empty stomach." They made their way through the crowded open office to the elevator without looking back. Having taken sustenance, they ascended to their 'office'. The top floor was empty but for a couple of painters' wallpaper pasting tables with trestles, and several emulsion cans, containing inches of solidified paint, which were scattered about. They looked at one another just as a junior officer arrived with two metal-backed chairs.

Black was unable to digest the probable fallout of the last half hour. Equally strange was Moss's confrontational attitude. Black could wait no longer. "How did this happen?"

"Obvious, surely," said Moss, "if this Sophie Redwood has tried to contact you, then someone has leaked details to the press. I haven't even discussed this case with my boss, simply because I was going to suggest to you that we should hand it over to the cold case squad. After all, it seems as if it was probably an accidental death which happened a long time ago. There are many people who could have leaked the actual incident, but most of such individuals would only have been angling for a bung, a payday for a gruesome story. For this to culminate in dragging in the intelligence squads, somewhere along the line, the detail must have reached the ears of a conduit to Westminster. What do you think?"

"What do I think? Well first of all, you obviously aren't up to date with some of our latest information, which may rule out accidental death. Surely you hadn't decided to ignore the letter which you haven't yet signed Sir? The skeleton is likely to have been a German airman, so why was he buried under a huge concrete slab when he should have been back in the Fatherland? There's also a ring which Constance Carr washed out of the hessian and fabric debris, and I haven't had time to actually log it in as evidence or update you on this find. But possibly most important of all, she has also indicated that there is evidence of trauma to the cervical vertebrae which indicates that we do have a suspicious death. I can't comment on the source of the leak Sir, but I still need an answer to my question – how did this happen, why do we deserve the attention of both MI5 and MI6? This mysterious person you believe has access to Westminster must know something we don't. I personally don't care who it is, but I do care about *why* they are trying to silence us."

"Inspector Black, you aren't thinking straight. You clearly have ambitions to become D.C.I. as soon as you can, and so far you're on track. The brownie points on offer in the current climate, I'm sad to say, are all in the sectors of this new drug Ecstasy, and related organised crime. Piddling about with the remains of an unknown foreigner, and a German to boot, who died forty years ago, is not exactly high currency. And that's a fact, even if he was bumped off. If it turns out to be an accident it will be considered as poor use of resource and poorer judgement to have authorised it. I'm heading for retirement, and although I was sceptical about your methodology when you came here, I have become a convert. Also, I have nothing to lose by being pensioned off early, whereas your career is just beginning. That's why I took these two bureaucrats head-on earlier. You should leave this with me."

"I'm not comfortable with that Sir, first and foremost I'm a detective, not a frigging ladder-climber. If further promotion comes that would be great, but I don't want to spend my best years arsing about with political hot potatoes. Something stinks here and I want to stay on the case, even if it means working with Laurel and Hardy from London."

"I fear I've misjudged you again Black. If that is really what you want, I'll have to transfer the Ecstasy related stuff to D.I. Horton. I do admire your stance, but you need to think this through." Moss was rather pleased that he'd misread 'Jet' Black's' career motives. He had never seen him as a moral crusader.

"I don't need to think about it. Give Horton the nod, if that keeps me on the Derwenthaugh case. Don't you feel it Sir? It makes no difference whether the skeleton was that of a German or an Eskimo, he and any living relatives deserve justice if he was murdered."

"Very well, we'll work together on this. I'll continue to be obstructive and you can sympathise with Stone and Wentworth. I had the case file copied and it's in a safe place, just in case any evidence from the original file goes missing. Now, about this ring, if it hasn't been logged yet, make sure it stays that way for now, after all we've been told we aren't running this investigation, effective as from half an hour ago. So, we're just doing our job."

"Thank you Sir."

"Well then, get moving, you'd better get Frank Reichert to send this letter himself. The spooks can't ask us to prevent a private citizen corresponding with a foreign organisation about something he believes may be connected to his family. He'll have to change the thrust of his enquiry, asking about his father's disc in the first letter. Then we can judge how the old enemy views digging into the past. We may have to lean on the fact that WPC Reichert is only supporting her father in this private matter, at least for now. Once he has actually sent the first letter 'without our knowledge' we should meet with him again."

Black was astonished at the emergence of this sudden rebellious character of Moss. He'd always thought of him as an establishment veteran. He now had to speak with Connie as soon as possible, in order to 'relax' on logging in the gold ring. He knew she would take some convincing, but in fairness it couldn't be proven to have belonged to the deceased as yet. There were dozens of other items retrieved from the mud, and they had been discarded as irrelevant. They could be legitimately forgiven for keeping such a valuable piece to one side until there was good reason to officially include it. One such mitigating fact was the inner inscription of the initials M.V. and that was why Freda Collins had already been asked to investigate this as grounds for inclusion or elimination. So, they couldn't be accused of sitting on anything, it was simply in process. He didn't think she'd buy into this but he couldn't think of a better plan.

*

Maggie Reichert was livid, but realised there was no longer a legitimate way of her father using the investigation as a shield to extract information from the

Abwehr. "Sorry Dad, I can't say why this has happened and we would understand if you don't want to go ahead on your own. I'm told that things could change if anything you find out throws new light on our case, but that seems to be a long shot."

"So this young man, he must have been very young at the time he died, is finally discovered in our country, and someone decides that it isn't worth pursuing. What about any living relatives he may have back in Germany? Don't they have a right to know? This makes me very angry Maggie. Two can play at this game. If I'm not allowed to refer to the disc you brought to me, I will go ahead and ask directly about your Granddad's ID code. I've put this off so long because of what I might find out, and this sudden change by the local police adds to that feeling of discomfort. You can tell Inspector Black that I'm very disappointed in him, and remind him that he came for my help, not the other way around."

"Ok, I fully understand your position Dad, and I only wish that I could explain the reasons for all this, but that's not possible, I'd lose my job."

"Yes I know love, so off you go, and don't you worry about me, I've needed to do this for a long time, I just didn't know that I needed such a kick up the backside to make me angry enough to get on with it."

As Maggie left she saw her mother gossiping over the back garden fence with a neighbour. It was a graphic illustration of how tongues could be loosened in the most innocent ways. Like Moss, she was keenly interested in *who* was responsible for the case being hijacked by two strangers on the top floor. Black seemed to be more keen to know *why*. She knew she hadn't been told the full story and grudgingly accepted that this was deemed necessary containment. That didn't prevent her from keeping her ears open and quietly trying to figure it out herself.

*

68

As soon as she entered the canteen and dumped her keys on a vacant table, she was accosted by Black. "Do you want tea or coffee Maggie?"

"Neither, I'm going to have fizzy water."

"So, how did it go?"

"It didn't Sir, he was pretty pissed off that you lit his fire then sent the emergency services to douse the flames."

"I can understand that, and I'm really sorry. Is he going to contact this Abwehr?"

Maggie had her chance. "Who knows? He just clammed up at first and then eventually said we were a bunch of pricks. But he'd always known that. He also said that for a fleeting moment when you visited him, he had maybe misjudged the force, but not anymore. You really put me in a bad position with my family and I would respectfully suggest you don't do it again."

Black had anticipated several possible responses, but not this. It was Moss's instruction which he'd carried out instantly, but without processing it properly. He made a mental note that this had to be addressed.

Chapter 11
High Spen 1945

Michael hadn't been so happy for many a year. It was a curious yet symbiotic relationship he'd formed with Karl. As a chosen way of life, being a hermit, a dropout, a tramp or any of the other expressions the community used to describe him, he hadn't a desire to avoid people per se. He just couldn't stand conversational small talk. The villagers all seemed to be afflicted with complaining about their ailments, the cost of living, the buses being late, the weather, et al. None of this did anything but alienate him. Karl was perfect. They couldn't understand a word the other said, so it provided company without baggage.

Things were progressing to the essential vocabulary for survival. Karl had mastered yes, no, eat, fire, clothes, and a few other monosyllabic words. One of the most urgent tasks for Michael had been to appropriate new clothing for his friend, mostly from unattended washing lines. The Luftwaffe uniform could then be used as blankets. The rest of the communication was achieved through mime, gestures, and drawing in the soil with a stick.

From Karl's point of view, his new friend had not only provided a safe dwelling, but had essential local knowledge which would help him move on when the search was abandoned. The semantics of Michael's attempts to explain that Karl's campmates were going home, failed to register. He'd tried every day, so he wasn't feeling too guilty that Karl stayed.

*

Meanwhile, the stranger who'd taken Harry's drawing of the disc, was now in charge of overseeing the departure of the remaining airmen. Theo Devlin had produced the schedule and interrogated each one until he was satisfied there was no connection with any known wartime agents or double agents of espionage, or purveyors of

70

disinformation. He'd deliberately kept one particular airman until last, so that the others couldn't be used as corroboration or denial of anything.

"Good morning Gunther. It is Gunther isn't it?"

"Yes, you must know this."

"Can I have the disc?"

"Oh yes the disc, it is in mein bag, sheiss, the bag – it is there, still at the tent."

"Right, well bring the bag please and give me both discs."

"Each man in der Luftwaffe has only one disc."

"Yes, but you have kept Karl's disc safe for him, surely?"

"Ah, I now see your mistaking, it is lost from me. I only can believe one other colleague has it. You can ask them, it must be with one of them."

"I see, in that case please go and get your own disc, and then I will question your friends."

When Gunther returned, groped in his bag, and felt the disc, he handed it over without looking at it. Devlin had to alter his carefully laid trap. "This is Karl's disc, not yours. You need to tell me the truth. Start talking."

"It cannot be correct, my number is 23...9, mein Gott this is impossibly, this disc has the number 277. I did not have two discs during this night, I was cleaning my own disc with old stocking. What can I do now? This is yes, the disc of Karl. Where is mine?"

Devlin thought his shock was reasonably genuine, but it didn't alter the need to get all of the airmen together in one tent, separated from their kitbags and clothes. They were marched naked, one at a time, from one tent to another, protesting vocally, until they saw the gathering crowd of villagers who had come to see them off. The males who'd been shouting abuse at the Germans now switched to mocking laughter, until they realised the women were enjoying an unexpected treat. Some of the women put their hands over the children's eyes while they taunted their husbands and boyfriends. The men then dragged their partners away in case there was to be a repeat performance.

Each airman was asked in turn and in the presence of all the others about a missing disc. Devlin by now expected a wall of silence, despite the shock they displayed when he asked the question in perfect German. *'So none of you know where the disc is? The disc of Karl Heinz Buchwald? Yes we know his full name, his German address, and where the rest of his family is located. We need to speak with him urgently or it may hold up the departure of the rest of you. Think about this please, because I do in fact know where his disc is, but not how it got there. I've got all the time in the world.'*

The first signs of panic in the ranks appeared just as one of the Home Guard officers brought the news that a full search of the kitbags and clothing had produced nothing. Devlin shook his head and spoke once more in German. *'I am afraid your return must be delayed. You can all unpack and return to your own tents unless one of you has suddenly remembered something of interest to me about Karl Heinz Buchwald and how I found his disc. Oh, and Gunther, I believe your family name is Klein, so we must now find your disc, otherwise you will have to stay here indefinitely. Your friends may be able to help you to find your disc, I really hope so. Have a talk amongst yourselves for a while, then we'll bring everyone's clothes back before it gets really cold.'*

Devlin wandered up and down their ranks, listening for any hint uttered in German which might offer a clue to who the phantom disc swapper might be. He heard snippets of accusations and subsequent dismissals, but they were based on nothing more than guesswork. The most common chatter was about the predicament of Gunther, who was by this time sitting, totally perplexed, while the rest were still standing in groups, and he was having difficulty in holding back a panic attack. Devlin relented and ordered the clothes to be brought back. The devastated Germans then filed back to their own tents, all except Gunther. Devlin suggested they had an honest exchange in German. *'I don't want anything to be lost because your English is rather basic. Can we do that?'* Gunther nodded.

'Right, let's recount everything from the time you were cleaning your own disc.'

*

The modest terrace house was bursting with anticipation. Harry had a brand new outfit, brought home from college by his mother. Hilda couldn't believe this day would ever come, her husband Jack was on his way back. It had been difficult to keep the faith all these years. Bella had used up the dividend money to put on a welcome home party, and although she couldn't say that no expense had been spared, it was a very special event. She'd secured a chicken from Mr Wilson, and a neighbour had given her lots of fresh vegetables. Even though Hilda's father had deteriorated further, he had insisted on making the journey by bus from Harrogate. He was shaken up a bit by the rough roads and was taking a nap. Harry frequently asked when his dad would arrive, approximately every ten minutes. Hilda was glued to the front room window, from where she could look up the street to the main road. The bus stop was directly outside Cumberledge's shop, and just out of sight. But she would be able to see it pull away from the stop, heading for Chopwell, and she'd be able to recognise most of those who got off. The Venture service came through the village at twenty past the hour and ten to the hour, every hour until eleven pm. Two had gone by in the afternoon and a cloud of restlessness settled over the household. Despite the cold, Hilda decided to take Harry up to the bus stop, to relieve the tension. Through the billowing mist, they spotted the ten to three chugging up the final few yards to the Road-End club, and past the

Palace cinema. The engine noise altered to a less strenuous pitch and swung toward the kerb. As it halted with a slight lurch, Hilda's tears streamed down her cheeks on to her emerald-coloured silk blouse. Jack threw his kitbag on to the path and picked up Harry with one hand, pulling Hilda close to him with the other. They hadn't spoken to one another for five years. The embrace continued without words until Harry nuzzled his face between them. The bus pulled away and the three of them walked down the slope to the waiting friends, Harry was swinging from his mum and dad's arms for the very first time. The bunting came into sight and Jack began to struggle with his emotions. He'd imagined and dreamt about this scene so many times. The cocoon was pricked for both Hilda and Jack when Harry revealed his secret. "Dad, I've got a new football, can we play with it today? I gave my old one to a German soldier called Karl, but he's lost now. He was my friend you know, you mustn't tell anybody."

In a microsecond, a montage of flashbacks whirred through Jack's mind. He stumbled, then put Harry down. In his inability to come up with a cogent reply, he settled for, "Well that was kind of you Son. Do you miss your friend?"

"Yes, but I didn't know him very well, the same as you," said Harry, turning to the gathering of Jack's friends, "who wants to play football with me and my Dad?"

A local photographer had volunteered his services to capture this special day. This was the first day of Jack's rehabilitation as a civilian. A task which was a lot easier said than done.

*

Devlin reached into the depths of his acquired German vocabulary. '*Now Gunther think carefully about how everything was when you began cleaning your disc. Had you already lost Karl's disc?*'

'*Yes, quite some time before.*'

'*Did you tell anyone else?*'

'Only those in my tent.'

'Did any of them leave while you cleaned your disc?'

'No, I don't think so.'

'You need to be sure. Think carefully. Did any of these men comment on Karl's disc being lost?'

'Torsten said it would show up again, and not to worry so much, because Karl had made his own problem by escaping. Now I remember, when he said that, Albert went to the latrine.'

'How long was he gone?'

'Only two minutes I suppose, not more, he didn't take paper with him.'

'Did any of the men dislike Karl for any reason?'

'One or two, they were probably scared that his behaviour would get everyone in trouble.'

'Was Torsten one of these?'

'No, he liked Karl, but he felt the same as I did, expecting you to find him and send him back to Germany later.'

'Who was the third person in your tent?'

'Herman, but he was already asleep when I started cleaning my disc. He can sleep forever.'

'Right, how long were you cleaning the disc?'

'About twenty minutes, not longer. I stopped when we all heard an argument outside.'

'Who was the argument between? Could you hear what it was about?'

'It was in one of the far tents, but I can't say which one. It happens a lot when you're in a confined space with people you didn't choose to be with. It sounded as if there was disagreement over who would be a spokesman when we arrived back home. Something about all of us saying the same thing about how our missions went wrong, how we were captured, how we were treated and lots of stupid stuff. You see, we expect to be questioned when we arrive, even though the war is over.'

75

'I do see, now could you recognise the voices?'

'No, there was such a lot of shouting from other tents for them to stop because they couldn't sleep. This has been discussed many times already by all of us and we thought the decision was made, apparently not.'

'Was this at the same time Albert was at the latrine?'

'I don't think so, but it might have been, Torsten was laughing about it, calling those who were arguing idiots. He couldn't believe they were worried about an interrogation when we didn't even know whether our families had survived. He referred to them as trained monkeys and said if there hadn't been so many of them in Germany, there would never have been a war. Just a minute, Albert mustn't have returned by then otherwise he wouldn't have used that expression. Albert was one of these monkeys according to Torsten, and they once had a hell of a fight about it.'

'But Albert's voice wasn't one of the voices you heard during the argument?'

'No, well I can't be sure, as I said there was lots of shouting. He would have been interested in the outcome if there was a change of spokesman though. Anyway he was back in the tent before I finished cleaning the disc, and the argument was still going on.'

'Did you all go to sleep after the argument and the shouting stopped?'

'We tried but it took a while. We were excited about leaving today. I kept turning over and prodded Herman because he was snoring like a thunderstorm.'

'Was everyone in the tent when you did this?'

'Yes, well Albert was at the door of the tent, and I asked him to turn Herman on to his side to stop the snoring, as he was the nearest. I'm not sure but I think there might have been someone else just outside. I didn't hear anyone speak but it could have been a shadow.'

76

'Fine Gunther, that will do for now. Try to relax and I'll speak with you again.'

Chapter 12

Freda Collins was enjoying her jaunt around the extensive list of local jewellers, but as yet she hadn't found anyone who was confident enough to be certain about the origin of the gold ring. One of the more well-known stores put her on to a little shop in Heaton, a fairly cosmopolitan suburb of Newcastle. It was next door to a bespoke tailor, who explained that the owner, Mr Hajek, was out to lunch.

"What time do you think he'll be back?"

"You never know with Milan, he won't hurry if the food is up to his demanding standards," said the tailor, "you are welcome to wait here if you like, he's been gone more than an hour so he should not be too long."

"Thanks, but I could use a break myself, is there a nice tea shop nearby?"

"The closest is just the other side of the traffic lights, it is mainly frequented by students, but they have lovely cream scones."

That was the clincher, Freda had a distinct weakness for such decadence. "That'll do me, thank you."

"I will tell Mr Hajek to expect you if he returns before you do."

The owner of the tea shop was Polish, and she thought the tailor was Italian by name, but sounded French. When she returned to the jeweller's shop, Milan Hajek introduced himself, and Freda added Czechoslovakia to the list of nationalities. "How can I be of service Madam?"

A promising start, as all the English jewellers had only begun with, 'Yes?'

"I'm trying to find out where this ring was made."

"Let me see it. Are you looking to sell it?"

"Not at all, but I would be interested in a valuation."

"Ah, well that might be more of a matter of opinion."

"I'm sorry?"

"Well, the origin of the ring is a fact, the value is what someone will pay."

"Oh yes, I see."

He looked at the piece over and over again with an eyeglass before he offered any comment. "May I ask where you got this Madam?"

"Well, I'm not sure I can tell you that Mr Hajek."

"You cannot or you do not want to?"

"Why do you need to know anyway?"

"Because of its rarity and the high probability that it has been stolen. I think it might need to be reported to the police."

She showed her warrant card. "I am the police. I just need to know where the ring was made, and if possible by whom."

"I meant the Czech police, not the British lot, excuse me I did not mean..."

"Just tell me what you know please and we can move on from there."

"Very well, the ring was made in Germany, but if it is genuine, and I think that it is, I am pretty sure it belonged to someone from the nobility in Prague. Many such valuable artefacts were taken by both German and Russian soldiers during the wartime occupation. It should go back to where it belongs. At the very least, you should have it safely deposited with a reputable company. It is worth a hell of a lot of money if I am right about the authenticity."

"W-What?" muttered Freda, "you can't mean it is that valuable? I think I'd better get back to the station. Now Mr Hajek, I'm going to need you to come to see us as soon as you can, my superiors need to hear this from you, because they can't rely solely on my word with respect to what you've just said. They may wish to have you there if the Czech police are to be contacted. The less people who know about this the better. Do you understand?"

"This is what I understand! People have been killed for lesser pieces in the collection to which this belongs. I agree that nobody else should know until this is handed to the Czech police, and that includes your officers at the station. I can come as soon as I close the shop."

"In that case, I'll stay with you until we can get an unmarked car to take you over there. Can I use your phone?"

"Yes, help yourself."

Freda's fingers were trembling as she dialled the number. When Black came to the phone and she summarised the information for him, he simply said, "I knew it, I bloody well knew it would be something like this."

"What?"

"Nothing Freda, just talking to myself. Right I'll get a car over there with backup, tell Mr what's his name to close up now."

"He doesn't want to do that Sir."

"Ask him again nicely, and if he refuses just wait until the backup arrives, they'll take care of it. Well done Freda."

*

Black went directly to Moss. They chose to take a brief walk amongst the traffic outside the building. "If this guy is right Sir, I mean about it being very valuable, and that murders have been committed to acquire others in a collection, we have a strong motive, you know, to go along with the other circumstantial evidence. It could also explain why Laurel and Hardy are in town."

"Indeed Inspector. But it also makes it more difficult for us to keep our investigation under wraps. At least it will if we have to speak to the Czech police. Interpol will also be on our doorstep, or more likely demanding we are suspended."

"Mmm, how do you think we should play it then?"

"In small steps, this jeweller might be wrong, or a crackpot. It would be helpful if we could get this ring verified independently. I know an old university friend in London whose wife works in the auctioneering world, in the very top end. I can make general enquiries about the process of authentication of rare pieces. If it looks tricky, then I suggest we give the problem to Stone and Wentworth."

"What? That's conceding defeat isn't it?"

"Maybe not. If I inform the fountainhead of the police force first, there may be surprise, he may not yet know that MI5 and MI6 have already muscled in on us. It wouldn't be the first time the left hand is told what the right hand is doing, but not when. In fact the spooks trade on it. I'm not talking about the regular side of the Met Inspector, I would make it clear that I want 'Scotland Yard' type clearance to discuss the situation with them. After all, we report to the head of police operations, not the intelligence agencies, and definitely not their bosses, the politicians. It's in the constitution. It's also a gamble, but the alternative of keeping potential evidence supressed risks the careers of too many people. Let's set them against one another. If the decision goes against us, we can still 'officially' assist your friends Laurel and Hardy. If they had wanted to do all the legwork within their own organisation, they'd have hot-footed it off back to London with the file by now."

Black stroked his chin and nodded ruefully.

*

Constance Carr stood back from her latest autopsy, removed her gloves and washed up. "Let me see if I've got this right. I found the ring amongst the hessian and rotted fabrics and you were overjoyed. Because I had an overload of other work I hadn't logged it in as potential evidence. You jumped to the conclusion it belonged to the unidentified person whose remains we are still testing. Then you ask me to leave it unlogged until you get Freda to check it out for whatever is brewing in that devious brain of yours. I said I'd intended it to be logged in my own time and just hadn't got around to it. You were happy once more. Now you're here to ask me to log it in immediately and pass it to you for inclusion into your file, without giving me a chance to do tests on it. You've never asked me to do any kind of evaluation of the ring, and I gave it to Freda on the strict understanding it was not to be taken out of the pouch. Is that an accurate summary?"

"Well yeah, but…"

"Let me finish. It is of course your prerogative to direct my work to some degree, targeting the priorities and so on, however, if I find something which in my opinion is relevant I am supposed to bring it to your attention. Once we are agreed that it is potential evidence, there is a requirement to log it with an *official* report. This isn't optional, I was always going to do this, but I have detoured from procedure by conceding to your request to let Freda take it out of the building, without a written request from you, signed by your boss. Now you've changed to reverse gear without telling me why. Don't I deserve some kind of explanation D.I. Black?"

"It's a very delicate situation Connie. You've heard about the people on the top floor?"

"My career qualifies as a delicate situation if I even bend the rules, never mind break them. I've only heard rumours about the two people occupying the attic. And you aren't going to enlighten me are you?"

"All I can say at present is that they are not from the Met, but they are authorised to look at the files. Come on Connie, just think about it and leave certain things unsaid, then you legitimately don't know. I'll put my request to release the ring in writing and date it retrospectively, so that you're clear of that irregularity. But please don't press me yet on why I want you to log the ring right now. Moss and I have to check it out further and then ask you to look at it before we have to hand it over to the attic people. Logging it now will straighten it all out procedure-wise, well from your side I mean."

"Mmm, you need to give it back to me with your predated release request, and the form filled in that you have actually returned it today, to be officially logged as relevant evidence, and a second request to pass it back to you whenever you decide to do that."

"Jesus Christ, we – neither you nor I, can categorically state that this ring belonged to the deceased. It could even be completely disconnected, the landslip bringing it closer to the skeleton than it was originally. Come to think of it, you can't say for certain that the hessian and rotten fabrics belonged with the remains for the same reason. You might have to put that in your report. Yeah, that's a neat way of handling all of this - 'is it or isn't it stuff', and the variation in logging times. Do we have a compromise?"

"This will cost you big time if it goes wrong you know. If you give me the documentation I've asked for, I will log it today, with an appended explanation that it is indeed premature to conclude that it is definitely a possession of the deceased. When do you think you can tell me to try and find out if it is? You know, so that whatever it is that you know already, can then be officially shared with me."

"You should think about a switch to C.I.D. sometime, you'd make a good detective and you already have that poker face."

"Get out before I blow the whistle on you!"

Chapter 13
High Spen 1945

Theo Devlin did not look up when Albert came to the tent he'd set aside for his second questioning of the airmen on an individual basis. He had not allowed Gunther to speak with him since the revelation about the shouting match. He sat there for another few minutes hoping to detect uneasiness or shuffling of his subject. Eventually Albert coughed. Devlin lifted his head and gazed past him to the guard at the entrance. "Could you get me a brew sergeant?" he barked in English, "wait, do you want anything Albert?"

"Only water please."

"Oh so you can understand some English then."

Albert smiled awkwardly and said almost apologetically, "A few words, since I am here, not more."

"Good, then I will return to your mother tongue."

The eyes told Devlin that his adversary had probably understood the words brew and mother tongue. *'So, Gunther told me there was an argument in one of the tents last night. Do you recall that?'*

'Yes, but not which tent.'

'Why was that?'

'It was far away.'

'From your tent?'

'Yes, I don't think any of us know which tent was the one responsible for the noise.'

'Of course, so you were all in your tent at that time then, good. Couldn't you recognise any of the voices? I mean you have been living alongside these colleagues for months.'

'No, I couldn't hear very clearly and there were others shouting for them to keep quiet. Can I ask what this is about, when we are ready to go home?'

'That's a fair question, and has a very simple answer. I am late in getting here to High Spen, as I should have been

here some weeks ago. We have to make proper records for our government and yours. I could have signed the papers by now if it wasn't for the missing man, Karl. I know we could have just let it pass if it was a simple escape, but he didn't take his disc, and now it is only right that we find him and give it back. But everything has just got more complicated with Karl's disc going missing, then reappearing in Gunther's bag, and now his is missing. It's a bit of a mess. Being a pilot, you should know that there always has to be reconciliation of those booked on the travel list and the passengers who actually turn up. And the paperwork, including passports, have to match. In this case, we are talking discs, not passports. Can you see my problem?'

'No, not really. It just seems ridiculous, Karl will be found, you have his disc, and when Gunther's is located he can come home as well.'

'I hadn't thought about it like that, you're right, so why did you lie about being in the tent with Gunther, Torsten and Herman. Only Herman can't confirm that because he was asleep, but the others can. Do you see my problem now?'

Albert was beginning to sweat and yet it was still very cold. *'Yes, yes that was correct, I forgot, it wasn't important. Going home was important, just one more terrible night sleeping here.'*

'So, if you weren't in the tent, where were you?'

'I needed the latrine.'

'But the latrine was considerably closer to where the argument was taking place. Anyway, why didn't you just piss outside your own tent? As you say the only thing which was important was leaving today. Pissing outside your tent would only really be unhygienic if you were all staying, instead of leaving the next day. That would actually make more sense than someone exchanging Gunther's disc. He'd already cleaned it so that it was ready for inspection by

*either myself or the German authorities. So you see, I want
to avoid your people in Germany having the same mystery
to solve as I do now.'* Devlin smiled and thanked the
returning sergeant for his tea. Albert stared at the glass of
water. Devlin resumed in English.

"Now drink your water Albert, and clear your throat.
It's me that needs to piss now but I won't take very long."
He stood over the German, hesitated and then yelled in his
ear, "And you'd better be ready to tell me the fucking truth
when I come back or I'll find enough irregularities to keep
you here for years." He then pressed his face right into
Albert's and whispered, "I've already got a list as long as
my arm of poor bastards like you who lied to me, and you
will be visiting them soon in the south of the country if you
don't start telling the truth. You won't like what they have
to say about life down there."

Devlin returned, stood in front of his prey, and only then
zipped himself up, saying, "That's me done if you have
nothing further to add."

"Ok, ok, ok. I took Karl's disc without Gunther's
knowledge."

"Why?"

"Because I was asked to do it."

"By whom?"

"I can't say. I'm no traitor."

Devlin's eyes lit up then took on a steely determination,
and his nostrils flared as he had scent of the kill. He picked
up in German once more. *'In that case it's you who will
take the rap. Get your things packed, we need to catch the
first train to London.'*

'No, wait, all I can say is his name, not more.'

*'I think you should know by now that I'll be the judge of
whether you've told me enough for a reprieve.'*

*'Otto Steinmann. He said it was important that Karl was
captured, very important in fact.'*

86

'*Now come on Albert, important that we capture one of your own? In that case you must know why he had to escape, and from what you're implying, it wasn't from the British.*'

'*He has done something wrong but I don't know what it is.*'

'*So why did you have to take his disc to Otto and then steal Gunther's, while you put Karl's back?*'

'*Otto took all the information from Karl's disc and then told me we had to exchange it for Gunther's. That's what the argument was about. It was me who was shouting at Otto. He said I could do it while Gunther slept. He wouldn't say exactly why I had to do something so stupid, but he has Gunther's disc, or at least I gave it to him. And when I did he said the problem was solved. That's all I know.*'

'*It seems like Otto isn't just a fly boy then, he is working as an undercover agent for someone.*'

'*I was beginning to think that myself because he said he could make trouble for me back in Germany if I refused to cooperate. Can you keep me for a short time until he is convinced that I have told you nothing, then send me home?*'

Devlin was now in a quandary. If he let Otto know that he was on to him from speaking with Albert, he might lose the entire game. He thought it better to authorise another search for Gunther's disc, issuing a further threat to all of the prisoners, that they would be shipped to a secure unit pending charges of withholding vital information after the surrender had been officially signed.

He addressed the group in their own language as he wanted no conferring about English words. '*This blunder of yours could possibly go all the way to the top of your new governing body in Germany. Why should you all need to suffer for something like this? All I want is Gunther's disc, ask yourselves – why should this be a big deal? It's*

87

not lost, one of you has it. Oh well, we must begin a new search, and I'm afraid that includes probing your bodies.'

One of the group held up his hand. 'And what is your name?'

'Sepp.'

'Go ahead Sepp.' Devlin kept his eyes away from Otto, and having asked Sepp's name, tried to convey the impression that he couldn't remember anyone else's, other than those of Karl and Gunther.

'It might be nothing, but last night, well into the middle of the night, I had to go to the latrine and I saw the outline of someone in the dark, they didn't seem to be using the latrine itself, but throwing something into it, downstream.'

'That's more like it,' said Devlin, 'if we can find it you can all go home, except the person who threw it away. I'm sorry to have to say that as it was a German who threw it away, it's only fair that you Germans retrieve it. I can't ask our people to trawl through your shit to find one of your discs, which one of you threw away. Ok get started.'

The group began remonstrating amongst themselves and this led to blows being struck. Amidst the mayhem, Otto emerged and held up his hand. 'Your name please,' shouted Devlin, 'quiet, the rest of you.'

'Steinmann, Otto Steinmann. I would like to talk in private.'

'About what?'

'Finding this disc.'

'I thought we knew where it is, well, approximately. Do you have more specific information?'

'I told Sepp to say it was in the latrine. It isn't.'

'Very well Ottto. Let's go to my tent.'

It was crunch time. Devlin dismissed the guard at the entrance. 'It's just you and me.'

'I buried the disc.'

'Fine, let's go and get it.'

'I might not be able to remember the exact spot, so it could take a while.'

'What you mean is that after a while you won't be able to find it. Ok, then let us cut to the chase. Just tell me why you did this, because to be honest I don't give a shit if Gunther can't go home. Anyway he'll have company – do you get on well with him?'

Otto stood up and was told to sit down. He frantically weighed up the consequences, finally asking for protection. Devlin laughed out loud. *'How the hell do you expect me to talk about that when I haven't a clue who it is you want protection from or why?'*

'Because it is some organisation within your organisation.'

'Look, you've consistently lied or have others lie for you. And that means the first thing you must do is gain credibility. Start with why all of the bullshit with the discs took place.'

'This could cost my life, either here or in Germany, so you have to believe it, or I will say nothing further. The German intelligence operation will not be disbanded just because the hostilities have stopped. There is a hell of a lot to gain from the re-settlement of Europe. I will not betray my country, but there are some who will still hold power with whom I don't want to cooperate, and if I make this known it will spell my death. They want Karl Heinz Buchwald back to extract his knowledge. He found out about this, and the stupid bastard escaped, directing the risk to the rest of us, if we didn't help you to find him. How could we? We are confined to this camp. I came up with the idea of taking the disc which the little boy returned to us after the escape. I had to send someone back to Germany with the wrong disc – as Karl Heinz Buchwald. They would find out it wasn't him and probably torture the imposter to no avail, if he didn't know about the swap. I didn't choose Gunther, he simply had both discs. His

misfortune would save the rest of us from suspicion and they would have to demand you to look again for Karl Heinz here. Now do you see why I need protection whichever way I proceed.'

'Hold on a minute, how do you know all this about Karl being wanted? There's no communication into or out of this camp to Germany.'

'You may believe that Mr Devlin, but ask yourself why Karl Heinz would risk being shot by escaping when he knew the war was all but over. It's true that no German officials have vetted this camp, but what about Nazi sympathisers? Think about it carefully.'

'Mmm, well you can get me in the mood by giving me Gunther's disc, as I already have Karl's.'

'I will, please take me to the furthest point of the latrine to the south, and give me a shovel.' They left together.

Chapter 14

Frank Reichert had finally got the monkey off his back. In a carefully worded letter to the Abwehr, he said he'd recently discovered his father's dog tag in the loft and although Ernst had talked infrequently about his detainment in the UK, he hadn't ever mentioned the previous period, except to say that he was involved in the Eastern Front of the Krieg. He played on the entire family's interest in completing Ernst's biography for posterity, nothing more. He recognised that records may have been lost, using this as the rationale for enclosing the actual disc, and politely requesting it was returned after any search they could justify. The letter was phrased in a truly nostalgic tone. He hoped it would elicit a response.

He told Maggie about it, but asked her to respect it as a family matter, not for the police to know of, or her mother either. He didn't want her to worry all over again about the past, as she'd talked him out of taking the first step on numerous occasions.

*

Moss hadn't elicited any helpful information about the ring from his London auctioneers and allowed Black to play the opening moves of the chess match with Charles Stone and Marion Wentworth. "I thought you might be interested in this," dropping the ring on the table, "it is part of the debris which we extracted from the mud surrounding the skeleton. We couldn't be certain it belonged to the deceased until we'd done some checks regarding its origin. We've now got a lead that it may have been made in Germany, so it is being logged as evidence. We need you to sign for it, if you want to add it to the file."

Unexpectedly, it was Marion Wentworth who spoke. "Is that all you know? How did you trace it to Germany?"

Moss answered. "Does that matter right now?"

"It does if we need to keep the information on a need to know basis."

Moss smiled and said without intonation, "Yes, thank you for reminding me, it seems that our omnipotent one, sorry for the internal jargon, - the head of the police in the UK, knew about your interest in this case, but was ignorant of your need to 'take it over' so soon. He understood you were looking for any surprises which may crop up, which you feel need to be treated with a certain sensitivity. He fully expects us to carry on with our investigation and if there are examples of disagreement on how to proceed, your bosses will clear any changes with him or vice-versa. I don't really care as long as my boss is in the loop. So, I hope that makes us all feel comfortable working together now. In reality I don't see it making much difference; we keep you informed on everything, and if you have concerns, we either thrash them out or delegate upwards. It helps us to be completely open with you on how we're doing and if we don't understand anything you propose, we have recourse to an official challenge. I do recognise there may be things you can't tell us and if we are instructed by our boss to go with the flow, then we will."

Stone and Wentworth looked at each other but said nothing. Moss continued. "In order to keep everyone on track, Inspector Black has this written update for you with some of what we think we know about this ring, so it would be nice if you can tell us what information has to be on a need to know basis. The ring is a perfect example of how to handle evidence, as there is an assertion that it may not have legally belonged to our skeleton man after all. As simple policemen we tried to determine if there was any direct connection to the remains. This seems to worry you. Perhaps D.I. Black should tell you the rest."

The apprehension was tangible as Black cleared his throat. "Apparently the ring may have been originally in the possession of someone in Prague. Our friend who was buried in the coke works may have purchased it there, or at least obtained it there. On the other hand, it may not have been in his possession at all, and there is some other explanation."

The dynamic duo asked for a couple of minutes of privacy. After conferring, nodding and shaking of heads, Charles Stone announced he would be leaving to head back to London. "If this information is reliable, it should be pursued by the Foreign Office. Things may change and Marion can always get hold of me if they do." He left looking like a relieved man, with warm handshakes for Moss and Black.

Moss got back into his stride immediately. "Well that was an unexpected twist. I get the feeling you weren't surprised at the possibility of the ring having exchanged hands somewhere along the way Marion."

"That all depends on whether what you say can be substantiated. Charles will do a few checks on this issue when he gets back to London."

"Excellent, will he be able to shed any light on the engraving on the inside of the ring?"

"I don't know, maybe. Can you be more specific on where you obtained your assertion that it could have come from Prague?"

"Absolutely, we were going to do that anyway, the chap is waiting downstairs. But before we bring him up, does the prospect of that being true worry you? I'm not asking why that might be the case, but if you need us to back off, we need to give our boss a reason."

"I'd prefer to speak with your man first."

"I thought you would. I'm a bit disappointed, but there we are. We talk – you don't, not a happy marriage. We could do with a modicum of mutual trust. Right bring our man upstairs Inspector."

Milan Hajek was acquainted with names but not Marion Wentworth's function. The potential purpose of the ring and its possible link to the Luftwaffe was explored, stressing the need for it to be kept secret until he was told otherwise. Before he could challenge this Marion Wentworth served him with notice of this secrecy being official, as from that moment. "You are now a British citizen, and as such you can be prosecuted under the relevant act if any of our discussion is leaked in any way, not just here, but in your original homeland. You'll receive this caution in writing before you leave."

Black took up the questioning. "How can you be sure that this ring belonged to a person in the nobility in Prague?"

"Because I am an expert in the field of jewels, precious metal artefacts, and pearls. As I studied my trade in Czechoslovakia, I have first-hand knowledge of rare and valuable items from my own country. I also know quite a lot about stolen valuables which have never been recovered."

Marion intruded. "Would you be prepared to test out your claims of the history of this piece against an expert of our choice?"

Hajek burst out laughing as he began to explain. "Madam, any true expert in the western world would tell you the same as I have. If you would like to make a wager to accompany your test of my veracity, I would accept on one condition."

"And what would that be?" said Marion.

"That it is not a German."

Moss was about to ask why he would disqualify a German when Marion cut across him. "We can leave that for now Mr Hajek, I am inclined to believe you. It's been very helpful to talk to you."

"But you have not asked me about the inscription."

Again Marion got in first, glancing at Moss. "I will, but at another time, I promise. Thank you for your time." She tried to see him back downstairs alone but was frustrated by Moss tagging along with an affable expression on his face. It turned to thunder when Hajek was gone.

"I want to know why you stopped him from saying more about the initials or I'm going to ring my boss right now."

"That would only complicate matters Superintendent. I will share with you what I can when we are alone."

Moss wasn't happy about excluding Black but fortuitously there was an incoming call. Freda had taken it, and now sought out her boss on the top floor. "Sir, there's an irate Eric Paisley on the line and I think you should read the evening edition of the local paper."

"Shit Freda, I clean forgot to meet with Paisley, and it was at my request. Ok, I'll come downstairs to take it."

He began with a profuse apology but was stopped in mid-sentence. "Inspector, I have no interest in your regrets, genuine or otherwise. I merely want to inform you that I went to the old coke works site and I can confirm that the landslide was where the engineering block used to be. One other thing did come to mind while I was there. It may mean nothing, but while I was standing on the precipice and looking at my predecessor's notes made at the time, the date of June the fifteenth, 1945 headed the page. And below was one word in capitals – FOUNDATION! At the bottom of the page however he'd made another note that I must have personally checked years later. He must have been curious as to whether the estimated volume of concrete proved to be accurate, for cost purposes, to keep tabs on the budget for the new building. I flicked ahead a few pages and there it was, he had expressed his concern. The initial quote was exceeded by more than seventeen percent. As nobody had mentioned this, he duly demanded an explanation. The contracted surveyor apparently placated him by stating that the soil report had been late coming in and it had produced a need for alteration of the specification. Last minute amendments were therefore made to increase the area of the slab, and include metal piles before pouring. I remember the exchange of memos in the file, my predecessor was incandescent with the surveyor about not being informed, but was quickly assured that it was a cost which would be absorbed by the construction company, and it would give everyone peace of mind. He also said that there would be minimal delay to the project. I thought at the time, even years after the event occurred, that something improper had transpired, backhanders in cash, or some such grubby behaviour.

"So, after closing my notebook, I looked again at the dislocated slab and I couldn't see any evidence of piles, but the area did seem to be larger than the original plan specified. I asked the security men on the site to make a proper measurement, as I was not dressed for such a romp in the mud. They reluctantly agreed and the slab is indeed considerably bigger than the original plan had called for. As far as I know, there was no amended plan submitted, which is strange, because the building regulations would have required it. I hope this is helpful and that you won't darken my door again." The line went dead.

Black was still mentally entangled in what this could mean when Freda pushed the evening edition under his nose. His jaw dropped when the headline had been assimilated.

Remains of Luftwaffe POW found at Northeast Industrial Site.

The journalist's name was familiar – Sophie Redwood. It was another slip up, Black had failed to respond to her request to speak with him. The rest of the story was just as worrying. As usual with journalists, they were prepared to suggest certain things and leave the denials to those who were involved in their own account of events. The dog tag was mentioned, and the possibility that it may end up as a suspicious death, citing the fact that the police were still investigating what was initially thought to be a forty year-old accident, and despite requests to speak with the investigating officer, there had been no reply.

It was an extract from a national publication which had been pasted into the local edition, and Black's first conclusion was a no-brainer. The shit was heading directly for the fan. He was in for an interesting discussion with Moss.

Chapter 15
High Spen 1945

Despite the continuing scarcity of life's comforts, their spirits were high. Bella was busy frying produce from Mr Wilson's latest slaughter of a pig. The pan was heaped and sizzling away on the open coal fire, Hilda was ironing near the door to the scullery and the two men were sat at opposite sides of the glowing coals talking about going to see the local football team play. Spen Black and White was a name which was both respected and feared by other local teams. Harry was on his dad's knee and wanted to go to the match.

"Will you promise to be a good boy and not run on to the pitch?"

An enthusiastic nod was followed by Harry's grandfather mentioning that they could go to Bella's sister's house for a cup of tea at half-time. Florence-Hilda lived right next to the ground. "What's half-time Granddad?"

There was no immediate reply as Bella asked everyone to sit up, the lunch was ready. Harry still wanted an answer and ran over to his granddad just as Bella turned with the frying pan. Harry's face and shoulder hit it head-on. His screams could be heard quite a way up the street, as the sizzling fat seared the side of his face and penetrated his vest. There was panic. Hilda rushed to the kitchen sink and turned on the cold tap. Jack yelled that she should not pour water on the affected areas and demanded to know where the tub of Vaseline, which seemed to be essential in every household, could be found. He had helped to treat burns on the battlefield on many occasions. He had been told that preventing air from getting to the affected area as soon as possible was important in reducing scarring of the skin. Bella was transfixed, glued to the spot, and seemed unable to function for the first time in her life. Her husband,

Cappy, told Jack where to look, and told Hilda to go for the doctor. Jack smeared on a thin layer of Vaseline and tried desperately to comfort his son, but the best he could achieve was to reduce the squeals to a pained wailing.

Doctor Mary Livingstone lived above her surgery about half a mile away, and although this wasn't open on Saturday, she would attend emergencies. Lucky that she hadn't gone out, Hilda pleaded with her to examine her son.

Her first action on seeing Harry was to explain what she was about to do. "His face is already badly blistered, we must attend to that first, but while I do that, please cut away his vest carefully from his skin, it will be painful."

The appearance of a scalpel terrified Harry and Jack had to hold his head still. The shrill screams returned as the doctor carefully pared away the blistered skin, and applied another smudge of Vaseline to the layer underneath. Little Harry was continually appealing for the pain to stop, but still had to endure the delicate peeling back of the cut strips of vest from his shoulder and upper arm. When this was completed, the doctor administered an oral sedative and he drifted off to sleep in his mother's arms. Dr Mary made them all aware of the prospects. "The time taken to strip the vest from his skin has unfortunately allowed the pattern of the fabric to hold, and then imprint itself on to his arm. The hot fat has then cooled, forming folds and this will also result in disfiguration. His face isn't so bad, but we won't know how much of the dermis has been damaged for at least another two days. You need to keep the dressing on until then. As much as Harry wants to take it off or scratch at it, you must prevent him."

Bella was distraught, replaying the incident over and over, every time concluding it was her fault. She couldn't be persuaded otherwise. The traumatic event had taken its toll on Cappy, and he had to be taken back to Harrogate. It was going to be a long two days.

*

Otto quickly unearthed Gunther's disc and handed it to Devlin. He then became emboldened, and unsettled the Englishman by a veiled threat in German. *'If you don't follow up on who could have been passing information into this camp you will regret it, whatever happens to us. We haven't had many visitors, but they knew everything about us. The information could only have come from Germany or someone who represented German intelligence in this country. They knew things about our flying missions which only those of us who were piloting the planes had invested in them. Your options are limited. You either have to find and expose these people, if higher authority allows that, or carry on our deception with the discs, or find Karl Heinz and get him back to Germany as soon as possible.'*

Devlin didn't reply and simply asked the guard to accompany Otto back to his friends. He then strolled around the perimeter of the camp, mulling over what the German pilot had said regarding someone having detailed knowledge of the Luftwaffe air raids. As he himself was employed in British Intelligence, ultimately accountable to the Foreign Office, albeit in a little understood and extremely convoluted way, he wondered why he hadn't been briefed about this aspect. He'd been asked to come to the Northeast, amongst other regions, to 'tidy up' loose ends in preparation for the official end of the second world war, and just as important, what was to happen next. He'd accepted the rationale that a senior officer such as himself should carry out these 'chores' simply because odd-ball situations could arise. The top brass didn't want the entire chain of command to be accessed for every little discrepancy, and the repatriation had to be done quickly and smoothly. He was that authority, and he was expected to be decisive. He'd had a few irregularities in other regions but only in terms of items of identification lost in plane crashes. This was different.

Theo Devlin ran the options through his analytical mind once more, not forgetting the expected time deadline. Finding Karl Heinz Buchwald was not a quantifiable choice. Allowing the disc deception no longer had merit because it depended on Gunther's ignorance of the scheme, and it was now known by all of the airmen. Even a hint of a suggestion that there could be an unknown German sympathiser in the ranks of British Intelligence would be squashed. It would be considered 'inconvenient' during the post-war period, unlike times of conflict, when complex covert investigation would swing into action. He would make a fool of himself and be diverted to the pathway of retirement or worse. Now was not the time to rock the boat. Gunther had his disc back, he had Karl's, and although the search had faltered, he would have it upgraded again. It wasn't as tidy an explanation as would be expected, but Karl had escaped before he got here. The repatriation papers were signed and the men readied for departure.

When the transport arrived and the airmen lined up to board, there was relief on every face except that of Otto. The German glanced at Devlin, wondering what now awaited him back in the Fatherland.

A Foreign Office car was also waiting to take Devlin to London, and it drew a line under his time in High Spen. The recapture of Karl Heinz Buchwald was the only event which would bring him back to this little village, which was busy recovering from the real damage of the war, or so he thought.

*

Michael and Karl could now gibber to one another in pigeon English, and there were signs that the German wanted to discuss moving on. Michael was torn, as these had been stimulating times for him. He felt important, something he'd never hankered after, yet it wasn't an unpleasant sensation. He had begun to see himself as the fulcrum of how the situation would play out. He had a swagger when talking with the villagers, which slowly groomed his self-esteem. There was also a certain mischief about playing both sides of the game. The only negative was the prospect of losing his new friend, but he couldn't delude himself, Karl could never stay indefinitely, and wanted to move on to somewhere that he could walk without risking arrest. It meant that he would have to become much more fluent in English and blend in to a city population. Michael accepted that he wasn't the right person to make this happen.

*

Miraculously, Harry's face was considered to be healing without much scarring. The dressings were changed regularly and he was to be kept away from school for a while longer. His shoulder was also improving but a large area of his upper arm had been grotesquely altered to look like a topographical snow scene. The vest had bitten deeply and twisted most of the flesh, but left what looked like footprints of small unaffected areas. It would be permanent. It could have been worse. His dad came in carrying a box. Before Harry could ask what it was, Hilda's searching look was answered. "I got the job! I start on Monday, labouring on a building site in Benton."

"Oh well, it's a start, but you won't be happy having to be a lowly navvy for very long."

"I won't have to, I signed up to be trained as a bricklayer."

"What's in the box Dad?" inquired Harry.

"It's a pile of wood. I'm going to make you a swing. We can put it on the garden gate. How about that?"

"When can we do it?"

"I have to measure everything and cut the wood, we can start at the weekend."

The positive vibes were checked somewhat when the postman arrived. Bella took receipt of a letter postmarked with 'Harrogate'. Her fingers could scarcely tear open the envelope. The news wasn't good, but not what she was dreading. Her husband had fallen while being helped out of the hot mineral bath, and had fractured his wrist. Of more concern was his post-traumatic respiratory function. It was thought that some dislocation of his shoulder was responsible for the physical pain experienced in breathing. As this effectively complicated his existing condition they were considering moving him to a regular hospital. "I'll have to go Hilda, we can't leave him on his own down there."

They embraced and Hilda made a suggestion. "I'll try to arrange time off, and we can take Harry with us on the train. Jack has to go to work on Monday, so there would be nobody to look after Harry anyway. It would do us all good, and my father would be so pleased to see us all."

Despite the considerable expense involved it was agreed. Jack nodded and picked up his son. "The swing should be ready when you get back kid. I'll start on it now."

"Ok," said Harry sheepishly, "will I be able to play on it with my bad arm?"

"Of course you will, I'll push you, you just need to grab and hold on to the ropes, and we might even give Grandma a ride on it."

"You'll need a lot more wood than that if you're going to get my backside on to your swing."

Chapter 16

He was kept on hold for a long time before he heard her voice. "Inspector Black, I thought you might eventually call back. I suppose the article did the trick?"

Sophie Redwood's diction was as near perfect as he'd ever heard, and although the intonation betrayed a hint of sarcasm, she had an extremely sexy voice.

"You know it did. I can understand your frustration when I failed to return your first call, but there was a hell of a lot going on, and I wasn't being rude, I just didn't get around to it."

"And this call is to express your concern at what I went to print with, or to try and figure out what comes next?"

"Both, if I'm honest. I'm not going to tiptoe around this, some of what you printed was information which hadn't been made known to anyone but the officers on the case. My only regret is that I didn't get back to you, and at least hear what your intentions were. Some of it is pretty unhelpful to our investigation, apart from causing us to wonder if any of our own people may have leaked it to the press. There are others who would know some of what appeared in your article, but not everything. Well anyway, that's not something I know for sure but it still bothers the hell out of me."

"What about your visitors?"

"Excuse me," Black stalled as he gathered his thoughts, "visitors, do you mean the winding down officer for the coke works, the ex-management personnel, or those university people?"

"Hardly newsworthy Inspector, any of them. Perhaps if we'd spoken earlier I could have forewarned you of the vultures from the Capital."

There was an uncomfortable silence while he digested this remark. She let him dangle, forcing a reply. "How do you expect me to answer such a question? Is this call being recorded?"

"I thought about it, but gave you the benefit of the doubt. There seems to be a lot of concern in the hallowed corridors of power that your investigation is spilling over into some events at the end of the war. It's not supposed to happen like that. Apparently, the pulses raced when certain files were declassified, but those fears were not justified. Then along you came with some old bones. You couldn't make it up could you?"

"Ah, those visitors. I could ask how...."

"You could, but it might be better to meet. If you're allowed to find out more by your own means, do so. But I've had to work really hard to convince my editor to run this story, and I have a source who will back up my assertions when the time comes. We could help one another, if you wanted that. I would be able to expose things which you can't, if you trust me."

"Mmm, ok. I'll get back to you very soon, as long as you realise I want to prosecute this case for only two reasons, the first is to obtain some kind of justice for this unknown individual, if there has been foul play. But there is also the compulsion to solve a puzzle which nobody else can. And that could get both of us into deep trouble."

"I'm fascinated, I look forward to your call."

Black put down the receiver, held his head in his hands and thought about the risks of telling Moss or not telling him of his entire conversation with Sophie Redwood. He didn't really like this pseudo-cooperation with MI6, and he instinctively felt that the police would in reality, be siphoned of knowledge, without receiving anything but roadblocks in return. On the other hand, he couldn't openly refuse to pass on information if either Moss or Wentworth knew of its existence. He opted for taking the flak right now on the article which had already rattled their respective cages, but at least for the present, he would not disclose any meeting with the journalist until he knew a little more about what he was dealing with.

*

Moss ushered Marion Wentworth up to the attic, invited her to sit, and in a clearly irritated tone said, "Well, you said you'd talk when we were alone?"

"Asking Mr Hajek about something prematurely is not our way Superintendent. I believe I know what the inscription means, who had it done, and where they are right now. I didn't see any virtue in engaging him any further unless we need him to confirm knowledge we think we have. Timing is critical in such exchanges, it is different in your line of work. It's both fortunate and unhelpful that you've unearthed Mr Hajek in such a haphazard, random or utterly improbable way. The same can be said about the remains having surfaced in the first place. Both events have occurred and we have to deal with that."

"All very interesting and enlightening, the cloak and dagger stuff of conspiracy. I'm afraid I need more than that, otherwise this becomes the first test of how our bosses will tell us how to proceed. I'm not going to be fobbed off with shadows and taboos every time we get a new lead. You could start by making a real effort to stop insulting my intelligence. I'd wager you're sitting there knowing whose remains were found, and to whom it's important that *we* don't find out, thus avoiding any connection to Germany, during the actual years of conflict. Your job is to babysit that information. It really does annoy me intensely that I have to accept such fanciful justification of obstruction. The political landscape has moved on in forty years and so has the cold war, so until investigating a probable homicide is no longer my duty, you'll have a pretty hard time here. Do you want to say anything else before I call Scotland Yard?"

"Go ahead, make your call. You are becoming increasingly paranoid about this. In a modern democracy, government is about containment, not the visionaries of previous eras. You should know how these things work, for example, if it had been necessary you would have been relieved of this case at the outset. It could have been transferred to London on day one. That won't happen because it could bring other unnecessary complications. For God's sake wake up Superintendent, if you want to conduct a neutral, politically-free investigation. And that's also what I want, so we actually have a common cause. Without insulting your intelligence, it's presently my job to ensure you do yours. Pointing out no-go areas and political detritus from long ago, if they arise. You can't just look at your responsibilities in isolation in this particular case, and I won't interfere unless I have to. That's why Mr Hajek's involvement has to be treated with caution, or if you prefer it, handled. Now if you will calm down I can reveal that the inscription probably denotes the initials of a person named Max Vogt. Does that help you? Not yet it doesn't! I can't say for certain whose remains you have found but they aren't his. I want to know whose they are as much as you do. I have a list of possibilities, but I want your investigation to take its course without undue bias. Are you beginning to get it or not? I hope so because if you make your call, you will soon be asked to step back from leading the investigation."

Moss twiddled his thumbs before taking out his pipe and lighting it. Through the smoke he spoke with his normal calmness. "Are you able to tell me how you know that initials M.V. belong to a Max Vogt?"

"Yes, I have a report with me from an officer of the crown which was produced in 1945. It mentions many things, one of which is a gold ring which has these initials inscribed on the inside. Written at the side of a photograph of the ring is the name Max Vogt, and other appended notes. Do you accept that this is all I can tell you at present? He may not be relevant to finding out who was buried in the coke works, or he might provide a crucial link. I'd rather Mr Hajek is monitored rather than courted, until we decide otherwise. I'm about to arrange the surveillance now. Are we done?"

"I think so, that wasn't so hard now was it Marion? I'll leave you to it."

*

Black braced himself for the worst. He was pleasantly surprised that Moss was deep in thought, puffing away on his pipe, and welcomed his presence. "Sir, I know I screwed up by not handling the journalist properly. I have no excuses to offer and it should have been prevented."

"It isn't the end of the world Inspector, just don't let it happen again, put her through to me if she comes back for more. I'm more concerned about where her information came from. Is there anything else?"

Black was so surprised that there was no hint of a reprimand, and he struggled to think of anything to say. He blurted out a garbled summary of Eric Paisley's statement that there was supposed to be piles driven into the foundation at the coke works to help reinforce the stability of the slab. "The surveyor's report said the concrete was to be poured on to these piles."

"And?"

"Sorry, I was just reminding myself of the actual scene after the landslip."

"Ah yes, your photographic memory?"

"Paisley couldn't find any evidence of piles because they'd have been on the underside. But he also said they should have scored the slope as it descended or be snapped off. He's right, I can see it now, and there were no score marks. I think we have to check the underside Sir."

"To prove what?"

"Well, firstly, why there were no amended plans submitted to further scrutiny by building regulations, and therefore why the surveyor's recommendations were ignored. It could help explain the incredible lengths someone was prepared to go to in order to gain time to place a body where it would never be found, or it simply offered up an opportunity at the right moment. Paisley did indicate a delay in the initial pouring date. Also, there was no extra charge for the serious increase in the area to be concreted. It stinks, seems like nothing, but details like this are important."

"Sometimes you amaze me Inspector. Carry on with the good work, I have to make a call, excuse me."

*

Moss was thinking through exactly what Marion Wentworth expected to achieve by shadowing Milan Hajek. He decided to look at it in a different way. A personal friend in the Inland Revenue was contacted. "Julian, Oswald Moss, it's been a long time. How is everyone?"

"Well, well, old Oz. We're all fine, including two grandchildren. Marjorie, and our daughter Alice are actually up in the Northeast with them at the moment. Her mum is over ninety now you know, and she's in care. Marge wanted a photo of all four generations. Her mother is doing ok, but she wanted to see the kids while she still has all of her faculties, and she is a bit too frail to travel. Anyway, is this purely social? I feel bad about letting the contact slide."

"Now you've made me squirm. It's a favour I'm after. How far back can you trace tax records of individuals?"

"Depends on a few factors, but there has been a kind of cut-off point for, shall I say, 'normal' people, if the revenue fails to collect tax. There are obviously exceptions if we're dealing with suspected tax evasion or avoidance. What is it you are after?"

"It's probably nothing but I was interested in a foreign national who may or may not have been registered for tax in this country."

"What period are we talking about?"

"I don't really know, that's the problem. It could have been any time from the end of the war until now, if he is still here and alive."

"I don't think there's much chance of running him to ground. Was there anything special about him?"

"He was German and may have had connections with the spooks. He was probably here under one or more aliases. Ok, just forget it Julian, it was a long shot."

"It's not the kind of enquiry which would go unmissed Oz, it's quite risky. I can do some background checking and that's about all, no specifics. What's the name?"

"Max Vogt, V-O-G-T. Now don't do anything stupid Julian, this is just a hunch I'm working on, it isn't crucial."

"Understood, I'll get back to you one way or the other."

Chapter 17
High Spen 1945

Michael was frantically trying to explain the change in the situation to his friend. "Karl, it has happened already, the Luftwaffe boys have gone home," he made flying gestures by spreading his arms and simulating aircraft noise, "yesterday, they go to Deutschland."

Karl's English vocabulary had expanded enormously, and grammar wasn't an issue. After all, the two of them had nothing else to do, other than eat and keep warm. "My friends, they are at home now?"

"Not just your friends, all Luftwaffe boys. It was on the radio."

"This is good, no?"

"Yes, it is for them but I heard from the village that they are going to send more people to find you?"

"For me? I don't want to go to Deutschland."

"Maybe it's not to go home. I don't like it. I think you must stay here longer. If you run they will catch you."

"But now I can go to the police and ask to stay in England."

"No, the radio said any German men who have escaped from camps will be kept here for questions, and then sent to Germany later. They won't let you stay."

"Something must change Michael. I cannot stay here for all my life."

Michael was crestfallen, and in this very moment it fully dawned on him that Karl was never going to be happy if there was no prospect of getting back to mainstream society. He'd hoped he might adapt and enjoy the wild. It wasn't to be. "You have to be very careful, but I'll help you. The problem is your English, it will give you away."

"In the city, Newcastle, there will be people sleeping in the streets, yes?"

"Lots of people Karl, but not Germans. They would tell the police about you if they could get money for it."

"But Newcastle has ships, and I can get work. I will go to Germany if I can do it with a trade ship. I still have my family there and they will keep me safe. It is only the German officers I must not meet. Yes, this is a good plan, can you help me?"

"I'll try to find someone who knows about merchant ships, but Karl, the war has just finished, so there might not be many going to Germany just yet. And I think the police will be checking them."

"Yes, you are right in this point. I will have to be – what is it? Some cargo? I will hide in the bottom of a ship. We must find one which goes to the north of Germany, Hamburg is good. I know people there. Thank you my friend, I would like to stay in England with you, but not living in the woods."

*

The news of the repatriation had spread quickly throughout the region and it suddenly occurred to Jack, that this continuing hunt for Karl would ultimately impact his own son. He asked Harry if he wanted to join the volunteers to find his friend. "If they find him, he will have to go back to his family in Germany. He might have a little boy like you. If we help the police to look for him, you can say goodbye. Would you like that? We can help at the weekends."

"Yes, and when he goes home can I go to see his little boy?"

"I don't really know if he has a son, I'm just trying to explain why he will want to see his family, just like I did when I was so far away from all of you."

"Ok, can we give him a present to take home?"

"Why not? I'll try to think of something for this weekend."

That night Jack went to the Field Club after his evening meal, tired from a hard day's work at the building site. The bar was crowded and the decibel output was verging on splitting ears, mostly because of arguments regarding the outcome of the forthcoming grudge football match between Spen Black and White and Chopwell. In the smoke-filled bar, Jack was telling one of his pals about taking Harry on the search for Karl. The smell of sweat from dozens of working men was extremely pervasive and yet totally ignored. Unaware that a bystander from a different group was eavesdropping, Jack mentioned that he had promised to take a present, in the event that they did find the German. The noise level faded as a man, not resident in the village, but temporarily employed there, began to bait Jack.

"We've only just got rid of these bastards from the village and you're talking about handing out gifts to the one who got away. Fucking Nazi convert."

Jack's friend, Tommy Hume, tried to restrain him from responding. "Leave it, this nutter is always looking for trouble."

Jack turned to the man and quietly asked if he had fought in the campaign. This caused the background noise to escalate again. There were obviously many who sided with this stranger.

"No I didn't, like many of us I worked the mines, to keep the bloody country's energy supply going. Now I have a trade to my name. What's it to you?"

"Then you made your contribution. But you have no experience of what it's really like being told to kill people. These German soldiers were told the same, and it wasn't so difficult to realise your own survival had to come first. It became more of a problem when we were told to clean out foxholes with grenades, even though we knew the people inside wanted to surrender. If you've never looked a man in the eye before you killed him, then you should reserve judgement on his character."

The man spat on the floor and moved closer. Jack prepared himself as he spoke, "Unlike this country, where there has been debate about conscientious objectors, the Reich made sure there was no such thing in Germany. Yes, I've spoken to young men we captured, and many of them didn't want to go to war at all. It's the politicians who wage war, not these kids. Now, what experiences are your comments based on?"

There was a short hiatus in the dialogue, during which the noise was completely doused. The big stranger produced a knife. "On the fact that my brother was killed by these filthy swine."

"I'm sorry to hear that. My own brother was also shot by Germans in 1918, just a few days before the fighting stopped. I know exactly how you feel. It doesn't change what I just said."

This actually enraged the man, and he lunged forward. Jack was nimble enough, and well-practised in avoiding bayonets. A group of the man's friends gripped him and relieved him of the knife, one of them saying, "Ralph, if you want to fight one of our soldiers, it has to be a fair fight, he's unarmed."

Confident in his size and strength, the stranger nodded. A ring of spectators was formed, while the barman despatched one of the customers for the constable. Jack had earned a reputation for this kind of combat, and it had been accompanied by an appropriate nickname. 'Biff' was derived from the technique itself, and conferred by soldiers in his regiment who'd suffered at his execution of it. Most fist fights, like wars were won before they were fought. Saturday night bar brawls were not much different, and Ralph depended on assets which would never come into play. Jack waited, coiled and watching his adversary's transfer of weight from one foot to the other. It came, and signalled a right hand punch. The auto-response was B (body) I (incapacitate) F (face) F (flatten). The natural tendency of wanting to immediately smash the opponent in the face drove Ralph to nullify his weight advantage. Jack feinted one way, side-stepped the other, not only avoiding the blow, but unbalancing Ralph, causing him to run on to a sapping right hand to the solar plexus. The momentum from both men was additive, and effectively cut off the big man's ability to take breath. His massive arms fell by his side and Jack delivered a crushing left hook to the jaw. His foe's legs buckled and he was in a heap on the floor. His friends carried him out before the police arrived and Jack resumed his chat with Tommy Hume.

It had done his reputation no harm. Word got back to his employer, Thomas Armstrong & Son. He was being depicted as fair-minded, modest, able to deal with trouble, and not least of all, a man who'd fought for his country. He didn't have long to wait for a transfer from labouring work to a trainee bricklayer.

*

Two days later Harry and his dad joined the search. The present Jack had mentioned to his son turned out to be a pair of fur-lined leather army gloves, as a barrier against the cold. Jack had an inkling that if Karl was caught, he'd be confined somewhere without heating. Nothing came of their efforts, and Harry was tired by the time the daylight began to fade. As they relished the supper Bella had made, she told them that another group searching for Karl had found a man hanged beside a bend in the river running through Chopwell Woods. Harry didn't immediately connect this to his German friend, but Jack said, "Was it Karl?"

"No it was that tramp who hangs about the village from time to time. But they reckon he did have some stuff on him which could belong to the airman. There's a watch for instance. Quite an expensive one they say, and it is a German make. Maybe he stole it from the airman and Karl killed him."

"I don't think so Bella. Soldiers wouldn't hang someone for a theft, more likely they'd strangle them, hit them over the head with a rock, or even stab them – not take time out to find a rope and hang them."

"Yes I suppose so. Anyway, they're now looking at all of Chopwell Woods, they think he's in there somewhere."

Nobody was to know that Michael had walked with Karl through the night to Newcastle docks, and they had bid each other a tearful farewell. Karl's watch was a gift to his 'landlord', who had lived so long before finding his first true friend. Michael had wept almost incessantly all the way back to the woods, and without any further deliberation, he entered the cavern, took the rope and chose the spot where he first set eyes on Karl. He couldn't rationalise why he was unable to go back to his lone existence after all these years. By taking his own life in this way, he'd unintentionally put the police on to the wrong scent. He had reasoned that Karl would never know of his suicide if he managed to get aboard a ship. Because Michael's death was being investigated as a murder, there was little information released, and no funeral would take place for the time being, with no next of kin to object. His passing changed nothing in the village, but indirectly improved the chances of Karl escaping the country. Then there was the matter of the watch. With nobody to claim it, the case file became its home for many years.

Chapter 18

Moss had engineered an olive branch to present to Marion Wentworth, without discussing it with anyone on the case. He'd roped in some of the uniformed staff to collect innumerable old files from a store room, and temporarily pile them in a holding cell which needed a facelift. By re-jigging the decorators' schedule, they spruced up the store room first. It was a pleasantly warm room, unlike the attic, and had a window on to a courtyard. The lawn had a central patio, and there were several architectural antiques scattered around the perimeter. The decorators were then despatched to the holding cell, as the old files were to be shifted up to the attic.

"May I ask what is going on?" said Marion.

"Come with me please while we finalise the transfer. I felt a bit guilty about you sitting up here all on your own."

She was very happy to see her new office but asked how she was expected to pay for it. "There's no such thing as a free lunch, I'm told."

"Just accept my apologies for you having to sit and freeze up there. It only took a bit of lateral thinking to sort it out. I'll still be asking the same awkward questions, that's not going to change. Since you've brought it up, you mentioned a report you had from an officer of the crown about events in 1945. Why can't I know his or her name?"

"If I believed I could tell you that I would have already done so. Things may change."

"Ok, just checking. I've convinced myself that it must have been a report about something in this region if it pertains to this case. I'll do a bit of digging."

*

Sophie Redwood had taken the flight from Heathrow to Newcastle. Black was nervous about being seen and whisked her away to a remote pub in rural Northumberland. He wasn't going to impress her with the reception of this venue; it was in need of a lot of work, but the place enjoyed a good reputation as a restaurant. She looked around the dingy, time-worn lounge and began to wonder what she was doing here. Black informed the barman that they would go straight to the table. It was a different world they entered – bright, clean and effusing a seductive aroma. After the waiter took their drinks order, he explained.

"My boss doesn't know I'm meeting you. That's why I chose this place, it's a busy day when they have six tables occupied."

"It's all a little melodramatic Inspector, isn't it? Why shouldn't your boss know?"

"He's a bit too cosy with the vulture from the Capital, as you refer to these people. The other one has gone back to London, but Superintendent Moss is being run by the woman who stayed. Let's order the starters before we talk any more shop."

They both perused the highly unusual selection available from the menu, and Sophie was impressed, so much so that she found it difficult to choose. Black watched her every expression, thought that her appearance certainly complemented her sexy voice. He had to force himself back to the case. Once they were free of attention from the waiter Black decided not to mess about.

"I know you aren't going to reveal your source, but can you tell me if any of our people are involved in leaking information to you? If the answer is yes, it might make our conversation today a little less productive, or even redundant."

"I'd figured that out anyway, and I wouldn't have needed to agree to this meeting if I felt able to get what I want by conventional contact with the Newcastle police force."

"You haven't ruled out other forces, or the Met in particular."

"None of my information came from provincial police forces, but nobody can ever rule out the Met, even though that isn't my source either. Look, if we are going to make progress it requires a certain amount of trust. I don't think I can get the whole story into print on my own, and I know you are being led to an 'acceptable' conclusion. Working together carries more risk for you than it does for me, that's true. But maybe I can provide you with just enough hints to feed to your boss to periodically swat the Foreign Office off his back. My article is a prime example. It isn't just you it has embarrassed, there are others who have made complaints to my boss. It's a fine line Inspector, and it could get very nasty. Could you top up my wine glass please?"

"I get the feeling that you didn't actually dig this information out, did someone come to you?"

"That's a strange question."

"Well, it's more of a statement really. The investigation hadn't even been of sufficient interest to the local rags, but you picked it up, and your information was disturbingly accurate. You know more don't you?"

"Yes, however, it requires proof, or should I say corroboration. Someone could have told me that a British citizen was a Russian spy, but I'd need hard evidence to be taken seriously."

"And why has your source volunteered this information about a Mickey-Mouse case in Newcastle?"

"Here's where some trust is required. It wasn't voluntary information. You don't need me to tell you that newspapers employ some pretty grubby methods of getting to the truth. I had some pretty reliable stuff which would have embarrassed a well-respected person. My boss wanted to go ahead, but when I gave this individual the chance to deny the claim, information on this case was dangled in front of me. So it was a question of trading rather than voluntary disclosure. You have to remember that it's not quite the same as a court of law. If the police are found guilty of entrapment, a case may be thrown out, and the punter walks free. Hoorah! Justice is done. Entrapment by a newspaper can mean that a person's entire way of life is shredded, merely by telling the story. Even if the court case was won by the said person, and the paper was forced to pay out compensation, the mud sticks. Also in a courtroom, the defendant can't be tried twice for the same crime, not so with a newspaper. Depending on how far they have to fall, repeated allegations can wreck the family. I sensed a bigger fish. My boss was still intent on spilling the sauce to the world, but I finally convinced him that this story had more stamina to run and run if we handled it in a certain way. The alternative of printing the sexy scandal would be over in a day. I have to trust this person to some degree and vice-versa. I get a snippet, you get it from me, we investigate its veracity and if we're happy, we print. I'm told it will make a lot of people nervous if we uncover what really happened in 1945, not just here but elsewhere in the country. I'm happy to admit I'm hooked by this story Inspector, a sex scandal is pretty poor currency by comparison."

"This is all a bit heavy for a country lad who grew up outside of Manchester. I'm still a bit confused, is this person claiming to know who was buried in the coke works?"

"I don't know for sure, but I believe so. Everything else I have been told so far has been confirmed by you, or at least not denied. Think about it again, you are working under some restraint and some guidance from the spooks. This source is or was involved in what was deemed to be the version of events with the least fallout. We have a classic double-edged sword Inspector. I can only repeat the sequence. I expect to get a lead, I pass it to you, it **has** to be checked, you get back to me and **we** decide if it can be released and when. In this way, the necessary trust evolves.

120

We all have a lot to lose, and you said you wanted justice for the poor sod who was entombed in concrete forty years ago. However, we mustn't be gung-ho in our approach, otherwise my source will become vulnerable, and we have to confine the revelations to the Northeast at this stage."

"You believe you've got a conspiracy on your hands don't you? So why must we, the Newcastle force, remain at the sharp end of such a big story?"

"Conspiracy maybe, but I prefer to call it an elaborate deception. If we make even the slightest suggestion that the evidence connects to other parts of the country, you'll see the case evaporate before your eyes. The Met will gobble it up and the story goes away. Ironically your visitor, Marion Wentworth wants the case to be solved up here, and put to bed again. That would make your boss happy too, and others would relax when containment was restored. Do we have a common cause Inspector Black?"

"Hold on a minute. You're saying you're prepared to go along with this alleged agenda of the Foreign Office, which is simply to tidy up a cold case, so that you can issue a challenge to the outcome?"

"Right, you're getting the picture. Apart from the people who orchestrated the events in 1945, others since then have become complicit by protecting the deception. The stakes are colossal."

"So your source is one of the people who you describe as complicit?"

"Uh, maybe, now you have to decide which way you're going to jump. I've told you about Marion Wentworth and her mission, so that's an example of something you didn't know, or didn't know that I knew. I'd like to recommend some bedtime reading for you. Here, take this file. During the war, there were many aspects to the conflict. Military strategy, logistics support, alliances, neutral nations, and technology, amongst many others. One of them was a means to deceive the enemy about our intent. You may never have heard of a man by the name of Tar Robertson, who worked for MI5. He suggested to Winston Churchill that deception could be sculptured to become a 'weapon' of immense power. Being able to plant disinformation inside the head of your enemy, and get them to believe it, means there is a possibility they will do what you want them to. The principle wasn't new, history is littered with tribal leaders employing such tactics. The degree of sophistication was the element of difference in Robertson's plan. Good examples were the D-Day landings in Normandy, and Operation Mincemeat – the allied landings in Sicily.

"Churchill was receptive to such an approach because he felt Hitler's character was to think in straight lines. Corkscrew thinking was Churchill's answer to this Achilles' heel. Allowing the foe to deceive themselves rather than over-egging the plot was the key. In the murky world of intelligence during the war, the British held the view that German espionage was something of a joke. The Allied spy network across Europe was effective, but they were also clever in turning German spies in the UK. In fact it was often said that all of them had been identified and became double agents because of the shambolic nature of Hitler's organisation. I've done quite a bit of research on this and although the Germans' thinking did rely heavily on having the best military leaders, the best equipment, and the best soldiers, that might not have been the full picture. There is the German view of themselves, to compare with our view of them. A reputation of incompetence in intelligence gathering didn't sit too well with their perceived notions of themselves. Our case is a perfect example, because my source insists that it involves a counter deception."

"Sophie, I don't think this is helping me to focus my mind on your offer to work together."

"Just read the book before you make a premature judgement. I'll give you a test to set for Marion Wentworth."

"I'm listening."

"In your efforts to put a name to this skeleton, which you believe was put in the ground forty years ago, what have you got? You think it's a male, probably German, with a Luftwaffe dog tag and whatever else. Even if the skull has lost some teeth it might be possible to use dental records to narrow the field? Why haven't you done this?"

"Because the medical examiner said there wouldn't be any record in this country, and although we could ask the German authorities – the Abwehr, to check it out, we'd have to narrow the possible candidates down significantly. In fact it would be the same problem we would have here. When she has a good idea of the identity she checks the dental records as confirmation."

"Right, so if you had such a candidate, even an imaginary one, you could ask such a question. If you ensured that Marion Wentworth knew about this before you intended doing it, I can tell you what would happen. She will say it's a bad idea until you have irrefutable proof that your suspect is the one. Why? Because she will say that merely by asking the Germans to send the records would produce an impasse. They would insist that the remains of someone suspected of being a German citizen should be returned. They'd want to check this out for themselves, not simply surrender a set of dental records. This would be the worst outcome for Marion, she must keep those remains here, or conveniently lose them. She would recommend that you seek this elusive, absolute proof of identity in another way. She would tap your desire to hold on to the investigation and you would fall for it. Come on, she's read the file, and knows you have a potential suspect. The dog tag, together with the dental information should be enough for the Abwehr to give you a name. She doesn't want the question to be asked. Do you want to put her to the test?"

"Maybe."

"Ok, I need to get back to London. You know where to reach me. I have to know very soon if you want to pull out of any cooperation with me, your only risk is that I will publish new stuff for you to deny."

Chapter 19
High Spen 1945

Karl had slept rough for a couple of nights amongst the dropouts on the docks. Then he spotted a Danish freighter, thought for a moment about asking for passage, but decided to wait for darkness and sneak aboard. It seemed to pay off when at last he heard the engines being primed. Another noise reached his ears. The meow of a cat. He lifted the tarpaulin a mere fraction to scare it away. It was a one in a million chance. At the very same instant a man with a torch flashed the beam toward the cat. The torchbearer saw two sets of eyes, and then the movement of the tarpaulin as Karl pulled it down. The man called for help, shouting incessantly. Two other crewmen arrived and asked what was going on. The whispering resulted in them splitting up and approaching the tarpaulin, each one wielding a boathook. Karl's heart thumped as if it was about to burst out of his chest. A long pole was pushed under his cover and slowly lifted. The game was up.

The most senior of the crewmen shouted and gestured for him to stand up. He did so, slowly, and then surprised them by asking if they spoke German. They all nodded cautiously. *'Can you give me passage to the continent? I escaped from a prisoner of war camp before the war was officially over, and I have no money or identification. I won't be any trouble.'*

The men conferred, and once again it was the most senior who responded, he shook his head and said, *'The captain must decide, we could lose our employment if you are found. We are responsible for such checks before sailing. Come with me.'*

The captain was sympathetic but not willing to take any risk of Karl being apprehended in Copenhagen. He delivered the instruction for the engines to be shut down. He, and two of the crew marched Karl to the Port of Tyne head office and explained the situation. The young airman pleaded desperately for leniency in English. "The war is over, I have a family and they do not know if I am alive. I will jump off the ship before arriving at the destination and swim to the shore. I will be happy to take my chance in the water. Please let me leave."

The Master of the Port was moved by his plight but simply shook his head and asked the Danes to leave. "I'm very sorry son, but I have to report this matter. I wish I could help you, I really do, but you must make a formal appeal." He phoned the police and asked for Karl to be collected. So near yet so far, Karl got into the car, with three policemen for company. The short drive was taken in silence and then he was registered at the station. Because he was such an irregular detainee, he was taken to the warm canteen, given a hot meal and then walked to the holding cell. He almost began to regret ignoring Michael's advice, but forced himself to think ahead rather than what might have been.

*

The news of his capture on the radio spread by word of mouth and Jack was saddened. Having escaped death or capture many times himself, he knew what it would be like for the curtain to fall upon one's hopes. Being stranded in a strange land far from loved ones was every bit as demoralising as the actual combat. Hope was the only anchor. As he replayed his weeks of hiding in a Dutch cellar in Venlo, his sympathy for Karl brought on a cold shiver. He pondered about visiting the police station in Newcastle, and was discouraged by almost everyone except his family. Bella and Hilda urged him to go, and he was finally persuaded, taking Harry with him.

"Yes Sir, how can I help you?" said the duty officer.

"I wondered if it was possible to see your German guest."

"Look, we've had lots of people asking to see him. Press, nutters, you name it. What's your excuse?"

"I don't have one. He was kind to my son who is right here with me." Jack lifted the little urchin on to the counter, and the officer was treated to a smile of enquiring innocence. "Harry met this German airman when he was a captive at the POW camp in High Spen, and gave him his football. It was an old ball, but it was his most precious possession, and I admire him for giving it up to help someone else. I just wanted to meet the young man and let Harry say goodbye to him. Having served throughout the war myself, I know what it's like to be away from any family or friends. I ached to see my son for the first time and he was already five years old. I'd liked to have known he was ok, even if I'd been told he'd made friends with Karl. You can't generalise about somebody because they're German any more than you can if they are English. I hear he's waiting for transport back to his homeland, and I just hoped my son could wish him luck. I'd rather Harry doesn't keep asking what happened to his friend for the next few months. I admit that I wish him luck myself. The war is over, we have to try to get back to being normal people, or we'll have to query what it was all for. Is it out of the question to see this young man for two minutes?"

"Just a minute Sir, I'll ask the sergeant to speak with you."

After half an hour's fidgeting by Harry, a burly man with a heavy moustache came to see them. "So do you think this Karl would want to see you? He has declined to see anyone else."

"As I explained, it's mostly for my son. If he remembers Harry but doesn't want to see him we'll be disappointed, but we'll leave without another word."

There was a broad smile on Karl's face as they approached. Jack's eyes met those of the German and there was mutual respect. "Hello, I am Harry's father, and I just

127

wanted to say thanks for making friends with him. I never thought I was going to see him."

Karl acknowledged this, summoned the entire vocabulary of English to ask about Jack's wartime travels. They exchanged stories and paused regularly to allow Harry to deliver his inexhaustible supply of questions. Jack nodded when the watching officer said the visit should come to an end. The two men shook hands, Karl lifted Harry up and hugged him quite emotionally before Jack asked the officer if he could leave the gloves he'd put aside for the German. The officer checked them out and agreed, even he was affected by the genuine feelings between two men who in other circumstances would have been trying to kill one another. Harry waved goodbye, thinking and hoping that Karl would come back some time. He put his arms halfway around his dad's waist and asked if he could have an ice cream.

*

Two days later, the paperwork completed at last, Karl was picked up in an official government vehicle and driven to the airport without any announcement of any kind. His departure was still controversial in certain quarters, and the various authorities wanted to avoid any demonstrations or worse. The German aircraft waited but the car never arrived. The local news bulletins picked up on the incident and described a car crash on the final stretch of the road from Kingston Park to Newcastle airport. The rest of what happened was unclear. Nobody had apparently been hurt or admitted to hospital, although an ambulance had been called. The driver of the vehicle in which Karl had been travelling, a government employee, said he had got out to reprimand the other driver, for careless overtaking, and cutting in, forcing him to jam on the brakes. He hadn't been able to avoid a collision and the front of his vehicle was badly crumpled, with water spurting from the radiator. During the ensuing altercation, the other driver came forward, full of anger and shouting profanities. He claimed the government car was swerving all over the road, lost his temper and punched the government chauffeur. He then grabbed him by the throat but relented, returned to his own vehicle, and drove off. The humiliated chauffeur later thought that there was a second person in the vehicle which took off at high speed, maybe a woman, but he wasn't certain. By now there was a traffic jam behind the damaged stationary vehicle and a couple of people left their cars to see if they could help. As the driver asked them if they got licence plate numbers, only then did he notice that Karl was gone. Although none of the following drivers could recall a single letter of the culprit's vehicle, they all said it was a foreign-looking car. One observant man noticed the altercation, but was distracted by a passenger in the other vehicle beckoning to someone, and saw Karl go around the back of the government vehicle. "He crouched, and you had your back to him. The rear door of the other car opened and he slid into the seat. I remember little about this other passenger, but I also think it was a woman. I couldn't understand what was going on, it all happened so quickly."

Four hours later, a burnt out car was reported near the market town of Morpeth. The German aircraft returned without Karl Heinz Buchwald, and the portents of an international diplomatic row were tangible.

*

Karl awoke in a barren, dimly lit room. He couldn't remember much after getting into the car. The people hadn't introduced themselves, merely telling him they were on a long journey and help would be at hand when they arrived. They'd suggested he should get some sleep. At first he resisted, but then he drifted into a very deep slumber, muttering frequently in German. When he had been prodded by the driver he had a clear recollection of switching cars, but no idea how long he'd slept. He pictured having walked from the car to a room which was so black he couldn't even see the door once it was closed. He felt slightly nauseous when he awoke and had trouble focussing his vision at first, even with the poor lighting having been switched on from outside. It must have been because of the water flask, handed to him by the female passenger. Before he slept he now did recall that his vision was affected. He had thought the water tasted slightly bitter. Despite banging on the only door, after managing to focus on it without it appearing to move about, he deduced that the people who'd brought him there had left, and shouting 'hello' over and over, did not bring them back. He was hungry but not cold, and the single radiator was very hot, gurgling incessantly. He was beginning to regret his knee-jerk decision to jump from one car to the other. He closed his eyes and tried to recapture more of what had transpired just after the woman beckoned him to join her. She was middle aged, perhaps about fifty, with streaked blonde hair. He remembered the dark lenses, not like most sunglasses, more like those worn by some blind people, completely hiding the eyes. She and the driver who'd punched the chauffeur, spoke in a kind of English dialect he'd never heard before, and he only understood a fraction of what was said. Mainly because of his relief at evading deportation, he had succumbed to whatever was in the flask and welcomed the chance to sleep.

His train of thought was interrupted by the faint sound of footsteps from above, first in one direction then the other. "Hello," he bellowed repeatedly. The footsteps stopped and then returned briefly, a muted voice called out some indecipherable reply.

"Hello, who is there?" responded Karl. Another silence was followed by a door clashing, and he heard descending feet outside his room, then nothing. Despite calling out continuously for a couple of minutes, still no one came, no one replied. He banged on the door again and the noise camouflaged that of a key turning in the lock. A uniformed man stood before him. Karl was pushed back and told he must keep quiet, and he could expect a visitor within a few minutes. He paced up and down the cramped room, looking frequently at the uniformed guard. The person arrived, dressed in civilian clothes, but Karl didn't recognise Theo Devlin.

Chapter 20

Moss was fiddling with the heating controls in his office, it was always too hot or too cold, and he disliked being controlled by equipment of such poor design. The phone rang.

"Moss, hello... Superintendent Moss, who is calling?"

The switchboard operator angered him further by admitting she'd accidently cut the caller off. "I'm terribly sorry Sir, we've been overloaded with calls today."

"They must have given a name, surely?"

"Err, yes, now let me see, I've forgotten the surname, Julian something. I can tr...."

"Never mind, it was probably nothing."

He used his direct line. "Julian, sorry about our operator hanging you out to dry."

"No matter Oz, listen, I was quite surprised to find that there are records for a Maximillian Vogt. I have to assume it's the same person – we don't have any others registered by that name. It wasn't so far back as you might have thought. His status changed as recently as 1975 when he retired."

"So he worked in this country for some time?"

"Yes, he must have been here during the war, which I thought was a bit odd. Anyway, he worked for a paint company in Crawley for a few years and then his records were moved to the Northeast Inland Revenue section. He worked for the National Coal Board."

"Don't tell me Julian, the coke works at Derwenthaugh?"

"How did you know that?"

Moss was annoyed at himself for not keeping his mouth shut. "I didn't, one of my people said that they thought they remembered the man from investigating a theft at the coke plant some years ago, and it is an unusual name, but I didn't take him seriously, and I didn't want to prime you with any predisposition. I guess that I owe my colleague a fiver. Well, thanks for clearing that up. I'd like to speak to this Vogt chap about another matter, can you give me an address?"

"I'm afraid he's dead Oz, his retirement pension stopped as he had no named beneficiary. Let me see, yes here it is, in 1977. God, two years after working all his life! It's unusual for us to keep records so far back as the time he spent in Crawley. I can only assume it was because of the war and his nationality. All Germans resident here at the time would be on someone's radar. So, that's all I can do for you on this, I shouldn't really have told you any of this – it stays unofficial."

"Yes, thank you Julian, it does shake you, thinking about hitting the buffers so soon after quitting the rat race. We must get together my friend. Give my best to the family. I'll call you soon."

*

Frank Reichert had received a curt but polite reply from the Abwehr. His father's disc was returned but there was no information that he didn't know already. The German authority claimed they had no record of Ernst after he went AWOL in England. There was an undertone of surprise that he had never returned to the Fatherland, and a slight accusatory statement that he'd never bothered to inform them of his intent to stay in the UK, as this would at least have made their records more complete. There was no hint of an apology or willingness to engage in any further correspondence. He rang Maggie and said he wasn't happy with the response. "I can't leave it at this Maggie. Has your Inspector Black found out whose skeleton it was that you pulled out of the mud at the coke works yet?"

"I don't know Dad, I was only helping out on that case, but anyway, I was about to ring you. I passed my promotion board, so I hope I can stay in Newcastle. I have to go now, I've just had an emergency call. Tell Mum I'll pop round tonight. Should I bring fish and chips?"

"Yes, yes, I could murder some fish and chips. See you later, and take care with that emergency."

*

Moss was rehearsing his pitch to Marion Wentworth about Max Vogt when Black knocked at the door, opened it a fraction and whispered, "Got a moment Sir?"

"Of course. Tell me you've got a new lead Inspector."

"Well, not exactly, but I think we need a change of emphasis. We haven't really got much justification for dwelling solely in the present. We seem to have exhausted evidence gathering from the site, the bones, and ex-employees. I know our friend from the Foreign Office is fixated on what we do next, but everything we've gleaned from the present points to the past. Maybe dealing with existing people in this Abwehr and Marion's sidekicks in London only shows up second-hand clues. We need *direct* access to records at the time of the suspected foul play. We should be studying anything and everything about Luftwaffe pilots, who were brought down and detained in this region in the latter years of the war."

This was Black's gambit to pry into why Moss's attitude to Marion Wentworth had softened so much. When there was no reaction he continued. "Don't you think Marion's dismissive behaviour toward Milan Hajek was unhelpful? It was a real lucky break for Freda to find the guy, and he's only been put under surveillance, her surveillance. I'd like your approval to pore through the official war records Sir, and that would mean a trip to London, where it's all in one place. I don't want the curators of these files to send me 'selective' data. It would be interesting to see her reaction."

"Mmm," mused Moss, "it can't do any harm to see if she tries to interfere. I'll suggest it to her."

"I would appreciate being there Sir, I'd like to observe the body language as well as the talk." Black wanted to put

Sophie's test to Marion after her leanings were expressed regarding him studying the centralised war records, by not giving her much space to think.

"Yes, in fact it was you who summarised your discovery of Mr Hajek. You're right Inspector, if for no other reason than we're keeping her up to date with everything we're doing or contemplating. That's what she asked for. Let's go and visit her in her new abode."

They caught her by surprise and she shuffled the papers on her desk into a neat pile then returned them to a red plastic file. "Sorry for the intrusion Marion, it's just a courtesy call to tell you in advance what we propose to do next. Inspector Black has a valid suggestion."

"Fine, do we need another chair? I just have the two."

"No, I'll stand," said Moss, "it means I can rest my rear against the radiator. It's all yours Black."

After the proposed foray into the war records was fleshed out Marion nodded wistfully and eventually spoke. "Good idea, I'll make a couple of calls to smooth the path for you. They won't just let anyone get their paws on these relics. Also, not every record is under the guardianship of the same office. There are matters which are exclusively to do with our own servicemen and women, which are protected by the Home Office, and then there are those covering incidents involving overseas personnel, both allies and foes, and they rest with the Foreign Office."

This was exactly what Black didn't want, filtered information, nevertheless he pressed on because he could check whatever he found with Sophie Redwood. "Great, I'd like to get stuck into it as soon as possible. And you've just touched on something which reminds me of another avenue which I believe we've neglected."

"Oh, well let me hear it Inspector."

"When we first brought the bones back for analysis, Constance Carr made a remark which I didn't pick up on at the time, but I think it's worth a shot. The skull was in decent shape and apart from her discovery of trauma to the cervical vertebrae, she said there were a couple of teeth missing. It was after that conversation that we found out that the metal disc was a dog tag – that of a Luftwaffe man. I then asked Connie if we could use dental records to narrow down the possible identity of the deceased, assuming it was his tag. You may have seen this when you read the entire file Marion." He paused until there was a response.

"Yes I saw the notes, I'm not sure I follow you Inspector."

"Well, Connie said we had to do it the other way around, you know, narrow down the possible identity first, because it would be mission impossible to run through every male dental record in the country to find a match. It's only now that the penny has dropped. We, the UK, can't possibly have the dental record of a German flyer, but if we assume for one moment that the deceased is the owner of the disc, we could ask the Abwehr to check it out."

Moss, hearing this for the first time, chimed in, "Damned good idea Black, it could save us a hell of a lot of time, or at least rule out that specific connection of the bones and the tag, well at least a direct connection."

Black detected furtive movement of Marion's cold eyes, and then a burst of false enthusiasm. "You may have hit on something here Inspector Black. I only have one concern."

"May we hear it," enquired Moss, "is it a disqualifier?"

"No, it's more a question of the best way to handle the request. I think we would all agree that we don't want to let the remains out of our sight, and I have my doubts that the Abwehr would be happy with just giving us a yes or no answer. It could become an emotive issue. In their position I'd want to see the remains, and if there was consensus that there was a match, I would be bound by a duty of care to any living relatives of the deceased. And I'd begin proceedings to recover the remains. The identity of the person may only be an inroad into discovering who may have dumped a body under concrete, and more importantly why? I hope you agree that we don't want to lose these bones until there is no alternative. I support your idea Inspector, I just think we could benefit from Constance Carr's advice – narrow the field before using the Abwehr in a confirmatory role. In fact your trawl of the war records may just help us to do exactly that."

Moss bought into this, so Black went along with the recommendation and asked Marion to make the calls to get him access to the war records as soon as possible.

As Black left, Marion made notes, but was interrupted by Moss. "This Max Vogt chap, of whom you know so much, can you tell me if he's still alive?"

"Yes, I can. And no he isn't. So, your next question is why was his ring found buried with our skeleton. I would like to know that myself, but as I did tell you, the bones aren't those of Max Vogt. He died over a decade ago, not back in the forties."

"That's a pity. How's the shadowing of Mr Hajek coming along?"

"He suspects he's being followed, and I expected that after we talked with him. When he's happy that he isn't, he might do something interesting. I will keep you informed Superintendent."

"Ok,"

When Moss returned to his own office, Maggie Reichert was waiting outside. She gave him her news about passing the promotion board and wanted to know if there would be a vacancy in Newcastle, or whether she'd have to move elsewhere. He assured her he wasn't going to let her go anywhere else. She was overjoyed and thanked him profusely.

"I'll attend to it with some urgency D.C. Reichert." She loved the sound of it, much more gravitas than WPC Reichert.

Chapter 21
Cambridge 1945

Theo Devlin sat looking impassively at Karl, glanced at his watch, stroked the previous day's stubble and then after several minutes, opened a file.

"I've been looking forward to meeting you for such a long time Karl Heinz. It's a pity you escaped from the camp in High Spen just before I arrived, we could have sorted out your problems there and then. Would you like a coffee?"

"Yes please."

"Where are my manners, I should have asked you in your own language, never mind we can now switch to German, because I want you to fully understand the limited options you have."

Devlin waited until the coffee had arrived and the door was closed before continuing in Karl's mother tongue. *'So, I understand there was contact between someone and the Luftwaffe men in the camp. Can you confirm this?'*

There was no reply. *'You'd be silly to pretend you don't know Karl. It would rule out some of your options. One being the possibility of staying in England for a while. Do you want to be sent straight to Bonn?'*

'No I don't, but I have no idea why I'm here. I was travelling to Newcastle airport to fly to Germany when there was what I thought was an accident. But it wasn't an accident, it was planned, and I am here. So you must know why.'

'Indeed I do, I also know that we can't help you if you won't tell us the truth. I will sit here for another two minutes and if you decide not to talk I will arrange for your deportation. You see, the aircraft at Newcastle was German, and we only intercepted your arrival at the airport to give you a chance to change your destiny by assisting us. If we were wrong and you have had second

thoughts about the whole business, I will be happy to let the people in Bonn ask you the same questions that I would. They may not be as tolerant of your answers as someone like myself. I am sure you understand what I'm saying, otherwise why would you have escaped when you knew the war was ending?'

'Ok, there was a man who came to High Spen to do some checks on prisoners, but only some, not all of them.'

'And you were one of them?'

'I was told before I left Germany that I would meet with someone with a code name and number in England if my airplane was shot down. But it wasn't shot down, others were, and some of the airmen did not survive. My friend and I were only told at short notice that we had to parachute out of the plane, but there was nothing wrong with it. All would be explained, the pilot said, and if we did not comply, we would face the Gestapo when we got back. We knew that unlike the bombers, our mission was reconnaissance, but we expected that to be from the air. We had to become POW's by choice. The contact we expected was from another one of the Germans in the camp, but in fact it was from a visitor. He spoke very good English around the camp, and we thought he was English at first, even though he spoke to us individually in High German. He said we would also be visited by a second contact, a local person, not inside the camp, but watching from outside. He would flick partly smoked cigarettes though the wire fence and we were to pick them up and keep them for the first man to return. We were not to inspect the cigarettes, just keep them safe and hand them over to him, the first contact, on his next visit when he ordered us to do so. It was obviously *some kind of information to be transmitted back to Germany. That's all I know.'*

'That's a start. Their names?'

'As I said, the first contact who came to the camp was only known by a code. He spoke the first part of a message and we replied with the counterpart. We were told that the second man would take off his gold ring before flicking any cigarettes through the fence, so that we would know they were the ones we had to pick up. This was necessary because there were some villagers who threw the odd cigarette to us, just as a smoke. The man would also whistle a certain tune when he took off the ring, but stop before he put it back on. It was a German tune, and then he was to speak only two words which would reflect his initials. The expression - Maximum Vorhang you will know, as you speak German, means Maximum Curtain, in this case denoting top security. He was then to take off the ring once more and roll it under the fence, as proof that he was indeed the proper contact. He never spoke to us again'

'That's a very interesting story Karl. Is there proof of any of these events you describe?'

'The ring is proof. I doubted some of the methods myself, but when I saw the ring, I couldn't believe it. Millions of Germans know of this ring. It's famous in our folklore, made in our country, but then there were allegations that it was stolen. It was thought that it ended up in Czechoslovakia, but it was never recovered, even after more than a century. It was then claimed that a German General had found it when the army marched into Czechoslovakia, and ransacked some of the homes of rich families. The original is apparently now in the hands of the Fuhrer's surviving staff. He had held it with great pride, saying it was symbolic of the justness of our cause. The ring was copied many times and 'individualised' with appropriate inscriptions. In this way, it attempted to connect ordinary soldiers directly to the importance of the mission, their mission, as part of that of the Fuhrer. It was reserved for intelligence work. I'm certain you'll hear more of these rings now that the war is over. I say that

because they were held in great respect, like a royal seal, except we didn't have a king, just Adolf Hitler. And as we all know now he was more than a king.'

'So where is it?'

'I hid it while I was on the run in the woods near High Spen. A friend who helped to hide me in his cave knows where it is. I asked him to take care of it as I was supposed to return it to the man whose initials were M.V. But he never came back. I panicked, thinking his cover was compromised. I thought I would be next, and that's why I escaped, thinking it would be better to simply disappear.'

'Fair enough Karl, I'll investigate this and speak with you again. You'll be given a more comfortable room until I return.'

*

It took several phone calls before Devlin eventually spoke with the village constable of High Spen. He asked about the man Karl claimed was a friend. "I'm trying to trace a vagrant who apparently sleeps most of the time in some woods near the village. Can you help me?"

"Do you have a name Sir?"

"Unfortunately not, nor a very clear description."

"The only person who comes to mind is a man who has sadly passed away."

"Oh, when was that?"

"Quite recently Sir, it was a hanging. We suspected that an escaped German prisoner may have been responsible. He was apprehended trying to leave the country at Newcastle docks. We told the Newcastle police, who were holding him, that our hanged man was wearing a German watch. This fellow has been on the loose for a while, and we think this tramp may have stolen the watch. This could have caused Fritz to string him up. However we weren't allowed to question him as he was to be deported as quickly as possible. But he escaped again, serves the buggers right for not listening to us. Just as well in the end though, because a lot of people up here would have tried to lynch him. Not that they cared much for this Michael, but he was considered to be pretty harmless."

"Thank you constable, that doesn't sound like the man I'm after. I'll just have to keep looking."

*

"Ok Karl, we're now going to speak in English. What was the name of this friend of yours?"

"Michael."

"And his family name?"

"I do not know."

"Then I think we must go and look for this ring ourselves."

"Why is this? Has he sold it?"

"No, he's dead."

Karl looked at Devlin, searching for something to say. The shock eventually caused him to throw up. "This cannot be true, how it was happening?"

"The police aren't sure, but he was hanged with a rope."

Karl's eyes filled up and he banged the desk. "Did the police have the idea that he helped me and punished him?"

"This isn't Germany Karl. But he was apparently wearing a German watch. That may have got him killed."

"Ah no, not the watch, I let him keep my watch for all he did to help me. If it has been the reason he was killed I am very angry about it."

"Well, there's nothing to be done about it now except find the ring. We have to go back there and retrieve it. You will need a disguise because apparently the local mob want to string you up now."

"Why can we not leave it there, where nobody will look?"

"I can't tell you that, but your freedom depends on its recovery, and tracing the man who gave it to you, with the initials M.V. I need to know who he is even if he's dead, as you suspect. Tell me Karl, exactly what do you expect to happen to you if we send you back to Bonn?"

"I will die, unless I have this ring and I can give an explaining why M.V. never returned to claim it. You see, the ring arriving back to the person who first sent it to M.V. completes the project. But it had to be the right one. There were always two rings for each project. One to say it was completed successfully, and another if something went wrong. I was sure something went wrong with M.V. The two rings were to look the same, but they had a slightly different style of initials, drucken in German, I think the English meaning is 'print type' or no, maybe it is 'font'. Even if I had the ring in Bonn, I can't know if the information in the cigarettes I gave to the visitor to our camp went back to Germany as it should. I would like to go back to my country but not in Bonn. I could get to my family from the border with Holland, they are living in Oberhausen."

"Right, well then, first things first, we need to get you ready to go back to High Spen. I'll get someone to visit you and start to alter your appearance. From now we'll speak only English, otherwise the locals up in the Northeast will suspect something. They'll know you escaped from the car which was taking you to the airport, but they shouldn't believe you would be stupid enough to return to that small village."

Chapter 22

Black informed Sophie Redwood of his impending arrival in the Capital. "You were absolutely right about the test of Marion Wentworth, and she has arranged for someone to 'guide' me through the war records. I'm therefore convinced that we should give this cooperation you suggested a workout."

"Good, then what I suggest we do is to take a few things which you extract, together with information you think is missing, and compare it to what my source has provided. If there seems to be censorship we discuss how you approach Marion for an explanation. I'll let the story lay fallow in terms of printing it, at least for now."

"Where should we meet?"

"Give me the name of your hotel and I'll suggest a café or something close by. We need to be sure about whether you're being followed."

"Fine, see you soon."

*

Moss summoned him to his office. "Inspector, before you disappear to the smoke, there are a few items we need to progress. This case of the 'man who never was' is taking up too much of your time. I said that a while back, and I need some of your other investigations to move forward. Your overall clear-up rate is not acceptable."

"I know Sir, I w…"

"No, don't talk, just listen. I have a dilemma and I want you to go with my suggestion otherwise we will be forced to downgrade the coke works case. Now, D.I. Horton is still weltering under the ecstasy caseload, and I need to help him out. It just so happens that Maggie Reichert is cleared to start as a detective constable. I could assign her to Horton, or transfer Freda Collins to him and you take D.C. Reichert. He gets an extra body and you get a rookie to replace her. Before you open your mouth, I've had Freda

Collins in my office a few times over the last year or so, requesting this move, and I told her that I couldn't see you being agreeable to it. She said that was part of why she wanted to switch, that she was stuck but not appreciated. This could be a neat solution. Now you can comment."

Black thought over the teasing Freda had put him through about being owed a favour, and that she'd recently decided what she would like. "Well Sir, I think you're right, Freda likes to be in her comfort zone, not working odd hours, but doing simple legwork, and she doesn't tend to think outside the box. Maggie is the opposite, and I would welcome the switch. Could I ask you a favour?"

"Maybe."

"Could you tell Freda that the move depends on her convincing me it's the right thing for the department? I'd like her to feel she's extracting something from me, and that I would normally have resisted it."

"That would also make her feel more valued, good idea. I'll speak to her soon and then she'll make her pitch to you."

*

Moss's next conversation was with Marion, whose stoicism was becoming an acquired taste. "I did some more checks after you told me Max Vogt was deceased."

"Oh yes, and what did you find?"

"Well he apparently worked at the coke works, isn't that a hell of a coincidence?"

He'd never breached her façade of 'handling' every contentious remark as if it was about the long term weather forecast. She always got the balance right between taking the subject seriously and appearing completely untroubled in steering it to a cul-de-sac. This hit a nerve. "Yes, what could that mean?" she drawled, marshalling the barricades, "do you think he knew who was buried there?"

"If that person is German it would be the first thing I'd be considering. It just shows how much we need to identify our skeleton Marion."

"I agree, maybe Inspector Black will find something in the war records which will give us a lead on that. Have you been able to find out in what capacity Vogt worked at the plant?"

"Yes I have," lied Moss, "but I need to confirm the information, I can't just take the word of one person, even though I'm sure he's right."

"So are you going to tell me?"

"Or you could tell me. Either would work, and it would give me a warm feeling if it was your turn."

"Let me check my old files, I might have missed something."

It took a convincingly long time for her to find the appropriate section. Thumbing through the pages, she eventually crowned her performance by 'discovering' an item in the appendix, rather than the main document. She even showed it to him, as she made a pencil mark in the margin. "Would you believe it? The complier of this report mustn't have made the connection. I'll be asking why pretty shortly, you can be sure of that. Mr Vogt worked out of the National Coal Board head office, and travelled to many installations around the country, but was paid out of the Derwenthaugh coffers. That should have raised a flag to all but a blind person. Look, he was an expert in fuel research and inter-conversion of various types. Jesus Christ, this has been right before our eyes for years." Marion had given an award-winning performance.

Moss perused the entry, but she didn't let go of the report. Appearing to run things through his mind, he suddenly produced a rapier-like request. "Let's call him Herr Vogt shall we? There is more and more evidence of a German connection about this case Marion. I think it would be helpful if you tell me all you know about the man who was buried. I fail to see why you declined to share the fact that Vogt is dead. It would have saved me a lot of time, and I thought you'd like this case tidied up to your satisfaction as soon as possible. Unless our relationship changes, I'd rather just work without your help. You may continue to interfere, even via my boss. That's your job, but you really should consider at least telling me as much as you know about the identity of the skeleton man. We will find out. And if that is achieved in spite of your suppression of information, it may be you facing the sack, not just me. Inspector Black is being monitored isn't he? He'll be guided around the maze, which has more than one exit. Think about this please. You probably knew that Max Vogt previously worked at a paint company in Crawley, and maybe you know some of his associates. Perhaps you can tell me how he got a job in the British energy sector, and who pulled the strings. I'm not interested in anything but identifying our corpse, deciding whether he died as a result of foul play, and who might have done such a deed. The grander scheme of things such as gunpowder, plot and treason are your concern. You'd like to wrap up the bones, pat us on the shoulder and disappear back into your caverns of mystery. But even your lot can't be so overtly covert can you? I'm just a policeman Marion, I can get away with a few mistakes, but you don't have such luxury. You would be making a serious error in underestimating Inspector Black. And then there's the media, we both realise that the press report was so accurate it could only have come from your organisation or ours. I'll be quietly looking into our lot and tightening the circle of those who need to know what I know."

They parted after a protracted silence, staring deeply into one another's eyes. Moss detected discernable discomfort in Marion Wentworth for the first time.

*

Meanwhile, Black was frantically gathering his stuff in preparation for the trip to London. The car was already waiting to take him to the airport. Freda entered the office looking a little nervous. "Sit down," grumbled Black, putting on a credible act of being let down, "I hear you have spoken to Moss about switching to D.I. Horton's team. I'm going to keep this brief Freda, I obviously would have liked you to talk to me first, but then I remembered you saying you'd decided what favour you were going to call in from me. It was in that roadside restaurant, and I cut you off, saying we had to get back to see why Moss hadn't signed the letter prepared by Frank Reichert. I realise now that I should have listened to you. Look, I don't want to lose you, but at the same time it's wrong to hold someone back in their ambitions. I've listened to Moss, and he made me see that the kind of work in Horton's section will bring the best out in you. So, you have my support. This isn't the proper time to say thanks for everything you've done Freda, as I have to leave in the next few minutes. Can we have a bit of a knees-up when I get back?"

"No hard feelings then?"

"Of course not. Que sera, sera! Can you put all your notes on the coke works case in one file and let me have it now, I have to dash."

"Yes Sir, and thank you."

*

Maggie couldn't wait to get started. That's why Black had asked her to drive him to the airport. The switching of her and Freda would only become official in a few days, but Black didn't want to waste that time. "Ok Maggie, in here you'll find the stuff Freda has just given me, and the other envelope covers the rest of what we know. Familiarise yourself with all of it, particularly the sequence of events. I know it will take a lot of time but I want you to transcribe a new timeline on to one chart. Don't let it out of your sight and don't do it in the open office. This is going to become our bible, no one else's. I'm sorry to drop this on you, and I don't want to be more specific. I want your input, your analysis, and your conclusions, all free from outside influence, even mine. Got it?"

"Absolutely Sir. It'll be ready when you get back."

"On another subject, how's your dad?"

"Not so good really. He sent his letter off to Germany, but I'm not sure if I told you he'd got a reply. Anyway, they stonewalled him. They sent his father's disc back but basically showed no further interest in updating their records. He was hoping that by offering to fill in some of Granddad's life in the UK, he would learn more of his service record in Germany. They don't seem interested for whatever reason. It's affected him more than he would admit."

"I think we should speak with him again when I get back, if he wants that. Does he think it's simply disinterest from the Abwehr, or they have certain policies regarding servicemen who don't return to the mother country?"

"All I know is that he has always tried to find out what his father was unwilling to tell him. The Fatherland, not the Motherland Sir, was a very different place back then. I get the feeling you think our case may be connected in some way."

"Not necessarily directly connected, but it is the same time period we're investigating and I'm going to London to look at war records, and they should cover people like your grandfather, as well as whoever was dumped in the coke works, unless it still isn't in the public interest to know about it. This isn't your usual Professor Plum in the library with a candlestick, Maggie. I'll keep an eye out for Ernst Reichert."

"I hadn't thought about it like that Sir. I can now see why you want this chart with the entire timeline on it."

"Good, and presumably you have figured out why it's for your eyes and mine only. The events forty years ago have to relate to those of today, they may even shape them to some degree."

Black hopped out of the car at the drop-off point and left Maggie with one further thought. "You can't take evidence home with you Maggie. You have to capture it in your mind and put it on the chart at home. Others seeing you looking through the individual statements and the rest of the file isn't a problem, the compilation of the chart is. Welcome to detective work D.C. Reichert."

Chapter 23
High Spen 1945

Karl looked in the mirror yet again. He was distinctly unhappy with his makeover. Devlin had really gone to town because he wanted to avoid any possible trouble with the villagers. The thick blonde Aryan hair had been reduced to a crew cut, and dyed chocolate brown. A theatrical prop, in the form of a Hollywood moustache, not only adorned his upper lip, but irritated his nasal apertures. The transformation was completed by applying a splint to his left leg, to make him limp without having to think about it. When they arrived, Devlin introduced himself to the constable, and merely referred to Karl as an underling who was to make notes. He whispered, "He is expected to be seen and not heard, in the same way we instruct children." Turning to Karl he then said, "Barrett, this is Constable...I'm sorry I have forgotten your surname, it is Edward isn't it?"

"Yes Sir, Edward Ferguson. Hello Mr Barrett, pleased to make your acquaintance." Karl nodded politely and Devlin continued.

"Now Constable, can you please take us to the place where this vagrant was found dead. I just want to search for any clues which your people may have missed. You see, the fact that you think he may have stolen this German escapee's watch intrigues me. I have to state right now however, that my business here during my first trip was simply to oversee the return of those airmen. The notoriety of the one who got away has increased with his second escape on the way to the airport. My job, as specifically stated by the government, is to find this interloper with the minimum of fuss. We all want him out of our country and that won't be achieved unless we track him down with methodology and not ballyhoo. I'm sure I can trust you to take care in that respect."

The constable touched his nose with the forefinger of his right hand, as if to convey the secret was safe with him. He led them to the spot of Michael's suicide, stopping a few times to allow the limping Karl to catch up. There was a wobbly moment when they reached the exact point on the bend in the river where Michael and Karl had seen each other for the first time. The memory came flooding back – both of them had been extremely cagey, and exercised appropriate caution. How could they have known that they would almost become soul-mates in the coming weeks? Karl struggled with his emotions, not least of all because he couldn't grasp the coincidence of Michael being murdered at this precise spot. He sat on a log and gesticulated that he needed a rest after such a hike. Devlin asked if he was feeling ill.

"Just tired Sir." The constable began his tale of how they'd examined the site, finding nothing to contradict the view that he'd probably been murdered by this German brute. After indulging the policeman for over an hour, and re-examining the immediate area, Devlin brought the search to a halt.

"So you have this German watch in a safe place?"

"Indeed we do, I am personally looking after it."

"Good, I need to see it and I may need to take it back with me for expert analysis. I will of course return it to you, as it is part of a potential homicide investigation. I wonder if you could retrieve it, while Barrett and I give this scene the fine-tooth comb treatment."

"Yes Sir, don't wander too far away, it's very easy to get lost in these woods."

As soon as he was out of sight Devlin turned to Karl. "He never mentioned anything about a cave."

"No, I am not so surprised. Michael said nobody knew about it. But Mr Devlin, something is not right about this whole story of my friend being killed here. This is exactly where I first met him. Look up at the tree, they have cut the

152

rope to get him down but the end is still tied to the tree. It is not a normal... how do you say, combination of events..."

"You mean coincidence."

"Yes, it seems more than a coincidence that he died exactly here."

"I tend to agree Karl but let's find the cave and the ring before the constable comes back."

Karl led Devlin to the disguised entrance and performed the habitual check that no one was to be seen in any direction, which Michael had emphasised over and again. The façade was removed and they entered. "My God," said Devlin, "this is unbelievable."

Karl knew exactly where the ring was buried and began to scrape away the soil. He stopped in his tracks when he saw a piece of wood upon which his name had been burned into the grain – K A R L. He jumped back. "This was not buried with the ring by me. Michael must have done it before he died. Mr Devlin, I think he killed himself, and it was because I didn't stay with him. I knew he was upset but I was sure he was to understand I had family. Now I feel so bad."

"You might be right Karl, but where is the damned ring?"

They couldn't find it even though they both frantically widened and deepened the dig. Devlin looked at his watch and was visibly concerned that the constable would be on his way back. In a moment of uncharacteristic anger, Karl kicked the wooden plaque with his name branded on it, yelling something in German which was obviously not in Devlin's Teutonic armoury. There was the ring, embedded in the reverse side of the tribute from Michael. Devlin's relief was palpable and Karl's containment of sorrow was finally breached. He sat with his head in his hands and said nothing.

"Come on Karl, we have to go, or PC Plod will be back. Look, put that plaque in my bag and when we remove the ring later, you should keep the poor fellow's last message to you, even though he may have thought you'd never find it."

They thanked the constable for the watch, and said they'd be leaving, having been satisfied about the prognosis of murder, at least until they caught up with the German fugitive.

"We'll be on our way now. I'll be in touch as soon as we have him Constable, and once I have had the watch taken apart you'll be the first to know if there's anything of significance about it."

*

Bella had received bad news. Her husband's condition had deteriorated and it was no longer thought that the spa baths would prolong his life, even though he did get temporary relief from the process. She was advised that he should stay there. It meant more financial and emotional pressure for the family. He needed the treatment, she needed to work, and she couldn't be with him. It had a ricochet effect on the relationship between Hilda and Jack, which in turn spilled down to Harry. Jack had been earning good money, with lots of overtime, and he agreed that some of it should go towards helping Bella to cope, including the odd weekend trip to Harrogate.

Before the war, it was quite rare for a married woman to work, even if she had no children. Victorian legacy was still strong in the rural north. A man was supposed to be able to 'demonstrate that he could take care of his family'. It was almost as symbolic as having an indoor toilet. The rub came about in a complicated way. Hilda was in what was seen as a 'profession' while Jack was just a labourer who was learning the ropes of laying bricks. It was a perception from outside the family, yet it was tangible. They'd also been on the council housing list and were getting near the top. Another custom was for working men like Jack, to compensate for a hard week's work, by a sanitised, ritualistic gathering at the local club on a Sunday lunchtime. However, most of Hilda and Jack's friends were 'normal' insofar as the wives didn't work. So, Hilda's hard week was rewarded with having to stew in a hot, open range kitchen to make the lunch, or dinner as it was in the local vernacular. Jack was always expected back at 2 pm precisely, and the timing was uncanny. On every Sunday, Harry was told that he should sit at the table and as usual, the next thing he could expect was that the dinner would appear from the kitchen at the same time as his dad would walk in the back door. But not this Sunday.

Bella, Hilda and Harry waited ten minutes and decided that the dinner would be spoiled by trying to keep it hot. They tucked into it, and cleaned their plates before Jack came through the door. He seemed a little worse for wear and the smell of alcohol was more noticeable than usual. He smiled and plonked a bottle of whiskey on the table. "Won the raffle," he said.

"You know the dinner is always ready at two, yours is in the oven and is ruined. It's long after 2.30."

"Oh well, I'd bought a ticket so I waited for the draw. I'll still eat it."

"Very gracious of you I'm sure." Hilda plonked the dinner in front of him and gravy spattered his shirt, some of it burned his arm.

"What the hell's got into you, for Christ's sake?" He stood up to go for a cold cloth and when he came back from the kitchen he saw Hilda hurl the plate of food into the coal fire. As he began to formulate a response, she picked up the bottle of whiskey, and it followed the plate into the fire. As the bottle broke, the ignition process reached the rug in front of the fireplace. Whiskey was an expensive commodity, and instead of attending to the blaze, Jack grabbed Hilda by the throat and began to swear at her. Harry was so scared he took refuge under the table. Bella came from the kitchen and emptied a bucket of water over the coals and the rug. It thankfully doused the spat as well as the flames. Sanity descended slowly and yet a rational discussion was needed.

Hilda's feelings were hurt, and so she complained that it wasn't difficult for her husband to walk a few yards to say he might be late. "I'm aware that it can be difficult for you to accept that I put more money on the table than you do at the moment. However, I'm sick of being treated as the quiet little mouse whose hero is back from the war. I don't mind making the dinner every week as long as it's appreciated. That obviously isn't the case."

"Hilda, I am sorry but you have to try and understand, appreciating my dinner and being here on the dot at the same time every week isn't easy for me. I've spent the last five years making decisions which might cost my life. How the hell do you expect me to equate that to being a bit late for dinner? It's the first time. I'd be happy to help you with the cooking and be a bit less rigid about working to a gong. I want to forget about being in the army, obeying orders or being punished for not obeying them. I can't live like that."

The heat of the disagreement had dulled, as Bella had put everything back in place. But there was one legacy they hadn't bargained for. Harry announced that if his parents got a council house, he was staying with his grandma. All strategies to talk him out of this declaration failed. They realised that his little world had changed so much too. From no parents to squabbling parents. From grandma and granddad to just grandma, and something they hadn't thought important. During these years he'd grown up amongst friends of his own age. They underestimated the threat of him living right at the other end of the village and losing contact with his playmates. Being outdoors and having total freedom was so important, as were his pals. Hilda and Jack deferred to this for the present, certain that it would pass. Bella knew him so well, she knew it wouldn't, but said nothing.

Chapter 24

As Moss entered Marion Wentworth's ground floor sanctuary she was placing files into two stacks. "Am I intruding?"

"Not intruding, but I'm in a bit of a hurry. What do you want?"

"I can't seem to get Max Vogt out of my head. And as I was turning restlessly in bed last night, I remembered your exact words, when I asked for the name of the officer of the crown whose report you quoted regarding the ring and Herr Vogt. 'If I believed I could tell you that I would have already done so. Things may change'. Well, have they?"

"Do I sense you have another little worm to dangle in front of me?"

"No but I was thinking of asking Inspector Black to check this out."

"He's looking at war records, I don't think he'll come across the author of the report."

"Perhaps, but maybe he will now find Vogt. If he doesn't, I'll know he may not have been given the help he asked for. You should have mentioned it to him."

"Am I to understand you haven't shared what I told you about Vogt with him?"

"I didn't say that. And you don't need to know. So this chap who wrote the report was indeed a spook then. And if that's the case he may have come to the Northeast to see Herr Vogt. If he did, and it was an official visit, I could look into the old police files, or more likely those of Mr Eric Paisley"

"Look Superintendent, I have to leave in a moment, could we talk about this another time?"

"Ok, I'll get Paisley in, he has only spoken with Black so far. He'll be more relaxed with a man closer to his own age. Am I allowed to know where you're going?"

"I can tell you why I'm going, but I don't know where I'll end up. Our patient surveillance of Milan Hajek has paid off. He boarded a flight to Cologne this morning. I need to get there ahead of him disappearing into the wrong hands. I have a contact in Koblenz who will shadow him until I get there. I have a car waiting to get me to a small chartered aircraft from Newcastle to Cologne. So I may be able to answer your questions after all."

"When will you be back?"

"I don't know if I'll ever be back here, but I will contact you. Now, can you help me to carry these files to my transport please?"

"It's the least I can do Marion, well, good luck!"

*

Black met up with Sophie Redwood at the café she had suggested. He was about to ask what she would like to drink but was stopped in his tracks. "I've been contacted by a German journalist who must have read some headline of my article in a rival publication. He then accessed the full story I published and he had something interesting to say. He apparently covers political stuff about the cold war, and particularly the partition of Berlin. He advised me or anyone wanting to investigate this case further, not to contact the German authorities direct. He says they will already be monitoring the situation, but didn't know how. He's tried on many occasions to access information on the circumstances which led to the ridiculous situation of a city being treated as an island hundreds of miles from the sea. Policed by the tightest security operation on the planet, this is a stalemate between former allies. He wants to come over here to discuss this in detail, not being certain that his house was free of bugs. He's absolutely sure that his newspaper staff includes undercover employees of the authorities. That's why he was calling from a public phone. I'm going to meet him to see what he has to say, and I thought I'd better let you know in case you want to change your mind about working with me."

"My head won't accept any more layering of this case. Focus is what I have to do. I'll be working with you until one of us decides that it's run its course. The German journalist is your call. I want to talk about poring through these war records. I think we need to check out any references to German servicemen known to have been in the Northeast around that time. I know your source implied that there is an ongoing cover-up, but even if that's true, I can't believe all POWs would be involved. That's a ridiculous suggestion. I can accept that our skeletal friend could be involved, if he needed to be disposed of. So as I said, I want to stay focussed on him. The period from 1942 to the end of the war, through to our man ending up in the concrete in 1945 seems about right. I've already done some background research, and there doesn't seem to be any Luftwaffe raids early in the conflict. Your stuff, espionage related presence in the country, is different, and there was early reconnaissance activity, so I'm leaving that to you. I'm afraid you'll have to get used to my obstinate way of working Sophie, it's the only way I can function effectively. Before I get shepherded through the tomes of information, I thought about who our man may have offended, and it occurred to me that the body being dumped where it was, in the coke works, might have more significance than we've given to it so far. If we were talking about a one on one personal homicide, I'd expect the disposal to be one of convenience as well as a safe haven. If it was part of an orchestrated killing of necessity, to shield some secret agenda, the means and location would have been meticulously planned ahead of the actual termination. Getting the timing right is important in this case. When does the concrete arrive? Who oversees the operation? How do they make sure that nobody in a plant which worked shifts suspects anything strange? This has bugged me since we found the bones. I found out recently that there was a delay to the original schedule, reportedly because of under-specification of the volume and piling of the concrete. But I'm told that these piles may never have been installed. I'm waiting on confirmation of that. You see Sophie, it's often insignificant things like that which lead me to the truth. On the face of it, there's no logic in taking such risks to dispose of a body, so there has to be a reason. You gave it to me when you talked about covert operations. The key is the Derwenthaugh site, and the examination of the war records has to guide us back there, at least as a new starting point."

"I did say that I have been given more allegations than have been printed, and what you've just said doesn't conflict with them. I wasn't given the detail you mention about the delay in pouring the concrete, but it was suggested that someone in the management of the coke works was involved in getting rid of a body. My source also said that there was an investigation of some kind at the time, but nothing came of it. I've tried to find out about this through available archives but there's nothing. I was beginning to suspect my source was padding out the morsels of fact with juicy treats. That's why I wanted to see if the information could be verified without me disclosing it to you. I think I'll keep this German journalist on hold for now."

*

Marion Wentworth was met at Cologne airport by her contact. Henry Middleton had been living in Germany for a number of years. The posting to Koblenz was under the guise of writing a historical novel which spanned the Habsburg lineage. He had references to show other books he'd written while resident in Holland and Greece.

"Hello Marion, everything is under control. My man has been following Hajek since he left the airport. He reported in to say that the target met with some German-speaking chap in a park. I will phone in again in a few minutes. I hope you had a good trip."

"Yes, it is good to get away from the investigation in Newcastle for a while. I need to remind you that I have to remain remote from Hajek, as he has already met me."

"No problem, Hans is very good at this kind of surveillance, and I have my 'secretary' waiting by the phone at my house in Koblenz for any calls he makes. Why don't we grab a coffee, don't you have luggage?"

"No, I travel light, and if I need anything, I'll buy whatever it is here. A coffee would be good."

Henry brought the drinks to the table and said he'd check with Koblenz. When he returned there was good news. "Hans doesn't recognise the man Hajek met, but tailed them to a restaurant, where he managed to get the table next to theirs. He's apparently wearing a highly sensitive set of hearing aids so he can eavesdrop on their conversation. Knowing Hans, he'll be putting on the act of being substantially deaf, when ordering the meal. I'll check in again when we get to your hotel."

*

Black hadn't been long involved in making out a grid sheet to record his observations. Those he considered worthy of questions he captured with his exceptional photographic memory. He thought he had managed to shed his chaperone, so he was frustrated when Percy Simpson crept up behind him again. "There's a call for you Inspector, you may take it at my desk."

Black couldn't believe that Sophie would ring him at this location, and yet he was surprised to hear the voice of his boss. "Hello Inspector, I trust you're having fun. I'll keep this brief."

Moss told him that their Vulture had flown the nest and why. "So that's important, but maybe more interesting is a snippet I got out of her about the artefact related to our jeweller. The inscribed initials, I assume you remember them, M.V. They denote a man by the name of Max Vogt. I thought you should look out for that name or even others with those initials. He started out his life in Britain at a Crawley paint works, but ended up with the NCB, you guessed it, at Derwenthaugh. He was some kind of expert in fuel technology, but he's dead now. She said he died in the seventies, and I have crosschecked this with a reliable source. He therefore can't be our skeleton, but he must have something to do with it, surely. I'm going to look at all possible police records at the time of the demolition of the plant, and I'm also going to bring in Eric Paisley. I wanted to make sure you didn't miss something just because it wasn't what you were primarily looking for - that being registered German servicemen. This guy might have been an agent of the Reich but not a conventional soldier."

"Thank you Sir, I'll keep that in mind. So this strengthens the case for the item being the connection between the bones and a contact from the coke works. It fits nicely with the timeline." Black had kept the conversation from his end vague because of the haunting proximity of Percy Simpson.

Chapter 25
Cambridge 1945

Theo Devlin completed his report and submitted it to his immediate superior. Whilst he wasn't preening about having shipped all possible POWs back to Germany, other than Karl Heinz Buchwald, he settled for the single loose end to be tied up. He had been careful in describing the ring in his report, and emphasised the need for a new investigation into the owner, a man in the Northeast, with the initials M.V. He was well aware that some, if not all the information passed from M.V. to Karl, then on to the unknown camp visitor, would be of great interest to his boss. There was a mole, if Karl's story was true. He desperately wanted to find out what the information was, and relied upon that aspect alone to ensure Karl remained in England.

It was therefore a total shock when he was congratulated for his diligence in completing his project, without any mention of the information hidden in the cigarettes. He asked for an audience with his boss.

"Theo, come in," said Bernard Compton, "are you so keen to know what we want you to do next?"

"No Sir. I wanted to ask why no one has even asked me about the passage of information from M.V. through our German detainee to an officer from this organisation."

"Oh, I thought you would have figured it out for yourself. It was intercepted, that's all that was important."

Devlin sat in silence for a short time, expecting more of an explanation. As it wasn't forthcoming, he ventured his own interpretation. "Intercepted, and then allowed to take its intended route to German intelligence?"

A nod was all he elicited from Compton. "So we don't have a German mole amongst us, we have one of ours amongst them. That's a relief. So what happens to Karl Heinz Buchwald?"

164

"You can arrange for his return. He has served our purpose well, even though it could have gone badly wrong. The sooner the better you can move him on Theo, then we can draw a line under this operation. We'll talk about your new assignment soon."

Devlin appeared to accept this, smiled and left the office. He still hadn't been offered any hint of what this precious information was, it evidently was very important to the Germans. Was it still important? He needed to grill Karl again.

*

Hilda and Jack had notification that they were about to be offered a council property, a bungalow, in a small development of pre-fabricated houses. They were both overjoyed that their marriage could now be the way they'd dreamt of it from way back in 1940. They had forgotten about Harry's protestation over the move. Bella was pleased for them but also saddened that the household would be broken up yet again. She'd worked herself to the bone to provide her husband with medical care, and simultaneously stood in for both of Harry's parents. It didn't feel like an appropriate thanks for making such a personal sacrifice. As they discussed which 'prefab' had the best view, they eventually noticed Harry under the table. It was his place of refuge when he didn't like the proposals on offer.

"You'll be right next to the woods in our new house Harry, the street is called Fell View," enthused Jack, "just think of all the adventures you'll have, and your school is just around the corner. There's going to be lots of children living in the street, so you'll have plenty of new friends. And you can have your own bedroom as well."

"I live with Grandma, I always live with Grandma, and I hate the other houses. I want my friends who live here, not new ones at the other end of the village. My Granddad will be coming home soon and I want to live here to see him.

He tells me exciting stories when I go to bed. You can't make me leave Grandma's house."

Bella was on the verge of tears listening to Harry's pledge of loyalty, but both Hilda and Jack insisted that the boy got dressed and accompanied them to the new development site. He resisted, and then cried as he was dragged out into the street. Bella's heart raced and yet she didn't intervene, but when the three of them disappeared up to the main road, she suddenly felt spent, redundant, helpless, and used. The avalanche of emotion resulted in her going early to begin her shift at the Co-op reading room, simply to avoid being isolated with her fears.

Hilda and Jack were busy imagining the décor and vegetable patch of the new property. Jack was already measuring up space for a proper tool shed, when Hilda asked where Harry was. "He said he was going to ask you where he could find a toilet or somewhere to do what he had to do."

They both checked the entire site together and began to panic when they couldn't find any trace of him, and none of the other folks around the area had seen him. Hilda was verging on hysteria. "God, do you think he's gone into those damned woods?"

Jack didn't think about it too long, he asked for volunteers to help look for Harry. There was a disappointing response, only a handful of people agreed to help in searching the woods. After an hour or so, the others drifted away and Jack decided to inform the constable. The woods had quite a few dangerous places to contend with, notably severe, hidden drops, and worse still, invisible river currents in which adults had died trying to swim to the opposite bank. The constable called in ambulance and fire services, as well as police reinforcements. The whole area was suddenly heaving with new civilian volunteers.

Out of sight and the spreading word of the missing little boy, Bella sat in an armchair in the reading room, cuddling

166

and consoling Harry. "There, there now, I'll talk to your mum and dad about this again as soon as I can." His thumb was uncharacteristically in his mouth and his chest rose and fell, keeping time with the sobs.

"Should we have a nice hot cup of tea?"

It elicited nothing more than a shake of his head. Bella tempted him with a piece of homemade jam sponge cake she'd brought for her mid-shift break. He weakly asked if there was any cream. "I might be able to get some from the grocery section downstairs, come on, we'll go together."

As soon as they set foot outside the large double doors, people began to point at them. They hurried to the grocery entrance and were surrounded by villagers who told Bella about the ongoing search. The Co-op manager took it upon himself to get to the woods and inform everyone that Harry was safe.

The incident itself negated the need for Bella's entreaty for Hilda in particular to reconsider the move, and the pressure it put on the boy. Bella tried to sum it all up for her daughter. "He's not had the same upbringing as other kids around here, and you can't expect him to adapt to this kind of change too quickly. He's only just got to know you and Jack as a couple, and already you want to change things. He needs time Hilda, and he doesn't understand the episode where you threw Jack's dinner and bottle of whiskey into the fire. The shouting, and your husband grabbing you by the throat really frightened him. You and Jack demonstrated in that moment that the two of you need space to adapt to the post-war situation, so if adults have hiccups, a child will have nightmares. Give him some time, and he has to see you and his dad happy together."

"You're right," said Hilda, "maybe we should decline this prefab offer."

"There's another choice. You and Jack are still relative strangers, take the offer and live together, like most couples do before they have children. Harry can stay with me. It's not very far to walk when you want to see him. He'll gradually adjust and it will be easier if his granddad comes home soon."

Bella and her daughter embraced and it was settled. "You go and tell him Hilda, he wants you to be his mother, even if you are a dreaded teacher." They burst out laughing as Jack came downstairs to announce that the runaway had drifted off to sleep.

*

Devlin gave Karl the bad news and it shocked him to the core. It affected his recently acquired English so much that he launched into a tirade, changing to German halfway through the first sentence. Devlin asked him to calm down and repeat everything in German in a controlled, quiet voice.

'I have helped you every way I could, even revealing things which would guarantee my death in Germany, and this is the reward I receive. Mr Devlin, I would rather be shot here so that my family doesn't have to hear any of the lies their new government would state as my crime, to justify my execution. If you people think that the roots of the Nazi organisation are just going to wither and die because they lost a second global conflict, you are wrong. That process will take decades, and I can't survive a year in their clutches, never mind a single decade. I have just been used and now I will be cast away like a dirty tissue. Can I ask you to help me to end my life? I have no acceptable future.'

Devlin held up his hand. *'I can't assist your suicide, they want you to disappear, not become a source of further controversy. Listen to me Karl. I want to help you, and I need to think how I can achieve this, because they will have to make me disappear if they suspect I collaborated with you in any way. You have to give me a reason to take such a risk. What can you tell me about the cigarettes you collected in which the information was hidden? You must have some ideas, surely?'*

'I was never told anything except that I must not tamper with the cigarettes. When M.V. didn't come back and I was planning to escape, I talked to one of the other prisoners about the possibility that he was dead. He agreed and took one of the cigarettes from me. He then tore the tissue paper very carefully and watched the tobacco spread out for a minute or so, and he had a spy glass which magnified things. He also had a pin, and very slowly moved more tobacco to one side. There was a film of some kind in the centre, and he pushed the pin point through one of many tiny holes along the edge. He teased it out, and looked at it with the light behind. He seemed to think it was a new kind of information storage system – microfilm, he said. He thought it could hold a lot of information, such as maps, plans, words, and even photographic negatives. We decided that as M.V. had not come back, there would be other information missing, and it was better to keep the one we had interfered with, rather than pass it on and be accused of breaking the rules.'

'Now this is beginning to make sense to me Karl, and you must think very carefully. Where is the cigarette you took apart?'

'I don't know, I left it with Gunther.'

'Jesus Christ,' shouted Devlin, *'I've been the victim of an elaborate sting.'*

'What?'

'Nothing, tell me, was this microfilm transparent to the naked eye?'

'No, it had a neutral, slightly opaque coating, and it seemed to be this coating which changed colour slightly when the sun was strong. Gunther said that's what enabled him to see the tiny letters and drawings, but they were too small to read, even with his spy glass.'

169

'Ok Karl, I'm going to work out a plan to get you out of here. First I have to have a reason to detain you a little longer. Don't do anything silly, I want to speak to someone who can shelter you when you escape, then I will tell you how and when you are going to get away from him. This time I won't be overruled by certain people to whom I nominally report. I may even have to come with you to Germany.'

Chapter 26

Black was becoming despondent after two long days checking the war records he'd been given. The task wasn't made any easier by the musty, oppressive odour in the archive chamber, with its row after row of light-blocking bookcases. An additional irritation came in the form of Percy Simpson, perennially perched on his right shoulder, offering no enquiry or help, merely pointing to the multiplicity of 'Silence' notices, every time he dropped one of the encyclopaedic volumes on to the desk.

He'd found nothing which was even remotely interesting, until the list of references he had checked accumulated sufficiently to alert him to certain gaps in the timeline. His extraordinary visualisation of these periods prompted him to write down the various dates. Percy Simpson showed the first signs of concern.

"Percy, I need an early break today, can I buy you a coffee?"

"That's very kind of you Sir." He summoned one of the clerks at the main desk. "Watkins, please return these volumes to their proper place until Inspector Black and I return."

Watkins began this apparently unnecessary task. "Wait, I'm coming back in fifteen minutes, just leave them there, left open at the pages which I'm checking."

Simpson intervened, "No Sir, they have to be returned, even for fifteen minutes, Watkins will insert bookmarks for you. Our system has strict regulation, you can imagine that several people in this organisation have need to take out volumes for all kind of reasons. It is very easy for disputes to arise if we do not log each and every event. The fact that we are leaving this hall of records means that the volumes you are researching must go back to their rightful place, in case someone else asks for them. It seems a little over-elaborate, but I assure you it is necessary."

Black conceded, and thought about it on the way to the refectory. As soon as they had their coffee and chosen a table next to a large gothic window, he hit Simpson with a question related to the system he'd described. "I have noted certain time gaps between the volumes I've checked, why is that?"

"That is perfectly possible Sir, you see we're also engaged in modernising our archival data. Some of it was already transferred some time ago to microfiches, but now we are well and truly in the age of computing. It will take years, but eventually all of this information will be compressed into dull, soulless megabytes of binary code."

The man was clearly upset at such a 'barbaric' edict. Black saw the first signs of rebellious potential in Percy Simpson.

"So, how do I get the missing volumes, in order to complete my search?"

"We have to check who has them and when they are supposed to be returned. Some could be in the process of transcription to hard disk, others could be logged out to certain people. This is a perfect example of why we have to return volumes to their rightful place, even for fifteen minutes, as we enjoy our break. Someone could ask for one or more of those volumes as we sit here. We need to know where they are, every minute of every day."

"Fascinating," said Black. "Right, I need to phone my boss, I'll see you back at the main desk in a few minutes."

"Very good Sir."

*

Moss did have a better rapport with Eric Paisley than 'Jet' Black. The former operations director of the coke works met Moss for lunch at a hostelry of his own choice. Moss wanted to avoid the man feeling pressurised in any way. The untreated internal stone walls and twisted beams seemed to gel with Paisley's tweed jacket and sienna slacks, trimmed by expensive brogues. Moss declined a double malt whisky opener, preferring a real ale.

"I appreciate you taking the time to speak with me Mr Paisley, and I regret having to pick through the recent events at Winlaton Mill once more. However, directly due to the information you provided for Inspector Black, we have an independent report which confirms your view that there were no piles driven into the earth directly below the concrete slab. We recruited a well-respected, reliable contractor to excavate the original location and they provided this report. It also details the condition of the slab in its current position, and again there is no evidence of piles, either intact or broken off." He passed the report to Paisley.

"So, there was some shenanigans going on, my predecessor was right."

"Indeed, and it's your predecessor I'd like to talk about. You see, we still have to find the identity of this person whose bones we recovered, and one way we may find clues is via any investigation which took place at the time. There is nothing in the official police archive which is even remotely close to such an event. However, it was during the war, and we can't rule out an intelligence study. There are two aspects in which you may be able to help us. The first is another possibility which could have occurred before your time as operations director, but might still have been recorded. This notebook which revealed the scam over the concrete, can you check it for any visits by people from the Home Office or Foreign Office? Alternatively, there could be something in the normal coke works files, if you still have access to them."

"I have the notebook with me, but the files which weren't destroyed I keep at home. Silly really, but it chronicles an important period in my life. You see Superintendent, I never married and I have no one to share my experiences with."

Moss nodded sympathetically and Paisley checked the notebook. "There's no specific mention of such a visit in here, but there are a lot of reminders to do things, speak to people etc. Regarding the files I have kept, I'll check them out and let you know, or you could follow me home and we can check them together."

"Yes, that makes sense. Now, the second question. Do you recall any of your employees during your tenure with the initials M.V.?"

He sat with his whisky in one hand, mentally checking familiar names by counting them with the fingers of the other hand. His eyes brightened and he triumphantly announced the name Max Vogt. "He didn't come to mind immediately because he moved around from plant to plant. But I recall him clearly because I had to pay his entire salary."

"Can you just check your predecessor's notebook again Mr Paisley, for that name or the initials?"

It was quite a thick book, littered with scribbles which would only be intelligible to the author. But there were exceptions, the concrete being a prime example. Moss came back from the bar with another malt. Paisley seemed to have had a personality change, he was devouring the pages with a fervour hitherto not seen. He swallowed the second malt in one, and waived the need for another.

"I knew something rang a bell, but I couldn't pinpoint it to a particular time. Here we are, my predecessor notes an offsite meeting between M.V. and a Mr Devlin, brackets London. I didn't like Max Vogt Superintendent, because he was like a cuckoo in my team, doing work which I hadn't authorised, and contributing almost nothing to solving problems in the plant. He was tolerated, no more. I seem to remember he died shortly after retiring. He was a very secretive person."

"What is the date of his meeting with Mr Devlin?"

"There is no date alongside the remark, but other stuff on the same page is all dated in 1945. My predecessor, Timothy Westlake gave me this notebook when he retired and said it may come in handy one day. You know, I have never thought about it like that until now. Will you keep me posted on how things turn out Superintendent? I have suddenly become disturbingly nostalgic."

"I'll try to do that Mr Paisley, and I would still like you to check the files at home for any further references to Vogt and Devlin."

"You can rely on that. I'll call you either way."

*

Moss called Black and asked him to ring back from a public phone box. Out of breath and with a thumping heartbeat he only managed two words.

"Black here..."

"What I have to say we must keep between us until I say otherwise Inspector, is that clear?"

"Yes Sir."

"Our friend Paisley has been very helpful. The initials on the ring not only belong to a Max Vogt as I told you when Marion admitted as much, but also he worked under Paisley, who disliked him intensely because he was extremely secretive and although he was paid out of Derwenthaugh, he was controlled by NCB head office."

"Another mysterious German connection to the bones."

"Yes, yes, but there's something else which is just as important as his connection to the coke works, he was visited there by a chap from London named Devlin. Now listen carefully, Vogt worked out of Winlaton Mill but according to Paisley, it was mostly for the benefit of other departments of the National Coal Board. I assumed this Devlin must have been working for the NCB or some other organisation. Paisley checked it out for me, and he wasn't an employee of the coal board. We need to know if he was investigating something in the Northeast, and I already checked the police records – he doesn't show up. You should check if there is any record of either Max Vogt or a man named Devlin during the period they met, which was in 1945. I ferreted a clue out of Marion before she left for Cologne yesterday. She has a report which she wouldn't let me see, but said it referred to a man with the initials M.V. and the report was authored by an officer of the crown. It's a mighty coincidence Black, and you may be looking in the wrong place. Check declassified documents from that time. I think your time at the war records should be targeted to POW camps in our region."

"I tend to agree with you about being in the wrong place. This museum may have information of use to us, but it will take me weeks to even scratch the surface of what is available. I'll call it a day when I've checked out the POW camps, that shouldn't take too long."

Black decided to try a short cut. He met with Sophie Redwood, and they strolled along the embankment in the moonlight. The odd foghorn sounded as boats made their way to the night's mooring. The lapping of the water from their wash was regular and seemed to synchronise with his cerebral pulse. "Can you get me solid information on all of the POW camps in the country during the war?"

"Yes, are you looking for any in particular?"

"Well, since you claim we're only looking at the tip of the iceberg in Newcastle, give me the ones in the Northeast."

"I'll have to get this kind of information from my system, but you're looking for the one closest to the coke works aren't you?"

"And that would be?"

"High Spen, have you heard of it?"

"No, I remember telling you I'm a Manchester boy, I've only been in Newcastle for a short while. It doesn't ring a bell."

"Ok, it's a small village only about five miles from the coke works, but apparently one can commute between the two by regular bus routes, and this was the case back in 1945."

"Great, I can start there when I get back."

"What about the war records?"

"Nothing in terms of names yet I'm afraid, and this guy Percy Simpson hovers around me all the time. I'm thinking about how I can get help on declassified stuff, you know, old government secrets and the like."

"Do you have anything in mind?"

"Yes, visits to the coke works during the war."

"Aha, you are beginning to believe me then."

"Well, let's say I've got a more open mind now."

"What kind of person are you looking for?"

"An officer of the crown, obviously."

"And the date?"

"Just after the cease-fire, perhaps 1945."

"You're looking for Theo Devlin then."

"Who?"

"Come on Inspector, remember we are trying to build trust. I'll give you the report tomorrow. When you are satisfied, you tell me what you know and we discuss the next moves. Goodnight."

Chapter 27
Cambridge 1945

Devlin had been persuasive in getting his boss to refer Karl to a psychiatric examination before despatching him to Germany. His rationale was that he would be subjected to comprehensive interrogation when he returned home, and it was in the interests of the crown to know exactly what was in Karl's head. "We mustn't lose sight of the fact that this man was a conduit, albeit we believe a dumb one. However, I was subjected to a clever deception by his campmates. It didn't actually work because they eventually broke ranks and wanted to get home very badly. This Gunther, the man I thought was being used by the others was in fact orchestrating the whole charade. He would have got back to Germany with Karl's disc, but we never truly found out why that was necessary. The fact that we fortuitously foiled the plan isn't the end of the story, and we should responsibly put Karl through a thorough screening to see exactly what he knows and does not know."

Bernard Compton gazed out of the window, then at a fly which had settled on his blotting pad. He crushed it with a heavy ledger, wiped the remains off with a tissue, and calmly put it in the waste basket. "Unfortunately I must agree Theo, but I'm a little disappointed you did not mention this 'sting' earlier. I will authorise a psychiatrist appointment immediately, and Karl must be detained until further notice. You must cancel his deportation arrangements."

"I only knew of the deception I suffered yesterday Sir, and it was because I asked Karl more questions. That's why I came to you as soon as I could. I would like to accompany him to the psychiatric session. This is our last chance to extract everything he knows."

"Very well, see to it, and I want to see the report before we have to brief anyone else."

"Certainly. That is a valid precaution."

*

Bella's husband Cappy had returned from Harrogate and was virtually bedridden. They decided to make up his bed downstairs, in front of the warm fire. He slept while Bella was at work, Harry was at school, and both Hilda and Jack called in after they finished work. With the family reunited, Harry was happy again. His teacher remarked on his dramatic progress in almost all subjects. The experience persuaded Hilda and Jack to save for a deposit on a house of their own, hopefully near to Bella and her husband. Then Harry would be able to live with them again and run to his grandma's whenever he liked.

The plan was almost thrown off course by another accident. Harry had been warned on countless occasions that climbing on the corrugated roof of the air raid shelter was dangerous. He was playing with Alan Crossling, sword-fencing with sticks. Harry was Robin Hood and Alan was always burdened with being the Sheriff of Nottingham. As Harry lurched for the kill, Alan sidestepped the sword and the momentum took Robin Hood forward, where his foot tripped over a protruding bolt. He was hurled over the edge and landed in the garden of the next door neighbour. Tizzie Goyne's husband had set out his vegetable patch with marker posts. Harry's full weight struck one of these two inch square posts at the back of his elbow joint. His scream was horrendously penetrating, and as Bella rushed to the neighbour's fence she felt her stomach recoil. His lower arm was lying at right angles to its upper equivalent. She could see the jagged end of a bone. There was no placating Harry. The ambulance arrived and he was driven to the Fleming Infirmary with all possible haste.

Jack was working away in Hartlepool, and Hilda went to the ward on her own. She stayed with him until he eventually succumbed to sedative.

Two weeks later Harry was re-examined and told the bones were knitting nicely and soon he could begin rehab exercises. It didn't go to plan. Even after weeks of religiously performing the painful routines, his arm remained grotesquely bent. Hilda ignored medical advice and took him to a bonesetter in desperation, the hospital having basically given up on him. Bonesetters were a last resort, and considered to be quacks by the medical authorities.

In a tiny, rickety office in North Shields, Hilda smoked several cigarettes in the waiting room during the half-hour in which the bonesetter arrived at his prognosis. He said nothing other than she should take a walk in the street for about twenty minutes. She protested but was accompanied by the receptionist and they walked back and forth past the entrance. She heard an ear-piercing howl from the upper floor and wanted to rush back to her son. The receptionist grabbed her arm and said they must remain outside for another few minutes. Her heart thumped as the lady explained what had taken place. "The bonesetter realised that the greenstick fracture had been incorrectly set. The only way of preventing Harry's arm from becoming calloused and unusable, was for it to be broken again and reset properly."

What she didn't tell Hilda was how it was done. Bonesetters weren't licensed to use general anaesthetics, and he had to literally snap Harry's arm without any kind of pain relievers. She sat in the waiting room, tears rolling down her cheeks, until the bonesetter came to see her.

"I've given him some sedatives and he's sleeping. His arm is now set properly and it will heal just fine. You need to get him home as quickly as you can, he will have pain when he is awake. It will last for a few days. I can call you

180

a taxi, he won't charge you a fortune, and I wouldn't recommend risking the bus."

It was another two hours before Harry woke up and complained about the pain. He was given more sedative and it was explained to him that he must keep as still as possible for a few days. He drifted off to sleep once more.

*

Devlin left Karl in the capable hands of Compton's chosen shrink and drove back to HQ. He'd only been back there for one day when the call came through to Compton.

"Mr Compton, it is Gerald Matthews."

"That was quick Gerry, have you finished with our man already?"

"No, I am sorry to tell you he has disappeared, well been kidnapped would be more accurate. I've informed the police and they said that they are treating the incident with some urgency."

"I wish you hadn't done that Gerry. Give me the name of the police officer to whom you reported this and I'll speak to them personally. Don't concern yourself any further."

He looked over the desk at Devlin. "What a cretin Matthews is, the Kraut has been snatched and he's roped in the plods. I'm going to speak with the regional chief constable, so in the meantime you'd better be prepared to get out there and bring Fritz back here. My instinct was to get shot of this man. Someone must have followed you there Devlin. Someone who knew what we were hoping to get out of the German. Did you tell anyone else?"

"Absolutely not, I didn't even tell Karl where he was going. Maybe someone thought I was taking him to the airport."

"That's possible, but they would still have to know he was here. Get ready to leave while I speak to the police."

Devlin paced up and down the corridor for over an hour. He was packed and kitted out for a spell of anonymity.

Finally Compton opened the door and ushered him into the office. "We are told that the abductors took our man in a dark green Austin, a large car but they don't have the model or the number, which was covered with a white paint. There were two men in the vehicle. One was obviously the driver and the other posed as a patient, waving an appointment card to see one of Matthews' junior partners. When the receptionist challenged this, he insisted that the appointment had been made for him by phone, by his father, who was waiting in the car. He asked if the receptionist would please check with the junior consultant, and she felt obliged to do so. Matthews' door burst open, the man had a gun. He ordered the German and Matthews to accompany him to the reception area, and the car moved to the entrance. Matthews was struck over the head with the gun and Karl was bundled into the car. Matthews wasn't unconscious but sufficiently traumatised to ring the police. In retrospect I suppose I can understand that. Anyway they have roadblocks set up around the county, so his call was probably justified, but there hasn't been any sign of the car. They are adamant it couldn't have got through in the time window, except by really minor roads. Perhaps you should start your search by talking with the receptionist, she apparently got a good look at the abductor."

"On my way Sir."

*

Devlin took notes from Matthews' receptionist and was amazed at the embroidery in her description of his hireling. He travelled around Cambridgeshire for a couple of days, looking out for any surveillance activity. He passed by the safe house twice and then parked near the village green. He walked the mile or so 'as the crow flies', and knocked at the door three times as planned. Karl was pleased to see him again. "Ok," Devlin said to the hired men, "I'll take it from here." He threw the rest of their fee on to the table and stayed while they counted it. They shook hands and went outside. The garage doors swung open to reveal a freshly repainted Austin seven, no longer green, but a stunning wine colour. One of the men backed Devlin's newly acquired black Ford car out from the adjoining space in the double garage, and threw the keys in his direction, then Karl was asked to get into this new vehicle. Devlin gave the man the keys to his own car, explaining exactly where it was parked in the village. The man acknowledged the instruction to drive it into the space alongside the freshly-sprayed wine-coloured Austin, as soon as possible after Devlin left in his new Ford. Devlin got into the driving seat and eased the Ford out on to the deserted road. No further words passed their lips until they were on to a minor road out of the county.

Devlin then explained that they had to exit Cambridgeshire, and if they encountered a road block Karl was to get out and walk over farmland to a ruin on the other side of the checkpoint.

"It could take you up to three hours to walk there but it's better to be safe than sorry. I'm pretty confident we won't have to resort to this plan, just be prepared in the event that I'm wrong."

"Where are we going Mr Devlin?"

"I thought you would have figured that out Karl. We have unfinished business in High Spen."

Chapter 28

When Black and Moss spoke again by phone, the intrigue kicked up a gear. "Let me just give you the benefit of my thoughts Inspector. We have Jerry number one buried at the same place which employed Jerry number two, and they were both being covertly investigated by a Theo Devlin, who must be a prime candidate for the author of Marion's report. It's not rocket science or guesswork. He has to be a spook. Marion said she may never be coming back to Newcastle. Her pursuit of Hajek over this ring is running her motor right now, so that connects in to Vogt, who is conveniently dead. You said the records show there was a POW camp in High Spen. So the answers are up here, in that village and the coke works. I think you ought to get back up here as soon as possible. We need to make hay while Marion is distracted."

There was no comment from Black. "Hello, Inspector, are you still on the line?"

"Err, yes Sir," mumbled Black, while wrestling with the ethics of having collaborated with a journalist, "I have to admit something to you Super. Once I'd got my lead, Sophie Redwood left a message at my hotel."

"How did she know where you were staying?"

"I spoke to her about her last article before I came to London, I told you that, and I was surprised you didn't tear my head off for ignoring her attempts to contact us. Well, when I mentioned that I was coming to the smoke, she asked if we could meet. I panicked a bit, because it sounded like she was ready to go with another piece on our case. I gave her my hotel address and I saw her last night. She does have some kind of an inside track on this Sir, and we ought to take her seriously. She confirmed the name of this Devlin without me asking. If you recall, when you told me his name, you didn't mention his first name, she knew it was Theo. She seems genuine to me. In line with your point about making progress while Marion is out of the way, I would like her to speak with us up North. I think she'll hold off printing more until we hear what she has to say. What do you think?"

He cringed while awaiting the verdict. "Fine, get her to come up here with you and you can extract what you can before I meet her."

"Right, right I'll get it sorted and call you back."

*

Marion and Henry Middleton waited impatiently for their man Hans to report in. They'd begun to attract attention because of the number of empty coffee cups they'd accumulated on their table. It was very un-German. At the fourth attempt Henry was able to report good news. Hans had overheard most of the dialogue between Milan Hajek and his unknown contact. Apart from the small talk, all of the conversation centred on the gold ring. It was all in German.

Hajek had insisted to this man that what he'd seen in Newcastle was the genuine article. This repeated assertion was met with a shake of the head on at least four occasions. Finally, the man said loudly, *'Enough Mr Hajek. We already have the original, have had since the start of the war. What you've seen is obviously a very good replica. There is also the inscription to explain.'*

'In that case why did you agree to meet me? You could have told me by telephone.'

'Come now Hajek, we have to verify who we are talking to, and we've now done that. Secondly, there is the question of loose ends which have to be tidied up. I am told there was such a ring in circulation in the north of England, and it was never returned to us, so your information is most valuable. We now need you to guide us to its temporary caretaker. Can you do that for me?'

'I can tell you where it is, getting your hands on it will not be easy.'

185

'Why?'

'I mustn't have mentioned it when I asked to see you, the police have it. They must be investigating its origin.'

'That is inconvenient. I now have to ask you what inscription you observed while you examined the ring.'

'I was sure I told you that already.'

'Indulge me, tell me again.'

'Wait a minute, you aren't the person who agreed to meet me are you?'

'No, he was my subordinate. I have to recheck your claims, it is procedure. Now, the inscription.'

'M.V. – the letters M.V. that's all there was. It was inside the ring. I suppose I should have known that nobody in their right mind would have done this to the original if they knew the history. But still, it could have been done in complete ignorance.'

'The letters, are you absolutely certain they were both followed by full stops? They couldn't have been marks which simply looked like full stops?'

'I'm a jeweller of some repute, not an amateur. They were initials.'

'Good, may I thank you for coming all this way Hajek? Is there any way you could procure this ring for us? We would offer a substantial reward.'

'I doubt it, but I will ask the police if they need my help again. Maybe they do, and if so I can contact you once more.'

'Not the same way of contact please, take this number, call it at any time. Thank you again.'

Hans had the entire conversation on a mini-recording system attached to his hearing aid. Marion wanted the tape.

*

Black was nervous as he spoke to Sophie Redwood, unsure as to how she would respond to meeting up with Moss. "I've been given a message by my boss that an ex-employee of the coke works has notes which confirm Max

Vogt worked under him, and many years before, his predecessor met with Devlin. So this ties up neatly. Superintendent Moss would like to meet you to discuss how we proceed from here."

"I thought I had that arrangement with you. You told him that I gave you Devlin's name didn't you?"

"He gave that name to me first, so it could be that we can make more progress by a more 'official' agreement."

"Didn't you say your boss was a bit too cosy with Marion Wentworth? That worries me Inspector."

"That's what I thought, but he was playing her at her own game. Anyway, she's gone off to Cologne and said she may not come back to the Northeast."

"Cologne? Do you know why she's there?"

"Yes, well Moss believes she is following this Czechoslovakian jeweller we found, the one who said the gold ring which was buried near the bones is worth a fortune. But that hasn't been proved yet, however Marion didn't deny it. Maybe it is true, otherwise why would she follow this guy to Cologne."

Sophie let this replay in her mind several times and said, "Ok, let's go and meet your boss. There's one condition though."

Black sighed resignedly. "Let me have it."

"We have to agree to print that you are investigating a murder. I have to make sure my source believes his trade with me is intact. The story has had a break and needs fresh impetus. So I want to see the evidence of trauma to the cervical vertebrae of the skeleton. Deal?"

"Deal," said Black, having no idea how Moss would react.

They took the first available train to Newcastle, and Moss said he'd be at the station to meet them.

*

Armed with Hans' tape, Marion Wentworth boarded the same flight as Milan Hajek, not to Newcastle, but to

187

Prague. She wasn't alone, Henry Middleton had tipped her off that Hajek would have company, in the form of two rather imposing heavyweights. The aircraft was half full at most. As the flight settled at its target altitude, she wandered toward the toilet at the front of the cabin, deliberately stumbled and said, "Hello again Mr Hajek. I said we would talk soon and here we are. May I sit?"

Visibly shaken, he nodded. Marion smiled and told him to relax. Again he nodded. "Just a few questions, may I call you Milan?"

"Yes of course. It must be about the same subject as when we last met."

"Indeed. Who was the man you met in Cologne?"

Hajek became extremely excitable. Marion offered him a set of head phones and switched on the tape. His face turned ashen. He was about to speak but Marion cut him off, and stopped the tape at an early point in the recorded conversation. "I am here to prevent you from getting into trouble. I'm sure you remember the secrecy documents I served you with in the police station in Newcastle. You did sign them and you can't take such things lightly. The rest of the tape is enough on its own for me to arrest you, but neither of us want it to come to that. Especially when there is an alternative, one which actually helps your country. That is of course, as long as we're talking about the same country."

"Do you mean Britain?"

"Do you still have Czech documentation?"

He froze. "Just hand it over," said Marion, "they still don't know you were a collaborator, do they Milan?"

His mind refused to comprehend how this situation had come about. How long had the British known? Why bring this up now? Was the Czech intelligence organisation part of it? How could he have lived a life under cover in the UK for so long? His natural reaction was to deny everything and call her bluff.

"Do you think you can arrest me in Prague? I'm not going to give you my papers, you have no jurisdiction on a Lufthansa flight or Prague airport. I have nothing more to say."

Marion got up to return to her seat, and the two hulks, mentioned by Middleton came forward. She had misread his message, she thought they were his back-up team. The larger one leaned over Marion's seat and flashed a Czech Special Service badge. The second went to head off a stewardess whose attention had been aroused by proceedings. He suggested he should speak with the pilot, as he presented his own accreditation. It all settled down again and Hajek handed over his papers to these men at last.

Marion asked if she could see the papers and was pleasantly surprised that they allowed her to check them over, and then one of the men put them in his file. They returned to their seats, and she spoke with Hajek again, to offer him a choice. "You can cooperate with me or take your chance with those two gentlemen. They obviously know of your duplicity with Germany, and they must be ready to charge you with all manner of things, leading up to treason. They also know that we, the British, have a vested interest in your wartime activities, which could lead the Czech Special Service to a bigger fish. They may be prepared to be patient, but only if I can tell them I have information from you which assists their investigation. What do you want to do? It's a short flight and I'm going to fly straight back to London. I'm sitting just a few seats behind you, so just let me know what you want to do. In the meantime, I'm sure your two friends will keep you company."

Hajek frantically searched his memory, trying to connect this accursed ring with information Marion could want. He knew of the bones in the coke works from the newspaper, but although it was implied that they were the remains of a Luftwaffe serviceman, he just couldn't make the link. He'd arrived in Britain long after the war, he had no idea that there had been a POW camp in High Spen, and yet he had known for a long time that death followed this ring. No, not this ring, the original – the one which his contact in Cologne said was still in their possession. He chose to speak with Marion again and gestured for her to come forward.

"Good. Now Milan, we both know that the ring which you examined is still in the care of the Newcastle police. We've also heard that the really valuable original is safe with the Germans. So we can forget about that one. It's the fake with the inscription with which we must concern ourselves, particularly its purpose, and who was involved in that chain of events. We need you to talk to your German contact again."

"You want me to go back to Cologne?"

"No, to your shop in Heaton. We will give you certain bits of information which will entice your contact to Newcastle. The rest we will take care of, now that isn't so difficult is it?"

"Err, no, I suppose not."

"Fine, so what is the name of your contact in Cologne?"

Chapter 29
Newcastle 1945

Devlin's vehicle, a 'blend-in' black Ford, had done well. He and Karl had avoided hotels en route, caution dictating they slept overnight in the car. They found a suitable temporary domicile far enough away from High Spen in terms of Karl being recognised, but close enough to get there by bus. Lemington was on the opposite side of the river Tyne, and there was a choice of buses available. The river could be crossed by using Newburn Bridge, and then services were available through either Blaydon or Ryton for the final destination. The other possibility was to cross the Tyne via Scotswood Bridge, and head up the river Derwent to High Spen. This public transport was important, because he didn't want his car to be noticed, consequently it had been garaged.

Devlin wanted to begin with M.V. and needed Karl to identify the man who delivered the cigarettes, and whose calling card was the gold ring with his inscribed initials. Even though Karl had escaped because he thought M.V.'s no show meant he'd been killed, Devlin wasn't convinced. He also believed that M.V. was the key to identifying the other government man who took the cigarettes from Karl. His belief in both of these things was rooted in Bernard Compton having declared that the embedded information was intercepted and then allowed to resume its journey to German intelligence. At no point did he show any sign that the flow had ceased, or the chain had actually been thwarted by Karl's escape. Gunther's shadow was still lurking over the whole situation.

'Karl, we must work quickly. Everything we discuss in the presence of others will be in English, but we will speak to each other in German when we are alone, like now. I telephoned my boss shortly after we left Cambridgeshire, to tell him I was checking all minor exits from the county,

191

but that won't fool him for long. I don't want to speak to him from the Northeast or he'll be on to us in no time. Think hard, what else can you tell me about M.V.?"

'He was probably about thirty, big dark eyes, hair parted in the middle, brown with some thin patches, and he had a faint scar over one eye, the left one I think."

'Was he heavily built or thin? What kind of clothing do you remember? Did he speak to you in German? What brand of cigarettes did he give you?'

'He was a bit on the heavy side. He never spoke at all, except what I already told you previously, two words during his first visit – Maximum Vorhang. This made me absolutely certain he was German. If he had spoken more in my language he would have attracted too much attention from the villagers, and he didn't speak to any of them. The cigarettes were from a red packet, but I can't remember the name. He usually came in a suit, but one day he must have been in a hurry, because he had working clothes on. It was an overall, a one piece overall. Blue, dark blue and...wait, there was a name across the chest pocket. No, there were three names.'

'Take your time, it is crucial that we get this right.'

Karl sat, imagining the scene again and again. At last he burst out with a single word – National, that was the first word. Yes, definitely. I can't seem to bring the others to mind.'

'It will come Karl, just don't push, it will come when you're thinking of something else. Let's switch to the other visitor, the one you only knew by a code. You said he spoke both English and German fluently. What else can you remember about him?'

'He always arrived in a car, driven by someone in a police uniform. It wasn't always the same driver. He also had someone else with him, an Englishman in some official capacity. But this person only signed some papers for the local constable, the man with the code walked around the

camp on his own. He only ever spoke to Gunther and myself about the cigarettes, but he talked with others about whether we were looked after well, hygiene, and stuff like that. When Gunther and I gave him the cigarettes, it was always when we walked by the latrine, because nobody wanted to go there except to shit. He was a man who was very confident about things, including the end of the war. He always checked to see if the cigarettes had been tampered with. He was tall, lean, and had angular facial features, a thin moustache, and was always impeccably dressed. I noticed he had a ring, but not a gold one, and not worn on his wedding finger. I am pretty sure he was younger than M.V. and yet he never seemed nervous, whereas M.V. often was. I've got it! – The other words - Coal Board – the name said National Coal Board. I remember it had to do with mining, but now I realise it wasn't just mining, there was another word and a stitched-on picture below the opposite pocket, one long word, which didn't make sense to me, but the picture was of a treatment type plant, with many buildings and chimneys, like an oil refining complex.'

'Well, that does give us a solid start Karl, there can't be too many installations of that size which are close to High Spen. We can start there and work outwards. As long as my boss thinks I'm still patrolling the borders of the county of Cambridgeshire, I'll be able to enlist the help of local authorities by using my current accreditation.'

*

Harry's arm was no longer really painful and the bonesetter was satisfied that he would recover full use of it over time. This had lifted everyone's spirits, not least of all those of his granddad. Bella read the letter from Harrogate many times, before she troubled her husband with its contents. The gist of it was the announcement of a new revolutionary treatment. She knew he was weak, but clung to the hope that some kind of miracle cure would be developed. She showed it to Hilda, as it contained far too many long words, which Bella could neither understand nor pronounce. Hilda didn't have the same hope that it would make a real difference to her father's condition, but wasn't going to deflate her mother's belief in the Harrogate expertise. Bella needed a lifejacket in these turbulent times, some anchor within credible reach, and Hilda gave her support, it was the least she deserved. "Let's ask Dad how he feels about going back there. We can take Harry because he's still not ready to go back to school, and we would all enjoy the break."

As soon as Harry was told about the trip he became hyperactive once more and asked his granddad to tell him stories about Harrogate itself. The two of them were only separated at bedtime for the next two days, before an early departure. Life seemed to have found some new banner to which the family could rally. Jack was doing so well with his bricklaying feats that he was unknowingly marked down as a potential manager of the future. His thirst for knowledge was more than matched with understanding of its application. He always volunteered for overtime and their savings were modest but mounted steadily. This also produced a new horizon, as Bella had heard of a bargain to be had. Currently, she lived at 1, Co-operative Terrace, and the Dixon family were moving out of number six. It needed quite some modernisation, but that was music to Jack's ears. They would apply for a loan. With their savings, Jack's steady earnings, and Hilda's 'profession' as a teacher, they stood a good chance. Bella's various burdens all of a sudden seemed just that fraction lighter.

*

Devlin was still remembered by the village constable from the search for the vagrant killer, and he explained why he had returned - to check out the death of Michael. He had also promised to return the German watch found on Michael's wrist.

"Hello Constable, I'm sorry it took so long, but here is the watch I borrowed from you. It is indeed of German origin, but I couldn't find out any more about previous ownership or where and when it may have been bought."

"Thank you Sir, I don't think it matters too much now that we heard the escaped airman managed to evaporate once again. Rumour has it he was abducted, and our coroner has ruled the vagrant's passing as an unexplained death. He said Michael's hands weren't tied and yet there wasn't any evidence of a struggle. So there we are. Did you come all this way just to give me back the watch?"

"Not really, you see, even if you've given up looking for the German chap, I still have to find him. I was going to ask the Newcastle police but maybe you can tell me. Are there any coal processing plants, oil refineries or coal-fired power stations near High Spen?"

"Yes, well I believe all the refineries in the country are near the coastline, so none are too near. But we have a coke works at Winlaton Mill, and there are several electricity generating plants along the river Tyne. Why is that of so much interest?"

"You must keep this under your hat Constable, but when I first came here to organise the repatriation of the POWs, I had reason to speak with many of them, personally, you know, about the conditions of their return. It seems there was a civilian who used to come and see them and they got the impression he was not from the village. If I can locate this person he may be able to help me. God knows, he may even have helped the airman to escape."

The constable could sniff a bit of fame, or at least his picture in the Blaydon Courier. "I see, do you have any more to go on?"

"Not really, it's a long shot, and in the dark, but I have to keep trying. Can you keep your ears to the ground for me?"

"You can count on it Sir." Devlin left to pick up Karl.

195

They took several buses from Lemington to get to Winlaton Mill, a necessary circuitous precaution. Another such item was the potential fallout if M.V. was an employee here and he recognised Karl. It was however equally important for Karl to verify or discount anyone as being the 'cigarette man'. Devlin asked Karl to stand at the bus stop shelter, and if there was a candidate, he would be told to walk outside the plant to answer questions. It would be explained as a security measure, for his own benefit. *'Take this newspaper, and stand as if you are waiting for a bus. You can obscure your face, and periodically lower the paper when you need to. Do not acknowledge me or try to alert me to any kind of identification. That can wait until we meet up again. If we strike lucky, I don't want to alert him. Not yet.'*

Karl sat patiently in the shelter, grateful for being able to borrow Devlin's long, warm black overcoat. At the reception a pleasant young lady asked Devlin if he had an appointment.

"No," he answered curtly, showing his ID card, "I need to speak with the head man urgently. He will understand when he knows who I am."

The Foreign Office watermark had got him to first base. The appearance of Timothy Westlake took several minutes and he was promptly shown the accreditation.

"To what do I owe a visit from the crown Mr Devlin?"

"Your office would be better Sir, I'd like to keep this to the two of us."

"Very well, follow me."

They arrived, and Westlake politely bade Devlin to enter first, asking him to sit. "I don't have a lot of time Sir. All I need to see is your employment register to begin with, and if I draw a blank, I'll leave, then that's the last you'll hear from me. You will appreciate that I can't tell you more, suffice it to say we need to speak to a certain individual, and that would have to be in London."

"This is very irregular, I must say, we are part of a nationally owned organisation too. I may need to make a telephone call."

"If you think that's wise, but I have explained the need for containment in my search. Go ahead, but don't say I didn't warn you."

Westlake thought it over for a few seconds and then asked his secretary to bring the register.

Chapter 30

Moss duly met Sophie Redwood and Black, the train was, as almost all trains were, running on time - twenty minutes late! They repaired to the Gosforth Park Hotel, and found comfortable seats at a corner table in the orangery. Sophie was first to get down to business.

"When do I see the injuries to the cervical vertebrae of the skeleton? Oh, and the report which deems them to indicate a weapon."

Black shifted a little uncomfortably, not having mentioned every little detail he'd conceded to strike a deal with a journalist. Moss did a pretty good job of intimating that he knew of the request. "Of course, we will get to that after we've eaten. I would however, like to talk a little about the next, and I assume, not the last chapter of your coverage of this case. Inspector Black assures me you have already been very helpful, and I'd like that to continue. So, would you indulge me in this respect? There may be things which we can't substantiate yet, but don't mind if they become allegations. On the other hand, as we're dealing with an old crime, the perpetrator may also be deceased, and if so, we may never be able to find them."

"Superintendent Moss, as I explained to the Inspector, we aren't just dealing with a forty year-old homicide, it has become a forty year-old deception. The murder is only one facet of this, and although I can understand that may be where your obligation stops, please be aware that mine doesn't. The purpose we have in common is to hammer home the proof of foul play, until it becomes an indisputable fact, known by everyone, including Marion Wentworth. If you don't want to stay with the complete ball of wool as it is unravelled, I don't mind, and I can extract enough collateral leaks to push for a full, independent inquiry. Look Superintendent, the implications of this cover-up in the current cold war period are very dangerous."

"How did you know about Marion Wentworth? Inspect…"

"No, I told Black that I knew about her some time ago. My source really does have scores to settle. I have to be careful in choosing which allegations to print first, but if it helps to convince you of the need to prove them, I can give you advance notice of one in particular."

Both Moss and Black moved closer, even though they were the only occupants of the orangery.

"I informed Black that Devlin's given name was Theo. You probably haven't found much information on him. That is, if you have conducted a search. You may have guessed that he was the author of a report which Marion has, and it identifies a number of targets he pursued. One of these was Max Vogt. There was no harm in her giving you that, because he died fairly recently. She therefore knows that the skeleton can't be his. Because Devlin has also passed on, he can't be asked to explain certain claims in his report. He chronicles a manhunt for an escaped German airman from a POW camp in a small village up here in the Northeast. A prisoner apparently told Devlin that Vogt passed valuable information to him. So, this report should have been declassified by now if it was deemed to be 'in the public interest', but not if it may prejudice national security. It's rather strange then that Devlin and this airman completely disappeared shortly after this interim report on the repatriation of German servicemen was written. There was no record of their deaths in the immediate years after they were deemed as having left the country. They hadn't turned up somewhere else either. There's more on that, but not now. What is it to be Superintendent? I came here with the hope that you could help me to get evidential proof of the monumental risk MI5 and MI6 are taking by continuing their denial. Am I wrong?"

Black stayed silent. Moss always lit his pipe when confronted with such a complex decision. It bought two minutes of thinking time. He was impressed with the cards she'd exposed, and wanted to see the ones she hadn't, but he had to set this against the probability he'd be told to back off, especially if Sophie's source was totally reliable. "Does your contact want to see the demise of a particular person, or bring the government down, or challenge the principle of national security, with all of its unfathomable motives?"

"He wants the implications of continued suppression to be placed before the entire cabinet, not just a couple of people who probably won't get re-elected anyway. President Reagan has been bleating on about SDI, some orbital capability with both defensive and offensive weapons of awesome power. Do we know what the Russians make of it, or how they will respond if they convince themselves that he has such unchallengeable dominance? Then take a step back and think of something of similar strategic shift in the balance of destructive force, independently developed in Europe. It would certainly disturb the Soviets, and it may even blow a hole in the 'special relationship' with the USA. It's a lot to get one's head around, but so was Oppenheimer's little chemistry experiment. The President at that time, with his infinite wisdom, decided to try it out on Japan. If this hasn't convinced you, I would like to see the skeleton with the proof of foul play and then we can call it a day. I could even catch a late train back to London."

*

Milan Hajek was in a difficult spot. He was single, lived alone, the proprietor of a one-man business, and now known to be a collaborator against his own country during the conflict. Not that the actual battle lasted long in

200

Czechoslovakia, but the occupation did, and was followed by annexation at the hands of the Russians. He'd always thought he could never go back there. He had now been linked to the gold ring by travelling to Germany, and that was both a dangerous move and one which hadn't been well thought through. He'd let his greed prevail over his expertise. Although he had seen the inscription, he determined there were two possibilities. The ring was genuine and some German thief had ordered the inscription in ignorance, which was feasible if tomorrow in the trenches could be your last day. The other possibility was just as intriguing, it was such a convincing reproduction that he could authorise the removal of the inscription via an expert engraver, and sell it in Prague, moving his jewellery business back there as a bonus. He answered Marion Wentworth's question with a question.

"What happens to me if I tell you my contact's name and leave it at that?"

"That wouldn't qualify as full mitigation of a potential leak of information, one about which I issued a warning - not to disclose it to anyone."

"I'll take my chances then. I don't know his name. Do whatever you think you have to. I'm a jeweller not an agent of espionage. My interest was and always will be in the ring itself. I have no interest in its role amongst spies. As you pointed out to me, via your tape, the one I examined was a fake. The Germans have the original, which belongs in my country, not in the hands of Westernised Germans, they are even worse than the Stasi in East Berlin."

"Your moral stance is reassuring Mr Hajek, first you entertain the idea of obtaining the ring in Newcastle for this 'Westernised German', and now you say you despise them. The reward he offered was unspecific, but you must have thought it worth keeping open, until you were confronted by my request to get this man to England. You would have had to meet him again for you to claim it, either there in Cologne or back in the UK."

"Yes, but that was before I thought it through carefully. I suspect that the loose ends he said needed to be tied up would include me. That's why I went along with the West German pig. And have you forgotten the conversation on your tape? I didn't meet the man I contacted, whose name I was given, but I'd never met either him or the swine who took me to lunch. Serve your accusation on me, I have no further interest in this fake ring."

"But they do, the West Germans, there aren't many people in Newcastle named Hajek. Is that a chance you want to take?"

"Are you going to protect me? What a joke! I will have to move, so if you are going to charge me you need to hurry."

"Right, so as my Czech counterparts know, you were a collaborator, they may ask for my help in your extradition. How would that appeal?"

"That was forty years ago, I could have been shot then if I had refused to help the bastards, so just like a lot of young German soldiers, I collaborated, but only to survive. There were many people faced with that choice, in Poland, Hungary, and even France. If we had made a different decision we would all have a gravestone, saying how brave we were. I'll take my chance with you, my own people or even the pigs. Now if you don't mind, please go to hell."

The pilot gave notice of the beginning of his descent into Prague, as Marion returned to her seat. She had a lot to think about. The Czech hulks would want satisfaction that Hajek wasn't just going to return to the UK, and escape further scrutiny by their security department. She quickly concluded that he carried less risk if he was held in Prague for now. He knew nothing of import regarding the true purpose of the ring. His failure to make further contact with the Germans might just lure them to his shop in

Heaton. It could be expensive in terms of surveillance of the shop, but it was probably the route of least potential damage.

*

Sophie was given a first-hand explanation of the hack marks on the skeleton, by Constance Carr, and was allowed to see it had been officially reported. Moss had thought about this irregularity of allowing a journalist official access, and come down on the side of the argument that it was an 'ancient' case, and that the perpetrator was probably dead. It did change the situation, because they were looking for help from anywhere they could get it, and not concerned about alerting a murderer who could react to their release of such information. Sophie was now able to quote this proof in her next article, and in the process, convince her source that the full story could unfold in this way. Those who would suppress unsubstantiated allegations would have to react in some novel way.

The accord between Black, Moss and Sophie Redwood was cemented in the knowledge that most attempts to get to the truth, with such high stakes, would fail. However, they parted, agreeing that people like Woodward and Bernstein had the tenacity and the guile to expose something which went right to the very top of the chain of command. Watergate became their watchword.

Chapter 31
Winlaton Mill 1945

Devlin found no sign of his quarry after checking the employment register line by line. He began a second trawl. Westlake interrupted him. "If you tell me exactly what you're looking for I might save both of us a lot of time."

Devlin put down the hefty tome and responded, "Fine, do you have any employees who speak German?"

"What kind of question is that?"

"Yes or no. I need to remind you Mr Westlake, if you are found to have withheld information pertinent to my enquiries you risk prosecution."

"The short answer is no."

"Is that your final word?"

"Well it is if we're talking about employees with whom we have an employment contract?"

"What alternative employment do you have?"

"None, strictly speaking, but we do have a chap who was foisted upon us from head office. He not only speaks German, he is German."

"So before you tell me his name, acquaint me with this 'arrangement'."

"He reports to the head of central research. We pay his salary and he conducts various projects around the country. You aren't connected to the tax people are you?"

"Relax, I'm not interested in little fiddles like that. Carry on."

"Well, because the central budget gets hacked apart every year, they farm out certain expenses to production units where the overhead can temporarily get lost in a bigger haystack. It gets refunded over time, and lets things like the research budget slip through the approval process."

"Ok, the name?"

"Maximillian Vogt, he does odd improvements for us, but most of his work is offsite."

"So who monitors where he goes and what he does?"

"No idea, but he seems to be in constant demand. Apparently he is a very capable man. He tends to specialise in development of new fuels and how to convert certain fuels into other types. It's pretty much top secret. When I asked what that meant I was told to think of electricity being produced by burning coke, coal or oil. I assumed they didn't want to mention future nuclear-powered stations, because that development process has such a bad press. Listen Mr Devlin, I can't really tell you more than that, perhaps you should speak with him directly."

"He's here right now?"

"Yes, we have a problem with one of the stripping units. I'll ask for him to come to my office immediately."

"I think it might be better for me to talk to Mr Vogt outside your main gates. I'm prepared to accept that his work could be confidential, so the less people who can eavesdrop the better, and it would appear to be less 'official'. Would that be acceptable to you?"

"Certainly, I'll send someone to find him and pass on the message to meet you there."

Devlin hurried to the gate after thanking Westlake for eventually helping him. He signalled Karl that the subject was on his way.

"Sir, you asked to talk with me about something? Who is it you are?"

"I work for the government and I'm looking for a missing airman who should have left the country. He was in a camp at High Spen, which I believe is not too far from here. I wanted to ask if you knew anything which could help me to find him, as you are also German I'm told."

"I did hear about some person who escaped, but that was quite far back. I'm thinking about it, but I can't help you, no – sorry for that."

"Didn't you ever see his picture in the papers when he went missing?"

"Not that I can remember." Vogt shrugged his shoulders and they turned back toward the gate. Karl had benefitted from a clear view. As they reached the gate, Devlin couldn't resist a parting dig. "I understand you work around the country most of the time."

"Yes, it is a lot of travelling, but I have a very nice car, so I am flexible. I don't live by the transport of the public."

"Well, thanks for your help, even if it wasn't really any help Mr Vogt. It's Max isn't it?"

He walked away without a reply. Devlin slowly wandered to the bus stop so that he was out of view.

"Well?"

"It was him."

"No doubt?"

"Not a single doubt. That was M.V."

Devlin turned about face, marched back to the gatehouse and asked the security man to inform Westlake he was on his way back to see him. He was met at reception rather than being allowed to intrude in another meeting.

"Please get Mr Vogt to come to reception. I'd like you to hear what he told me. It will be of interest to you."

A confused Westlake complied and began to get irritated when there was no sign of Vogt after two minutes. He strode angrily toward the stripping plant, followed by Devlin. They bumped into Vogt as he came through the sliding door. "Sorry to bother you again Max, I just needed to be sure about something. I forgot to ask if you had ever been to High Spen."

Westlake was about to explode when Devlin spoke again. "Please think carefully, it is very important."

Vogt shook his head lazily, but did not reply.

"I need Mr Westlake to hear your answer."

"No, what is your problem? I do not know even where this High Spen is. I want to see your ID again."

"I was just going to do that actually, because I have a man in the gatehouse who swears he saw you at the camp in that village. He has no reason to lie, as he is the escaped airman, Karl Heinz Buchwald. He identified you as we walked outside the plant. Here is my accreditation of office, you are a witness Mr Westlake. Maximillian Vogt, I caution you that anything you now say can be used in evidence. I am arresting you on suspicion of acting in a way which is against the interests of the crown and the state. Please come with me."

Devlin deftly handcuffed Vogt, left a speechless Westlake trying to work out what had just transpired, knowing that he would get straight on to the chiefs of the National Coal Board. They would in turn ring alarm bells in the security service and Devlin's boss, Bernard Compton would now need to see him urgently, realising that the combination of Karl and Max posed a different kind of problem. As soon as the three of them were alone, Devlin suggested it would be in his interests for Vogt to surrender his car keys, so that they could be on their way. He drove to the hotel in Lemington and removed the cuffs, explaining to Vogt that all three of them would become the focus of a massive manhunt. He spoke in German. *'You may wish to consider your position carefully. You are the man who passed the cigarettes to Karl. He could only tell me that there was hidden microfilm in them, but not what was on the film. He was obliged to pass on these cigarettes, without inspecting them, to another man. The British security force knows this from my report. They wanted Karl out of the country because they believed he was just an ignorant conduit. I persuaded them Karl should see a psychiatrist as insurance, because whatever he might know would surely be extracted by the Germans. Now they are about to discover that I was responsible for him being abducted, while in the care of the psychiatrist. Having added you to the mix means they must find all of us. Why?*

Because they intercepted the microfilm before allowing it to follow its intended course. They are aware that the ring must be returned to Germany to confirm the completion of the project. Now, Max you need to tell me why you stopped delivering the microfilm to Karl.'

Vogt was shaken by these revelations. *'I knew my deliveries were to be collected and passed on to another person, whose name I wasn't given, but I was approached by a different German airman. He had evaded capture when he parachuted from his aircraft. He carried very high levels of authorisation and he told me who would collect the cigarettes from me, he mentioned both Karl Heinz Buchwald and Gunther Klein'*

'Shit,' said Devlin, *'so Gunther really was at the centre of everything. Please go on.'*

'I got an alert from this airman to disengage from the deliveries for a period. He would let me know when to begin again. When I did go back to the camp Gunther told me that Karl had escaped. I had no further contact from the other airman, so I stopped visiting High Spen altogether. I had other deliveries to remote parts of the country which were running smoothly, and Gunther said the unnamed collection man had also stopped his visits without giving any explanation. I put it down to the war coming to an end.'

'What was the name of this other airman?'

'Markus Emmers, I think he must have got back to Germany somehow. I never saw him again.'

Karl interrupted the conversation. *'Mr Devlin, you must remember me saying that when my friend and I parachuted out of our aircraft, there was nothing wrong with it, and we were expected to be captured, after which we could begin this flow of information from Vogt to the man with the code.'*

'Yes, I do recall you saying that.'

'Well we jumped out after a set time gap from each other. I never saw him again, and he wasn't at the High Spen camp, so I thought he must have been at a different one. His name was Markus Emmers.'

They all sat with blank expressions while trying to piece together how this Emmers person fitted into the puzzle. Devlin brought the contemplation to a close by producing a pistol and turned to Vogt. *'Karl will retrieve our stuff from the hotel, you have until he returns to tell me what was on the microfilm. Your chances of survival without my help are close to absolute zero.'*

*

Jack and Hilda's offer had been accepted for the house up the street from Bella. She had also been influential in persuading the Co-op to advance a small, short term loan. They drew up plans for its makeover, and a new bathroom with an inside toilet was the priority. Jack was going to do all of the work himself. Even Harry was glowing with enthusiasm, the prospect of a bedroom of his own filled him with all manner of ideas. His arm had shed its plaster and the rehab exercises were gradually restoring its original functionality. Things were looking up, except for the further decline of Bella's husband 'Cappy' and it was all down to his many years of working in the pits. The new treatment had shown no signs of halting this decline, and yet Cappy's letters remained upbeat. He had made new friends in Harrogate, and he was an avid reader of political doctrine. The library there was overflowing with books which he could never have accessed from home, and they were free to all patients. Cappy's letters to the family served two purposes. They helped to bridge the gaps in the expensive trips from the Northeast, and they were a defiant counterbalance to the official medical reports. Bella put on a brave face about this, it was what folks did at the time, but she frequently wept in bed at night when she was alone. She wasn't about to kid herself, her life had taught her that praying to the almighty never seemed to change anything. She knew her husband was dying, and constantly thought about the worst scenario, that Cappy would pass on without her being there. She knew he had been relatively content there while he appeared to be improving, but that was no longer the case. She determined to bring him home, it was only right that he was with his family when the time came. She wanted to write to the hospital to begin the process, and enlisted the help of Hilda. Bella had never had the time or opportunity to fulfil her literary potential.

Chapter 32

Moss brought forward Maggie Reichert's assignment to Black officially, and told him to get her on to this little village in the Northeast referred to by Sophie Redwood. His own trawl of the police files had shown nothing of interest, so it needed a new pair of eyes, and a fresh line of attack.

Black explained the reasoning without telling Maggie they'd been tipped off by Sophie. "Beginning in 1943, and going all the way to when the concrete was laid, we're looking for any German connection by name, profession, domicile, or whatever. We have the names Devlin and Vogt to go on, there will be others. We aren't just looking at crimes or investigations which are typical of today. They could be absolutely anything, missing persons and the related searches, people trying to leave the country without proper documentation, follow your nose Maggie. I realise it's a big net we're casting, and that's why we want a pair of eyes which won't be predisposed by what we know already."

"Err yes Sir. Do I include Lord Lucan?"

"Great idea, that's the spirit."

Moss and Black worked together on checking out the POW detainment facilities Sophie had hinted at. The actual records were either missing or never existed in the police files in Newcastle. All of a sudden that wasn't too much of a surprise. The Home Guard, even if they had been charged with such a responsibility would have surrendered all data after the war. Black suggested that they should 'begin at the beginning'.

"What do you mean by that?" challenged Moss.

"We first got involved at Winlaton Mill. I recall the man who found the skeleton talking about how the village had its soul ripped out when the coke works was closed. He frequently talked about the 'community' spirit. Let's talk to the villagers in this hamlet which Sophie mentioned, the closest one to the coke works – High Spen. We should do it door-to-door."

"Another one of your assertions about attention to details, no matter how small?"

"Absolutely. What have we got to lose?"

It didn't take long to get multiple claims of in-depth knowledge regarding a POW camp at the bottom of the valley separating High Spen from Greenside. The vast majority of these claims were nothing more than hearsay. What the two policemen could see was a village whose purpose had all but vanished. The closure of the mine, many years ago had conferred a kind of death sentence on the infrastructure, but not all of the people. Although the population had dwindled steadily, following a Category D notice being served by county planners, the community somehow clung together. Green shoots of small businesses setting up had eventually produced reconsideration of permission to build more houses. Although the present feel of the village itself could not compare with its heyday, the people were now winning their battle against those wielding the axes. There were acorns of hope looking to take root. The mention of the redundant village constable was a recurring sense of injustice.

"It looks like we really did have nothing to lose Inspector. We should check what happened to the local police records, now that we've been informed that there used to be a village constable. It would help Maggie in her weighty task. I'll make a call from that public phone box over there, there must be a section for such archives which ceased to exist because of the obsession with centralisation."

"Ok Sir, I'll keep knocking at doors until I find someone who was not only living here at the time, but has direct knowledge of the camp."

Moss returned and Black recognised the triumphant smile. "Did you strike lucky?"

"Not complete luck Black, you're not the only one who delves into the nitty-gritty. Our records man knew all about these files, but quite rightly pointed out that I hadn't asked for stuff from outlying villages which no longer have a dedicated police presence. The files for this village are apparently in Durham, by deed of county boundaries at the time the post of constable ceased to exist. I'll go and retrieve them while you try to unearth your eye-witness of the POW camp."

After three long hours, Black found someone who was credible. An ex-pupil of Hookergate Grammar school knew of the camp but didn't visit it. "But a boyhood friend of mine went there regularly. In fact, there was a lot of fuss about people trying to talk with the prisoners, but his grandmother wasn't put off. His name is Harry Smyth."

Black's hopes soared. "Where can I find him?"

"He doesn't live here now, and I lost touch with him some years ago, but I know he played local football until recently."

"Do you know which team?"

"Oh, lots of them. Highfield, Crawcrook, North Shields, but I think he ended up at West Wylam or Prudhoe. Just a minute." He called for his mother. An elderly lady came to the door and was asked about Harry Smyth.

"Oh yes, now I do know that he and his father bought some land to build themselves a house apiece. I'm sure it was in Prudhoe, they bought the land from the council a few years ago. I remember his grandma being quite upset that they were all going to move away from the village."

"Thank you for your help, most appreciated."

Black immediately used the village call box to contact Prudhoe council. He punched the air when he got the name of the estate and the number of the plot which Harry had purchased. He shot over to Prudhoe, a small but thriving

213

town virtually on the border of Northumberland and Durham. He knocked at the door of 16 Paddock Wood, but there was no answer. A neighbour, James Hall came over and asked if he could help. Black was told that Harry's mother, Hilda lived two doors down at number 18. He was invited in, and soon had a cup of tea, as he sat on the cosy living room sofa.

Moss drove directly back to Newcastle with his booty and gave the files to Maggie. He was astonished by what she'd already noted. There were missing numbers in the report sequences and no reason given. "All of the reports should have a reference number even if the report has been logged out or transferred to another force. There are many instances of this, for all kind of reasons, but there are a few gaps in the actual references and there is no file, so it's not just a clerical error when there is duplication of a particular number and then the next one is skipped. There aren't even empty files without numbers. It isn't right Sir."

"Brilliant Maggie. Leave that for now, just give me the missing numbers and start checking these files from Durham which cover the village of High Spen, where there was a POW camp. We need to look at anything out of the ordinary. Have yourself a coffee break and then see what pops out at you."

Moss wasted no time in calling the Met. He eventually got through to someone he recognised and could trust. He explained the situation and asked if their files could be checked to see if there had been transfers from Newcastle which matched up. He didn't ask for priority treatment of his request, as that always threw up a flag. He hinted that there was a clear up in progress and he wanted to enforce internal discipline at the station. "You know how it is, your own people will close ranks when old files are moved about or put on to disk."

As soon as he put the phone down he exclaimed, "You absolute oaf Moss - moving old files!! Some of the buggers are upstairs, from when we cleared out the ground floor room for Marion."

He wandered up to the attic and was horrified when he saw the decorators at work, but no files.

*

Hajek's bravado had worked on Marion and as she fastened her seatbelt for landing, she saw him approaching her. He had not really convinced himself. He wanted to talk again. She invited him to sit and buckle up. "Listen, I have reconsidered and I believe your plan might work. If I can convince this contact whose name I do *not* know, that I have been asked to examine the ring again, but this time with the purpose of identifying the engraver, it could be believable. You already know that it has suffered some distortion, and I could tell him that there is a small area of pitting. This would not be perceived as unusual if the ring is gold-plated rather than the pure metal. I can examine it again, now that I know it is a fake, but it would result in damage to prove it. The pitted area can be explained as the engraver's mark, a breach point for the soil attack over a period of forty years. If my contact in Cologne accepts this, I will tell him the police want to find the man whose initials are M.V. It doesn't matter whether he actually knows this person, or believes I do, as long as he thinks the police don't. He may be happy to come to Newcastle. I don't really want to get involved with an obviously transparent lie with this contact I had in Cologne, I just want to get back to my business. If you can arrest him, then I may be left alone. I remind you that he wasn't the person I was told would meet me. I can only agree to this if I can be protected until this is all over. Is this of interest to you?"

"It could be, but we are about to land, so it's you who has the decision to make. I can't mess these Czech officials about. They would have to be sure that you were trying to make amends for cowardice during the war, and that they may, like my people, be able to put this ring stuff to bed once and for all. I agree that this will only be achieved by apprehending your contact from Cologne, who will also be looking for closure, but maybe not the same closure."

"Very well, I will do as you say."

"Fine, then you must not contradict anything I say to the two Czech officers when I tell them I need to take you back to play your part in the lure. Do you understand?"

"I do."

The rubber tyres squealed as they hit the tarmac and the attendant puff of fumes dissipated quickly. The plane decelerated and swung around ninety degrees, heading for the terminal. They all disembarked as a group, and it was time to talk to the two hulks. Marion had expected to get this over and done with in Cologne, and was not expecting a third Czech intelligence presence to be awaiting them. She reminded Hajek to agree with whatever she might have to say. "Talking, isn't doing Mr Hajek, keep that in the front of your mind."

The welcoming smile from the Czech official in in the arrival concourse was quickly partnered with the declaration that there was a car ready to take them to 'an appropriate place' where they could discuss arrangements. There was a firmness which was confirmed by his brusque order to his two obviously junior colleagues, that there was a separate channel for Hajek to pass through customs. Marion had hoped that they could have boarded a flight to London within the hour. She needed to make a private call as soon as possible. The senior Czech official replayed his sickly smile and said, "In good time Madam. We have to speak to this man first and you need to be there. We have booked a hotel for you. Everything can't be done over a cup of English tea. It will be good use of your time, of that you can be sure, and maybe a nice surprise for you, but not for this collaborator. You may want to stay longer in our beautiful city, let us see."

Chapter 33
Lemington 1945

Vogt stared down the barrel of the silencer. Devlin stared at his watch. He burst into German again. *'Don't think I won't do it Max, your treachery has put all of our lives at risk. As I said a few minutes ago, the only trade you have left for your life is what was on the film. Even that might not save us, it's down to you.'*

Vogt saw Karl returning and began to tremble. Devlin disengaged the safety catch. *'Ok, ok, I gained my employment in Britain through a recommendation from a tutor in the University of Aachen, and I was soon acquainted with a serving German intelligence man, who was actually English. I was young and naïve. He told me that I had to support the needs of my country or I would soon go back there in a box. For a while, during my time in Crawley, I was given the task of getting information on paint research. This was, in retrospect, to check if I was up to the job, and whether my cover had been established. I was then told it was a dummy run and the information I obtained was of no value. Then I was put forward for a position in the National Coal Board. The travelling remit was to enable me to gather the desired information. It was all to do with creating new fuels. I got very scared when I was told the real reason for this. They had been testing me again, and now had to explain the highly specific research work they needed access to.'*

He seemed to hyperventilate, but recovered his poise, and then he swallowed repeatedly as he continued. *'You know of the employment of the German V Rockets toward the end of the war. Well, they were introduced prematurely to soften the defences of this country prior to any plan to invade. The Reich was researching more devastating weapons at the same time, but there were technical roadblocks. They were identified as being able to create*

217

the necessary type of fuel, and to somehow alter the slow advance of electronics. In terms of aeronautic technology they already had an enormous projectile ready to go into production, but were continually frustrated by these two drawbacks. Now that the war is over, I expect the prototypes to be destroyed. The information on the microfilm was all in this field of research. And now you say that the theft of this data is known to your people. So how did you not know what it was?'

'Because it must have been decided that I might jeopardise the deception in some way. Your people in Germany must have been given bogus information.'

'No, all of the data was valuable and highly pertinent to the projectile development. I am an expert in this field and I could get access to every source in the country.'

'I don't doubt that Max, but we're dealing in sophisticated deception here. I was told the data was intercepted before allowing it to continue on its way to the Fatherland. That kind of deception worked, not just on your people, but on me. The fact that the cease-fire hasn't ended the horse-trading on this project can only mean it isn't going to be stood down just yet. When the victors sit around the table to carve up the map of Europe again, there will be new alliances up for grabs, which will in itself create foes from former friends. We have to think how to avoid becoming an anti-lubricant to this process. I am inclined to let you go Max.'

'You really mean that?'

'I do, go if you think that's in your best interest.'

He certainly didn't need a second invitation. *'But we need your car, a small price for not blowing your brains out.'*

Max walked away, slowly gathering pace until he was running full speed toward Scotswood Bridge. Devlin and a mesmerised Karl took off in the car.

*

Bella's letter to Harrogate had crossed in the post with one coming in the opposite direction. It wasn't from the spa medical staff, and she put it down before reading it all the way through. Once she'd stopped shuddering with grief, she picked it up again. It read:

'Royal Bath Hospital
Harrogate.
To My Dear Family,
This I think will be my last love letter to you all.
And this is the end of a Perfect Day. Couple it with Harry Lauder's Keep right on to the end of the Road.
Also, I hope the friendships of Florence Hilda and Lillian and Jack….This is a fine morning and it takes me back to us getting the children to the pleasure trips.'

It was unsigned, and Bella couldn't quite work out why the hospital hadn't contacted her if the end was so near, apart from which the constable hadn't been sent to tell her Cappy had passed away. She rushed to the village phone box and made the call to the hospital to say she was making preparations to leave for Harrogate. She was told that Cappy had descended into a coma the previous day and the doctors were trying to return him to consciousness, but had failed so far. Bella contacted Hilda via her school secretary and she was given compassionate leave of absence. When Hilda read the letter, she knew this wasn't her father's normal style of writing. He was fastidiously pedantic about grammar and punctuation, yet it was his handwriting even though it was wobbly in parts. She knew he must have been already losing the ability to concentrate when he had written the letter.

Jack had to cut back his working hours, pledging that he'd make them up, so that he could look after Harry while the others made the trip. It wasn't thought to be proper to ask anyone outside the family to step in.

They were gathered around the bedside as Cappy Henderson passed away without regaining consciousness, and the letter had indeed been his farewell to all of his loved ones. Bella could not forgive herself for failing to get him home, where he'd have dearly wanted to be. It wasn't that his passing was unexpected, it had even been predicted. The utter frustration of not being able to turn the clock back gnawed away at her, eclipsing the consolatory support of Hilda and her brother Andy. The ruthless need for arrangements to be made so quickly after the moment of that last intake of breath was so cruel. Seeing the transition from a person struggling to inhale oxygen, to a corpse with a fixed motionless form, is a shock of immense effect which will live in the memory for the rest of one's own life.

Harry was walking to school, humming some popular tune. As he passed Robert Terrace, not far from the school gates, he could see two women on the path. They were both talking at the same time, as was often the case, he'd observed. When he was within a few yards, he noticed that one of them stopped talking. The other, known by his grandma as Gobby Lizzie, turned, saw him, and raised her voice. "They say Cappy Henderson got away then. It was to be expected. I don't think many of our men or Bevan boys will miss him."

As Harry passed by them, he replayed these words in his immature little mind. 'Cappy Henderson got away then.' It surely meant that his granddad had escaped from that awful, smelly, bath place. He must be coming home for good. He could see more bedtime stories becoming the order of things. He radiated with excitement and ran eagerly through the school gates. The devastation which awaited him when he got home turned to anger when his dad explained what Gobby Lizzie had really meant with her well-chosen words. Harry began to hate this woman with a vengeance.

*

Devlin and Karl headed down the eastern coastal route to Hull. The Humber estuary offered the opportunity of small boats for hire. They could easily move amongst the thriving mass of fishing vessels spread across the North Sea. Devlin had anticipated the need to leave the shores of his country, and had brought his entire liquid assets with him. He hadn't bargained for the extent of duplicity within his own organisation. Nevertheless he was philosophical about it, he had often employed such tactics himself. He could probably have returned to base with Karl, claiming he'd recaptured the German, but exposing Max Vogt had changed the bigger picture. He'd grown to respect Karl, but he also put that out of his mind for now. He scented the *value* of what he had stumbled upon, the other side of the coin. That value to the new West German governing body could allow early retirement in some kinder climate.

He knew a trustworthy man in Rotterdam, a former resistance leader during the occupation. If he could get there from Hull, he was almost guaranteed a safe domicile until the hunt died down. This would also give time to plan their route to Germany and in particular to the remnants of its intelligence organisation. Karl would be crucial in this respect, a loyal servant of the Fatherland, even more important – carrier of the seal of the ring, who was rescued by none other than a former intelligence officer of His Majesty.

It needed a lot of haggling to close the deal for the boat. The owner had to be familiar with the Dutch coast, and how to avoid immigration, by disembarking at night. Eventually he settled for someone who claimed to have participated in the Dunkirk evacuation. Horace Pattinson had the experience of concentrating while riddled with fear because of shells raining from the sky. He also had his sons as crew, which limited the 'loose tongue' risk. A necessary precaution was to avoid Karl being introduced as himself, he was Devlin's deaf-mute son, with learning difficulties.

The ruse was rooted in a new educational approach for such people, which had been developed in the Netherlands, and the red tape in getting the British government to issue a passport for the boy, so soon after the war. Horace Pattinson warmed to such disregard for authoritarian intransigence, after all he didn't have a passport when he was asked to put his life and livelihood on the line, and in a fog of anonymity at Dunkirk. Devlin and Karl had to mimic basic communication with sign language. They pulled it off admirably, and Devlin thought it was because Horace and his sons actually *wanted* to believe it. Karl's performance was largely truncated because he was constantly leaning over the side, depositing undigested porridge into the heavy sea. It helped the deception and instilled an atmosphere of good humour during the seemingly endless journey. They anchored well offshore, roughly between Noordwijk and Katwijk aan Zee, and waited for night to fall. It would be a tricky and slow inward journey. With the engines finally silenced, the elder son of Horace, Sam, launched the dinghy, and was joined in the rubber air bag by his brother. Karl, and then finally Devlin, made their ungainly transfer into the bobbing craft. They got within fifty metres of the shore and Devlin said they would make it from there. It produced a smile from Sam, and a shake of the head. Another few minutes and the two fugitives made landfall. No one spoke as the dinghy headed back to the lightless boat. Step one had been achieved.

Chapter 34

Hilda said she would ring the factory where her son worked and tell him that Black wanted to speak with him. "Can you just leave that for now Mrs Smyth, I'd like to ask you about some events which occurred in the distant past. Don't worry, it's nothing serious, it involves the POW camp at High Spen, specifically in 1945."

"Oh, I see, in that case Harry may not be too helpful, he was only five at the time. It was his grandmother, who would have been most use to you, but she passed away in 1972."

"Did you visit the camp?"

"Very rarely, but Harry used to keep me up to date on things, he was fascinated with the airmen. So I have heard every story."

Black's anticipation was verging on cerebral salivation, if there was such a thing. "Can you remember any of the names of these airmen?"

"I did know quite a few, but I can only recall two. You should speak to Harry when you can, he'll probably remember them all. His favourite was Karl, because he had his identity disc for a few days and felt important for the first time in his young life. The other man was called Gunther, and he took Karl's disc back from Harry, because Karl had escaped in the meantime."

"I'll just write that down. What about their surnames?"

"I hope I can get them the right way around. Harry wrote them down. Let me think. Yes, I'm pretty sure now, Karl Heinz Buchwald, it's a strange family name – it means 'Bookforest'. The other man I'm not sure about but it will be in the old records of the village constable."

"Do you think Harry would remember the details on this identity disc?"

"He almost certainly will, but anyway, he drew it over and over. It's probably amongst his old toys, in the box. I have them in the cupboard under the stairs."

Hilda scratched around for several minutes before she found the box she was looking for. She took out the toys one at a time, as if they were the crown jewels, handling them with great fondness. Here we are, his favourite drawing book."

When Black saw the meticulously copied dog tag, his brain immediately summoned the one they had recovered from the coke works. The word 'match' flashed before his eyes. Every detail was clear, because this was drawn forty years before the disc had been pulled out of the stinking mud.

"May I borrow this Hilda? It would really help us."

"Of course, would you like me to ask Harry to call and see you at the station?"

"Yes please, and thank you again, lovely cup of tea, made the proper way, no damned tea bags. I'll be in touch."

While he was on his way back to Newcastle, Black was bristling with the aura of nailing a key element of the case, convinced that they had at last found the name of the man whose skeleton had clung on to its secrets.

Concurrent with this joy, Moss and Maggie had made their own little discoveries. Maggie had unearthed a complete list of names of the airmen from the High Spen camp, nestled away in the village constable's records which had been spirited away to Durham. Moss had wasted no time in threatening the decorators, if they had disfigured any of the files he'd virtually abandoned in the attic. He needn't have worried, they were under a gigantic dust sheet. He instructed one of the juniors to begin carrying them down to his office. He began to spread them out on his desk, pulling a couple to one side which had interesting descriptions on the covers. He stopped at the first page of the thinnest file. A transcript of the transfer of a German stowaway on a Danish freighter caught his eye. As he avidly devoured the content, he sat back and reflected on the name on both the Master of the Port's sheet, and the police interview statement. Karl Heinz Buchwald was described as a Luftwaffe serviceman, who'd escaped earlier from a POW camp in High Spen, been on the run for some time, and finally tried to get back to Germany.

Maggie put the list on Moss's desk without saying anything. Moss showed her his discovery, and they were engaged in self-congratulation when Black walked in wearing a mischievous grin. His drawing completed the focus-lock on Karl Heinz Buchwald, even though Black felt a tad less buoyant, being one of a trio rather than a solo hit.

*

Marion Wentworth was mulling over all possible aspects of Hajek's value now that they had been escorted to an expensive hotel overlooking the iconic King Carlos Bridge. The senior of the three Czech intelligence officers knocked on the door of her room.

"Before we speak in detail with Hajek, I thought you might be interested in what our man from Cologne has told us."

Marion's jockeying of all acceptable scenarios was put on pause. "I should have known you had him followed as well, shouldn't I? By the way you haven't introduced yourself."

"Yes, that is correct, neither have you, but I know who you are, and your reputation is very high in my country. It would be a pity to throw dirt around. My name is Pavel Banved, at your service." He showed his ID for the second time, but on this occasion, left it open for her to digest as much as possible.

"On this assignment, I report to the highest rank in our service. We are still plagued with fallout from the war, notably with the Sudaten population. You will be aware that our position with the Soviets is not much better than the occupation by the Germans. The Sudatenland is always complicated, and Hajek has things to answer for in that respect. However, during his conversation in Cologne, we were pleased with what we saw, more than what your man or ours actually heard. We have been monitoring Hajek's contact person for a long time, but this is a real breakthrough. He is now quite elderly, but has not lost much of his influence. It is mostly behind the scenes, but very – shall I say – persuasive. Maybe you know of him, he was a prisoner in your country until the end of the war, a Luftwaffe pilot, by the name of Gunther Klein. Do you have information on him?"

Marion mentally scrolled through various summary documents and recalled a hit with Devlin's report. The name Gunther Klein had been underlined several times, she thought, but the clearest recollection she had was the comment that Klein was at the centre of the dubious activities in High Spen. She'd therefore known that he wasn't the man in the muddy coke works, as Devlin's list had clearly shown he had returned to Germany.

"I've heard the name somewhere. The North of England I believe. He was sent back to Germany after the cease-fire."

"Impressive recall, I must say. He wants to carefully erase all events of espionage which took place in England without, how do you say it – no rocking of the cradle?"

"It's the boat actually, not the cradle. But the war has been over for forty years, why is that so important for an elderly ex-pilot?"

"No, not the boat, he wants the baby to go to sleep without rocking the cradle, the boat would be too obvious. I suppose he wants the same as you do, or am I wrong? You have been watching Hajek recently, and it isn't all about a silly ring, which means it may have another purpose. I have a proposal which I would recommend you consider carefully. Eastern Europe still has quite a few Soviet satellites, but the uprisings will continue and someday the Russian domination of these peoples will come to an end. You would do well to imagine how things will be shaped then. Hajek is a small cog in this murky political evolution, but he can help us with certain problems in the Sudatenland. He has little value to you really, both of our men heard him tell Klein that the ring is in the hands of your police. You don't need Hajek to spring your trap, it would be more convincing coming from a deception that he divulged the means to obtaining the ring and whatever goes with it - but from one of our Sudaten-domiciled people. After all, he is one of them himself, and they still believe they are German in their roots. I can see by your face that you didn't suspect he was more than a collaborator, and you didn't know his real name. He did a good job on you. Listen a little more please before you decide. We will make sure that Klein hears that Hajek has been interrogated here, because the Germans will have followed you both to Prague. They will hear that his shop in your country lies abandoned. They will know we have forced the truth out of him, but which truth? Maybe one in which the police do not have the ring. They may wish to believe that his story was just to guarantee his protection. We will inform you when the bait has been laid, and you can put surveillance on his shop. Or maybe you aren't interested in Gunther Klein?"

Marion said she would need to make a phone call. Banved said it would not be wise to do it from the hotel. He agreed to let her use his office. They left and Hajek was in the safe hands of the hulks. Banved's office was in a classic, old building and as she waited to be put through to the number she gave to the operator, a glance upward disoriented her. The room was of modest floor space, but the incredibly high, vaulted ceiling made her feel as if some invisible, weird anti-gravitational force was pulling her up from her chair.

The main question for Marion, when her call was put through, was in relation to Hajek's British citizenship. Pavel Banved had also hinted that Hajek was possibly registered in the UK under a false name. This could affect his status in the immediate term. There was also the small matter of how Banved seemed to be so certain that the police in the UK didn't actually have the ring, when she was sure that they did. Her mind went back to Devlin's report and that Karl had led him to it in the woods near High Spen. She couldn't remember any entry which said he'd disposed of it. This had always intrigued her.

She was cleared to leave him in Prague, while his history was checked more thoroughly than it had been when he applied for citizenship. The consequence of this call was bad news for the jeweller from Heaton, whoever he really was.

*

The combined efforts of Moss, Black and Maggie, for a fleeting moment, brought a showdown with Marion Wentworth into focus. It was Moss who shook his head. "We owe her nothing, and I prefer to speak with Sophie Redwood again after we see what the reaction of the spooks is to her printing 'that the police are treating the case as murder', even if they hadn't made this declaration themselves. All Marion has ever said about the identity of the skeleton is that it's not Max Vogt. I'm being terribly cautious, but why didn't she tell us it was Karl Heinz Buchwald when she saw the disc with his identity plastered all over it, top and bottom? Sophie will have to give us the answer to that, if she has it from her source."

Reluctantly, Black and Maggie nodded. The party was put on hold.

*

While Marion waited for her flight to London to be called, she caught sight of the headline of yesterday's Clarion on the adjacent table, which was not yet cleared of the food debris left by the previous occupant. She picked it up and read the whole story. Sophie Redwood was becoming a nuisance, and she would be more difficult to silence than the police. She needed to swat and discourage two pests without leaving a corpse.

Chapter 35
Noordwijk, Holland 1945

The journey to Rotterdam wasn't free of risk. Despite the liberation of the Netherlands, and the uplifting of spirit which came in the wake of it, there was a dedication to cleanse what remained of German presence and influence from society. Karl was still a problem, but at least he could respond in his best English. He had to be mindful of certain words. He'd been briefed before he left for his mission in England, that in the event of being shot down or being forced into emergency landing in Holland, there was one particular taboo. The Dutch resistance were able to hunt down German spies by manoeuvring them into mouthing the name of a town in the west of the country. Apparently the embedded Teutonic linguistic capability failed most of them when trying to articulate 'Scheveningen'. They couldn't quite handle the guttural 'ch'. Karl warned Devlin of this verbal booby-trap as they changed a small amount of English money into Guilders. This wasn't risky in Holland so soon after the war, because the allies were held in such high esteem, and were not to be insulted by over-officious bank clerks, while they were presumably making an inventory of their fallen on Dutch soil.

The train from Noordwijk chugged its way to the city of Leiden, a well-respected seat of learning, where they changed for Rotterdam. The journey had been accomplished without incident, but the sternest test now faced them. Asking for directions to the residence of a resistance man was not considered to be a good idea. They didn't want to be continually stopping to peruse a tourist map either. Devlin went to one of many canal-side information cabins. He apologised for his inability to speak the language, and merely tried to pronounce the name of the street where he could expect to find Cees Verdel. The obliging lady offered a city map, and when he'd paid for it, she marked the quickest route to get there on foot, and circled famous landmarks like the Feyenoord football ground which had been fallow for so many years. He thanked her and they set off having memorised the first few major street names. Although they headed off in the wrong direction at a couple of the canal bridges, and a stop for coffee, they made it. The moment of truth arrived. They pushed one of the five intercom buttons but received no response. Rather than involve any neighbours Devlin suggested that they passed the time by buying bread and cheese, and sit by the canal for lunch. It wasn't quite that easy, as the food supply was still chasing the post-war demand. The shops were emptied almost as soon as they opened, and there were queues at every one. Loyal customers were given precedence, having goods reserved. Devlin and Karl had to decide, a very expensive hotel, or the residual scraps from the street vendors. They both needed a bath and their grubby clothes would have attracted undesired attention, so they ruled out a hotel. They sat on a seat by the canal and chewed away at half a loaf of stale bread, which was speckled with mould. They looked at one another and laughed as they took turns to spit green-flecked crumbs to the ducks. The vigil finally came to an end when Devlin spotted Verdel entering the apartment block, four hours later.

*

It became clear to Max Vogt that he hadn't thought the situation through carefully enough. It hit him like a sledgehammer, the instant he stepped off the bus and tried to pass through the gates of the coke works. It was no consolation that he had been influenced by the gun barrel, and his humiliation at having to use public transport was now the least of his worries.

"Can you wait here please," said the gateman respectfully, "I am instructed to inform Mr Westlake that you have returned." The man put down the receiver and said Mr Westlake would be down immediately.

Having then ascended to the inner sanctum together, the edict was delivered. "I have been given extremely clear instructions from the Central Board regarding your future."

Vogt was ready to sit down and explain away the arrest by Devlin. He was told to remain standing. "This won't take long. You are to remain at the plant until you can be collected first thing tomorrow by car. They will drive overnight so they should be here around daybreak. You will not go home, you will be accompanied for the entire time between now and their arrival. You won't speak to anyone, including those who will guard you. I have decided that the board room will be the most appropriate location for this temporary confinement."

"I must be given a chance to tell you what is going on here, you have no idea of...."

"No, I am instructed that I must not listen to you, not one word. I'll have you know that this is most inconvenient for me, not least of all because the pouring of the concrete foundation of the new engineering block is scheduled to commence at 6 am tomorrow, after all of the damned delays we have suffered. Now, I will walk with you to the boardroom, as I have to report back to HQ."

Vogt's mental processing of this draconian behaviour spelled the need for urgent action. He knew what he had to do, but at present he had no idea how to accomplish such a task. Perhaps the solitary confinement would become an ally, rather than a restriction, in terms of how to plot his course.

*

The funeral was dignified in its simplicity. Cappy had always been an atheist, not to the point of trying to convert others to his view, just a passive non-believer. The service reflected this, the humanist thread wasn't eclipsed by the obligatory church minister detailing the glorious afterlife.

The gathering of friends back at the house produced the relief of having had to watch the coffin disappear, cutting the physical cord of the here and now. It also produced a pivotal moment in the life of Harry, who hadn't been allowed to attend the service, because he 'wouldn't understand'.

When the last dregs of the mourners drifted away, Harry hugged Bella and said he was going to look after her now. Jack and Hilda experienced a compulsion to laugh at the same time the tears formed.

"That's nice Harry," said his mother, "and you can pop down any time you want." Jack tousled his son's curly blond hair. Bella said nothing but realised that wasn't how Harry saw the situation though his eyes, mature well beyond his years. She could see that the boy had lived for the vast majority of his life with her and Cappy. This was his home, and number six was where his father and mother lived. He could always visit them, which was much better than it used to be, as they were usually in places he had never heard of. He had just lost his granddad, and he knew it was forever. He wasn't about to live somewhere else in case he lost the one constant presence during his five tender years, Bella.

"No, I want to live here, with Grandma. You and Dad will be at work in other villages. I can help Grandma when I'm not at school."

Bella could not intervene. It was Jack who relented first. "Hilda, he's right in a way. Neither of us will be here when he comes home from school, so he knows where he can find Bella, here or at the Co-op hall. It makes sense, at least for the time being."

Hilda nodded reluctantly, and apart from the practical arrangement, she confessed that her mother would be impacted by losing Harry so soon after the sorrow of Cappy's departure. "Yes, it will help to keep the family together, rather than splintering it."

There was another aspect which was of great importance to Bella, she had to continue to feel needed, to be an important cog in the family life. Of course she still had her paid job, but the chance to make the evening meal for Jack, Hilda, and Harry gave purpose and self-esteem. It also helped her to fill the great void which was Cappy, only to be preserved now by memories. Harry was a ready conduit to those days. She hardly slept that night, but the horizon was punctuated with handholds and new dreams.

A spin-off benefit for Jack was his clear path to modify the parts of number six without having to worry about Harry having further disruption to his life. There was considerable demolition and rebuilding to accomplish, and not having to worry about working around a child would shorten the period of pain for Hilda and himself. He would start in three days' time, even though the planning approval was lying on the sideboard. It would be more respectful to Bella.

*

Vogt waited patiently for his chaperone to need the toilet. He grabbed the telephone and rang the number. He spoke in German. *'Meet me at the coke works, tonight after midnight. You can slip in when the shift changeover is in operation. I am being guarded in the boardroom on the third floor of the main office block. There is an external fire staircase. You can prise open the door to the third floor with a chisel or something. It is not alarmed. The boardroom door has that name on it. If you burst in suddenly, you can overcome the guard before he can contact anyone. He isn't carrying a weapon, and he is pretty fragile, just a security man who is a heavy smoker. Once you have disabled him, I can pay you the rest of what I owe you, and we can take off. We have to get to a man in London to sort out a mess, otherwise we will both be arrested. I have to go, he's coming back.'*

'Got it. Midnight it is then.'

Verdel didn't answer the intercom alert with a question. Years of experience guided him down to look through the small lens in the external door.

"Theo, what the hell are you doing here?"

"Can we come in Cees? I'll explain in a minute."

Inside the apartment the Dutchman repeated his question and Devlin replied. "I'm in a bit of a spot with my boss. It's one of those situations in which you can't win. He's up to something but I can't go over his head in case the deception goes further up the line, and I think it does."

"Ok, I know the scenario. In that case who is your friend?"

"That is a really long story Cees. He is a German airman who helped me to expose this entire deception. You can trust him."

"Maybe I can trust him, on your say so, but any German in Holland at the moment is in extreme danger, and I am afraid I cannot get involved with him. Don't tell me his name or anything else. He has to leave now. I can help you, but if that is not enough you will have to go with him. Sorry."

Karl smiled wistfully and patted Devlin on the shoulder. "He is right Sir. I will take my risk upon myself." Turning to Verdel he asked, "Can I get to Oberhausen by train?"

"You are mad to even think about that. Relations are not normal, and any trains which are allowed to cross the border will be crawling with security, it would ensure your capture. Your safest way is to make your way to the outskirts of Rotterdam on foot. Steal a bicycle and take a few days to reach the eastern border. You must then take extreme care, keep off the roads and proceed by a rural path at night, until you are certain that you are well into Germany. You must avoid any kind of checkpoint. Don't worry, bikes are stolen all the time now, because nobody has any money for anything but food. The police cannot handle so many reports of petty crime."

Despite Devlin's protests Karl was unmoved, he embraced the Englishman, who was quite shaken by such a gesture of familiarity. Devlin put his hand into his pocket and gathered a pile of guilder coins of multiple denominations. He gave them to Karl, and surprised him with another gift. The dog tag which had caused so much fuss in the camp and beyond, was dangled and then reunited with its Luftwaffe owner. There was an unspoken sadness at the parting of their ways as Karl said, "I must leave now to get out of the city before it is dark." He scribbled the last known address of his family on a piece of paper and gave it to Devlin. "Maybe it is not goodbye forever."

Chapter 36

Both Moss and Black travelled to London, leaving Maggie to action any tasks in the Northeast which may result from their session with Sophie. They were pretty sure they would learn something new, but had no idea of the import of what she was able to reveal.

The hotel room was only a marginal upgrade from 'Spartan' and they felt a little bit like market traders trying to woo established Harrod's clientele. The carpets were tired and the plumbing was pre-war. Grotesquely flowered shades did exactly that, blocked most of the light from the flickering bulb, casting pockets of shadow, even at dusk.

The seating options, or lack of them, meant one person was obliged to sprawl on the bed. Black's room was even less comfortable. Sophie looked them in the eye, first Moss, then Black. "You both remind me of Cheshire cats. A worrisome, choreographed smile. Let's have it then."

Black was given the honour. "The Luftwaffe disc buried with the skeleton is that of Karl Heinz Buchwald, of that there is little doubt. We also have a full list of the prisoners who were kept in the High Spen camp, and documented evidence that the same man was detained in the Newcastle nick after having tried to leave the country on a Danish freighter."

"Yes."

"We believe that it means that he is our man. There is too much converging evidence, which can't be ignored."

"Well Marion will be happy."

Moss made his first comment. "Why would that make her happy Sophie?"

"Because they aren't his remains, you're just supposed to conclude that they are."

Moss had his teeth around the bone now and wasn't going to let go. "So explain how you know this, not just by telling us that your source says so."

"I will, but I'm glad you have drawn this conclusion, because we can print it at the right time. It is useful that you have put a name to the disc. Do you mind if we eat early? I'm finding this room very oppressive, and not appropriate for celebrating with a glass of champagne."

They followed her to a bistro in which she was patently well-known. They settled down and the bubbly was delivered. Sophie asked the owner for privacy for fifteen minutes before they'd be ready to place their order.

"Very well done gentlemen. I will attempt to put your hard work into a wider context. Marion will endorse your conclusion and won't express dismay that we printed it. When you find new evidence that Karl Heinz Buchwald lived long after the concrete covered the body at the coke works, she will be furious, but hopefully we will be ready for her. I need to sketch in more background detail for you. Karl Heinz and Theo Devlin got out of the country and then split up. Devlin never came back from Holland even after he died. He had no family and was buried in Holland, his adopted home. His gravestone is still there, and here is a photograph of it. Karl Heinz made it over the German border and lived with his surviving family for a number of years, waiting for certain regulations to be relaxed, before contacting the Abwehr. He was treated with suspicion, and the British authorities were asked once more if they could trace this man after his escape from the camp. MI6 stonewalled the question and the man was told he would be charged with some strange law on their statute which dealt with obstruction of post-war reconciliation of lost servicemen. Karl Heinz insisted that he was who he said he was, and produced his birth certificate. They took him a little more seriously and asked him to come back in a few days. Now, the bigger picture. If you recall, I said at our last meeting that there was a major deception programme at play. My source claims that the Germans already had blueprints for a concept, which *will* be realised, even though today's state of the art technology still comes up short. Please reserve judgement for a moment, and think of men like Einstein who visualised the theory of General Relativity, but died before inventions were developed to test it out by observable evidence. The V series rockets were but a crude stepping stone in the path to something much more sinister. What do you understand by the term 'drone'?"

Black's reflex response was, 'a bee whose purpose is defined at birth, and solely but unconsciously providing balance, ultimately helping to ensure the queen flourishes, yet distinct from the workers, which have an inborn, direct drive to do so.'

"Right, and if I continue to use your analogy, a dumb, pilotless projectile can be used as a platform for a huge range of weapons. The very large can deliver unprecedented carnage and a very small one can seek out and kill an individual. Anonymous assassination of power brokers, or hell beyond anything we have ever seen. The problems back in 1945 were considered to be microelectronics and efficient, safe fuels. The main drawback today is the lack of something which has been labelled as GPS, or a Global Positioning System. Now, back to the immediate post-war period. The list of items to be taken, shared, destroyed, or hidden was almost endless, as I said last time we met. This Drone concept was high on that list, especially as the American-Russian brinkmanship was predicted, and verified by the Cuban missile crisis. The contributors to the Drone research, whether or not they had been allies or on opposing sides during the war, had to be identified and either harmonised to the cause or made to disappear. One small facet of this 'restructuring of trust' involved the various espionage programmes, which had to percolate through the revolving door of the intelligence organisations. There were potential loose ends which needed to go away - either by manipulation or be guillotined without remorse. Successive generations of MI5, MI6 and their German equivalents, have become complicit by inheritance, the latest being Marion and Stone. My source, you should have guessed by now, preceded them by some years. He will know when we reach the point of no return for them to save their careers, bringing an end to his own. Being a whistle-blower is a dangerous path to tread. He would rather go down for this, a belated moral stance, than lose his family. Every day brings a risk that something will happen to push the human race toward self-destruction. Balance is fragile, as we've learned from the proliferation of nuclear warheads. This Drone technology is assessed as being strategically important because of the incredible flexibility of scale, accuracy, and altitude capability of near-ground and stratospheric manoeuvers. During the war and in the immediate aftermath, the espionage activity was one of a duplex nature. But later, as fast as loose ends were tied up or amputated, new tentacles were created, and it is not known for certain if this technological thrust is being replicated by the agglomerate known as the Soviet Union. There is a tacit agreement between the former main protagonists, Britain and Germany, plus other members of the European Common Market, which states that all vulnerabilities by which the Soviets can begin or continue to fast track this research, should be nullified. Easier said than done. So, isn't Marion doing what is best for Britain? That's one way of looking at it, unless you believe that real deterrents are a product of mutual balance. Furthermore, spying won't go away just because it becomes more difficult, it merely ups the stakes. My story will never reveal this scenario, I can promise that, but I need Marion to know it lurks out there in a safe place, unless she helps us to conclude a truly independent investigation of our case, and the others which have occurred around the country. Protecting the interests of national security doesn't have to mean that individuals who have ordered the deaths of British and German citizens should escape murder charges. Some of the deceased were actually working for the people who had them eliminated. Marion and her immediate superior should face up to that responsibility, just as high-ranking members of the Third Reich were pursued as war criminals. Theo Devlin was one such person, and exhumation would prove he did not die of natural causes, they finally found him, and they killed him. We may even find the ring with his remains. Obviously not the one you found in the coke works, he had the counterpart ring. My source is adamant that he never surrendered that ring to his boss when he left the country with Karl. Do I need to go on? You are both very quiet."

Black's rationalisation was straightforward. "My job is to bring criminals to justice, plain and simple. It doesn't make any difference to me whether they are scallywags or royalty, I want closure without distraction. I admire your stance Sophie and I still want to work with you, but that's also up to Superintendent Moss. I'd like to think he agrees with me."

Moss was more circumspect. "We can be seen to have worked with you, but not for you. I do agree with Black's succinct summary of his personal leanings. The political stuff is a step too far for mere plods, Sophie, but I also support your reason for pushing this all the way, nobody is above the law. I'd like you to guide us to the identity of the man under the concrete, if you are sure it isn't Karl Heinz Buchwald. We aren't in a position to check your claim that he was still alive after the body ended up under the concrete, but if you can provide proof, it would surely help when we have to admit we were wrong. Even better would be the name of the man who *was* buried with Karl's dog tag."

"I will be able to reveal the name which belongs with the skeleton, and proof that your evidence that it was Karl is suspect. Surely you both realise that an investigation which is exclusively conducted by a journalist does not have the gravitas to spark an independent inquiry. The 'artillery' of national interest would be assembled to discredit me. The people must see the very same evidence verified by an apolitical organisation such as the police. Murder is murder isn't it? Can we meet again tomorrow?"

It was agreed as the waiter asked if they were ready.

*

Back in London, Marion wasted no time in debriefing her boss. The emergence of Gunther Klein was another example of how poking a stick in precisely the right spot in a wasp's nest can destroy the illusion of control. "Sir, I'm of the opinion that we may have to begin to be seen to go with the flow on this one. The long-standing objective of keeping certain things in cold storage has been compromised by this damned incident at the coke works. It could have been contained but for this journalist. I'd hazard a guess that she has not only fuelled intense public interest in the mystery, but hasn't yet published everything she knows. It's a strange coincidence that Gunther Klein has resurfaced. I have given serious consideration to this Czech offer to lure him to Newcastle, but now I recommend taking a step back. We suddenly need a flavour of humility, and a credible reserve of deniability, in the event that other names re-enter the fray, Devlin in particular."

"That is sound advice Marion, when one's name and signature hasn't been added to certain documents. You are speaking from such a privileged position, but that luxury doesn't apply to everyone. Hindsight provides a wonderful vantage point, but doesn't afford a magic wand to rearrange the present. If I don't have your support any longer, I must make preparations to step aside on another pretext, such as ill health. I will defer to this advice, and recommend you as my successor in my letter of resignation. I would benefit from a spell in warmer climes with the family. Don't say anything more to me about this Marion. That would only complicate matters if you are promoted to this post. I appreciate having worked with you, and wish you all that you would want, but think it over very carefully."

Marion Wentworth was stunned by this apparent knee-jerk capitulation, until she let it flow over her again. He'd seen this coming and had been preparing for it. It wasn't just the discovery of the skeleton in the mud, and its implications.

Chapter 37

The second meeting between Sophie and the two detectives was a defining moment in the whole saga. The first revelation produced an inversion of just about everything the Newcastle police had come to believe.

"Here is a set of photographs. Gentlemen, I would like you to study them all before asking questions. Just reflect on how you now interpret all of the evidence."

The first was a picture of Sophie and an elderly man, in which she was holding up a German newspaper with a recent date prominently displayed. The second picture was obviously the same man, but from when he was in the Luftwaffe, and in his uniform. The third was very similar to the first, but the newspaper had been replaced by a close up of a dog tag. Black's photographic memory immediately confirmed it was the one from the coke works.

Moss said, "How can that be?" But Black was ahead of him.

"He and Devlin escaped the country. Devlin had custody of the dog tag sometime after Karl escaped. They split up in Holland according to Sophie, so Devlin must have given it to him then."

"Well done Inspector, but that alone does not explain how it got back to the coke works. Think about it again. Take your mind back to a conversation you told me about at our first meeting. You spoke of the information displayed on these tags. Apparently, you found out what it all meant from the father of one of your police officers, a woman."

Sophie let them stew on this while she went to the ladies room.

*

244

Winlaton Mill 1945

Max Vogt's plan had succeeded so far. Markus Emmers had entered the boardroom and easily overpowered, then rendered the security man unconscious.

Since Vogt was first contacted and primed by Emmers, the situation had become very strained. Emmers had evaded capture, had German-forged papers to assist his 'integration', and spoke excellent English with just a hint of a Dutch accent, conferred by his roots in the Netherlands. His papers had been neatly produced in the name of Mark Emmerson, and he had no trouble finding a 'cash and no questions' domicile of anonymity in a cheap, dilapidated tenement block in Gateshead. The money for the rent and his subsistence was paid to him each month by Vogt, but supplied by the man with the coded name. After quite a while, the comparatively opulent lifestyle of Vogt really got to Emmers, and he demanded more, because in his view he had taken all the risks. This was why the deliveries of cigarettes containing the microfilm were interrupted, Emmers wasn't as dedicated to the cause of the Reich in the same way as Vogt. They had a showdown which resulted in Emmers being promised more money, but Vogt had extracted a very important favour.

'We have to hurry, I have the money, Have you brought the replica disc?'

'Of course, here it is, now, I want the rest of my payoff before I hand it over.'

Vogt put the pile of notes on the table and Emmers began to count them. He felt the thud of the blade strike the back of his neck several times. He couldn't speak, because by then Vogt had one hand over his mouth. He then felt a chilling intrusion to his lower back and rapidly lost consciousness. The improvised weapon had been taken from a framed artefact in the boardroom, a prized ancient discovery when the original site had been excavated. The razor-sharp, hand-chipped stone-age axe was unemotionally left embedded in Emmers' body. Vogt rushed to the janitor's cupboard in the hallway, and grabbed a set of overalls and a large sack. He wrapped the body quickly and made sure that the security man would not wake, by giving him another whack on the head. The final act before using the opportunity of dumping Emmers into the massive hole, was to place the duplicate of Buchwald's disc and **this particular ring** in his pocket. This second ring was the signal to the Reich that the project had faltered. He had failed to recover the other ring from Buchwald because of his escape from the camp. This had become a problem, because he was supposed to get it safely to the man with the coded name, otherwise it would not reach Germany by the stipulated route. Its sole purpose was to announce the mission was a success, and his life depended on this. He could never have imagined it would end up in the possession of a vagrant named Michael. He had to gamble. The concrete would ensure that the ring denoting failure would never be found, or so he thought. He no longer had any influence over the destiny of that 'Ring of Success', but at least the war was coming to an end, and he prayed it would be soon.

The dead of night allowed the body to be hidden amongst the hard-core of the foundation without further incident. It had gone well, considering he originally had other, very specific plans. Emmers had been scheduled to 'disappear' the following week, ending his blackmail threat to destabilise the project. He should have been found in the upper reaches of the river Derwent. But without Vogt's car, now in the possession of Devlin, and the pressure of the impending arrival of his escort to London, he'd had to improvise. He faced an interrogation by the Coal Board in London, there was no other choice. The time had come to help revive the security man and sympathetically remind him of the intrusion of some criminal. He was totally convinced that Vogt had actually tackled this person and scared him off, indeed he may even have saved his life. They both gave a description of the intruder, but had no idea what he was looking for. When dawn approached, Vogt could hear the rumbling of concrete mixers. As he was taken to the awaiting transport, he nonchalantly peered into the foundation, proclaiming that they had at least been blessed with dry weather. Soon the liquid slurry would encase the body of Markus Emmers in a grip which would endure forever. Max Vogt would die with the fervent belief in such certainty.

*

The man with the code name, who collected the microfilm from all over the country had been the real architect of the plan to plant the second ring and the duplicate dog tag on Emmers, before he was thrown into the river. He had been apprised of Emmers' increasingly unpredictable behaviour, by Vogt. When the man with the coded identity was unwittingly approached by Emmers about how to obtain new dog tags, he said he could help. Neither Emmers nor Vogt had any idea that he was a double agent, intercepting the information, altering it and passing it on. He was a perfect example of how it was possible to help the enemy to convince themselves of the veracity of such data, obtained by espionage. His genius was to engineer the honour of being asked by the Germans themselves, to participate in a project they thought to be a deception of their own. Ernst Johan Reichert could never enjoy the gratitude of the British people for the part he played in helping to delay improvements to the V series rockets and their offspring. He died with that secret, keeping it from his family. Another important aspect of Ernst's counter-deception was the incoming instructions from Germany with respect to their obsession over fuel research. The British knew for certain that Hitler's scientists were ahead of the allies in pure theory. It would have been easy to shut down German infiltration of British knowledge, but it was felt to be of much more value to learn of the Reich's direction of priority, and at the same time alter the return flow of the detail provided by Vogt.

*

In London, Sophie had carefully led Black to recall Maggie Reichert's father explaining that during the later stages of the war, some units had to make their own tags for reinforcements arriving at the front line. Frank Reichert knew this because his father, Ernst, had told him of such expediency being forced upon the field commanders. That was the elusive clue, indicating the leap of logic to Ernst having access to British back-up to reproduce such discs, solely to entrap the maverick who could ruin the entire operation - Markus Emmers, She related the whole story to them, mentioning Markus Emmers as the unfortunate individual who was never expected to surface. He is just a pawn really, but pawns can sometimes win games, depending on how they are deployed. You will find that there is no record of a Mark Emmerson living in Gateshead in 1945. You will also be told by the Abwehr that there was no Luftwaffe serviceman with the name of Markus Emmers despatched to England at that time. So he didn't really exist, but despite that he has inadvertently opened the door to other cases which can now be investigated. Now, I had a phone call last night from Marion Wentworth of all people, she said that it is time for a total shakedown of this case. She also said her boss had resigned, so we might now get the independent inquiry which is so badly needed. Rather coincidently, my own source called me this morning, confirming that he'd resigned – a bit of a connection there, don't you think? He asked if I was going to honour our agreement. I must say I expected a real cat fight to get to this point, but he was as good as his word. Oh, by the way, Karl Heinz Buchwald confided something to me as well. The watch which he gave to this vagrant, presumably still somewhere in the constable's files in the village of High Spen, had a message stuck to the inside of the back cover. It mentions Vogt as the reason for his escape, he thought he was lying about something. Pity nobody opened up the watch, after all, it was evidence."

"Moss turned to Black and said, "Let's get back to the boring old Northeast, I told you this was about the 'Man Who Never Was'.""

As they travelled back to Newcastle, Moss said, "That young journalist is a brave woman Black. And I never thought I'd say that about someone in the press. So, where do we start again now?"

"I got a message this morning at that bloody awful hotel. I rang Maggie back and she said Harry Smyth wanted to know if I still wanted to speak with him. So she fixed up an appointment for today. That reminds me, what the hell are we going to tell Maggie about her grandfather's role in all of this?"

"Nothing as yet, the inquiry will deal with the greater scheme of things. We just carry on with the identification process of this Emmers, and who killed him."

"But it sounds as if Ernst Reichert was involved."

"We don't know for certain. First things first – the dental records of Emmers Inspector."

*

Harry was already waiting for Black when he arrived. "Thank you for coming Mr Smyth, I just wanted to follow up on one thing from the conversation I had with your mother. What do you recall about this Karl Heinz Buchwald?"

"Only that he was a flyer, and I liked him because he loaned me his disc. I was only five at the time and I thought he was my friend. I must say I was devastated when I found out that he'd escaped, and that the search party might lynch him. Everything is a drama at that age."

"Do you remember him wearing a watch?"

"Yes, apart from the disc, that fascinated me more than anything else he had."

"The records show that you and your father visited him after he was caught, here in Newcastle. Did he have it then?"

"I can't remember for sure, let me think. I would say that he didn't, but I just can't be certain. My Dad would have known."

"Would have?"

"Yeah, he passed away in 1979. He noticed things about soldiers, having been one himself, and he got on well with Karl. Is it very important?"

"It could be. It was supposed to be in the file, probably some opportunist copper sold it as a souvenir. Never mind, I just had to be sure. When you say your dad got on well with him, I expect they never met again."

"No, we thought he must have forgotten about us."

"I think not, he would have good reason to keep his head down when he eventually got back to Germany. However, we now know he's still alive and well."

"Really, that is fantastic news. You know, I'm married now with a son, and it's time we Brits recognised that all people from a particular country aren't the same. I would love to see him again. He will be sad to hear of my Dad's passing, but may be glad that I still think of him as a best friend. Are you able to give me his address?"

"Not right now, there is still an ongoing investigation to identify the skeleton found at the coke works, but perhaps in a few weeks I can help to put you in touch with him."

"It's a pity I couldn't take his watch back to him. Wait a minute, the watch was found on the wrist of the vagrant they thought Karl had killed. So he couldn't have had it in the Newcastle jail."

"Brilliant deduction Harry, in that case it might be in the High Spen constable's file. I'll get back to you about Karl's address, give me your home number again."

Harry walked out into the sunny street and inhaled deeply. 'I wonder what Jack and Bella would have made of Karl still being alive and well. I can't wait to tell Hilda'.

When Harry and his father had built their bright new houses in Prudhoe, it was an experience he would never forget, for two reasons. The sheer joy of finally appreciating the expertise Jack had accumulated to become a respected General Supervisor of massive building sites, thereby constructing a legacy which would survive him. That's how he felt about his new home. Everywhere there was contact with his dad. Secondly, the downside was a feeling that they had all let Bella down by moving away together, leaving a large hole in her everyday life. She only lived for a year or so after the move. He couldn't help seeing a connection. The prospect of a re-connection with Karl-Heinz Buchwald would bring back those memories of seeing his father for the first time. The scene in the prison cell with Jack and Karl was so poignant, a graphic cameo of the futility of war.

*

Before the independent inquiry began, a news bulletin caught the attention of Moss. Sophie Redwood was one of seven pedestrians killed when a van lost control and mounted the pavement in central London. The many witnesses all claimed that the driver simply got out and ran off from the stolen vehicle. The subsequent investigation was quickly concluded and stated that it was a straightforward case of hit and run. Although the victims were named, there was no hint of Scotland Yard disclosing it may have been a **professional hit**. Without Sophie's testimony, the inquiry had to be rescheduled, and yet there was still no accommodation of a possible link to the intelligence agencies. Her editor tried, but was instantly made aware of the dangers in rocking the boat. Therefore, a compound fracture in the pursuit of the full extent of the cover-up was considered complete, but then another significant event was reported. Her newly-retired contact had seen the news and knew immediately that they could discover his connection to Sophie, and then find him in Australia. He didn't know they already had. Alistair Crawford told his wife that they must get the children to safety. They argued about how best to achieve this. She had never been enlightened by Crawford as to the precipice on which he conducted his remit within MI6. Naively, after he filled in the detail, she insisted that the safest route was to fly back to the UK and become a whistle-blower. She favoured hiding behind the barricade of a public declaration. He tried to explain how things really worked, and at the same time, pleaded with her to trust him. He struck fear into her by emphasising the importance of proceeding with extreme haste. She reacted uncharacteristically by refusing to discuss the matter any further. Crawford drew on his long experience in the job and it delivered clarity. He left their temporary home without saying another word, not even where he was heading. Two long days of driving around in wide circles, following the London 'accident', convinced him that he was being followed. His shadows assessed that the altercation with his wife meant he hadn't enlightened her about Sophie Redwood et al. Crawford had deliberately signed the motel register in his own name, as an additional lure. He didn't have to wait long to meet the nameless hirelings. He could only hope that his deliberately erratic behaviour would spare his wife and children; he could do no more. His body was found in the motel swimming pool after dark, clad only in bathing shorts, and he was presumed to have drowned.

*

Upon hearing of the death down under, Moss and Black didn't take more than a few minutes to connect the dots. They didn't really need to discuss the matter; they knew they could well be next. They proceeded with all haste to end their involvement once they had identified Markus Emmers as an unfortunate victim of circumstance. The case in Newcastle was closed once and for all.

*

Meanwhile, the research on Drone technology had never broken stride, and had serendipitously been partly funded by the windfall assistance of public clamour for all manner of future products from branches of the same research – GPS. Satellite TV, cars with satellite navigation, and mobile telephones were just around the corner. This thrust would ultimately lead to the internet, something which would change the way we live our lives, for a very long time. Even espionage would be forced to adapt to instant everything. The independent inquiry, for which Sophie had worked so tirelessly, gradually lost momentum, eventually becoming a sideshow to the birth of new kind of terrorism.

Newcastle 1989

Harry Smyth's pestering of DI Black finally paid off, a few months after the independent inquiry had faded to obscurity. Having obtained the address of Karl, he initiated contact with the ex-Luftwaffe pilot and arranged for the whole of the family to visit Dusseldorf. The exact timing was unclear because Hilda had become quite unwell. Multiple examinations and diagnoses proved fruitless, and she deteriorated steadily as the weeks passed. By the first of November she tried to explain that Harry needed to let her go. "My quality of life is at a low ebb, and I know my time is short. There is something I want you to know. Your birthday, in August 1940 is just six months after…"

"Yes Mum, I know where you're going with this. I figured it out before I was twenty-one. You and Dad didn't get married until February that year. I just assumed that it was a circumstance of the war. He may never have returned, and procreation was more important than the 'fuddy-duddy' Victorian morality of the villagers. Who am

I to comment on such impropriety? I wouldn't be here otherwise."

Hilda had finally shed a burden which had lasted a lifetime, and somehow this made the prospect of impending farewell a little easier for both of them. She passed away quietly on the next morning, just after 10.30 am. For Harry, her final breath dispersed the expectation of departure, as an immense shock wave hit him. The utter finality of losing a second parent.

A month later he stood in the concourse of Dusseldorf airport, waiting expectantly. He was alone; it no longer felt genuine for the whole family to make the trip, so soon after Hilda had passed on. The figure approaching him with a smile and an outstretched hand was not overly familiar. Back in 1945, they'd both been recognisable by their shock of blond hair. The intervening years had thinned Karl's thatch, and turned the remnants a snowy white. But the smile, and exposure of the prominent gold fillings produced waves of emotion as they embraced.

Back at Karl's house, he was introduced to Frau Buchwald and their two daughters, plus a few grandchildren. After a wonderful welcome, and bedtime for the young, the reminiscing began in earnest. Finally, everyone had retired to bed other than the two of them. Harry produced a wrapped object from his pocket.

"I managed to recover this from the police, and I know that my father and mother would be pleased that this reunion is marked with such an appropriate reminder."

Karl's facial expression was a mosaic of curiosity and anticipation. He was speechless as he revealed the watch, and his thoughts leapt back to the bend in the river where he had given it to Michael, his saviour. The tears trickled slowly downward and a couple splashed on to the face of the timepiece. The shared feelings of the two men, representatives of nations at war all those years ago, were in stark contrast to the building tension of the current clash of ideologies of the Superpowers, previously bound as allies against fascism; obviously it had been a veneer of convenience. The two friends eventually conceded to the need for sleep.

It didn't seem like farewell as Harry departed, he felt as if a missing piece of his life had been impossibly retrieved, against all odds. Karl made a solemn promise to return to High Spen. Harry knew that the mysterious stranger with the gleaming disc, who had turned from a POW into a true friend, would never break such a pledge. It was important to him, as it indirectly bridged a gap of several decades back to his early life in High Spen, particularly his parents and grandmother.

*

The reunion was poignant. The POW site, the refuge Karl shared with Michael, the docks where he was apprehended, and not least the coke works. When Harry and Karl chatted about those times, the German was able to state that he'd left Britain without knowing that his friend, Markus Emmers, had died in Winlaton Mill. "Theo Devlin and I took Vogt's car and left him to talk his way out of the British discovering that he was a spy. When we flew over this part of your country Markus jumped out of the aircraft ahead of me, and never explained that he was to work with Vogt and the man with the code name. I thought we were to be captured together. It all seems so pointless now, but I sometimes wonder what the Reich was actually trying to achieve with that research mission."

Harry and Karl could never have made the connection, even though they remained good friends until Karl passed away in 2001.

2001-Legacy

The warnings were not heeded, and the loosening grip of governments around the world eventually bore witness to the horror of asymmetric warfare, as hijacked aircraft struck at the very heart of New York, and therefore American society itself. Pilotless weapons were very high on the agenda of Nazi Germany. As history has since recorded, when such concepts are combined with the currency of martyrdom, the boundary becomes blurred. Without the anonymous, untraceable means of communication – the internet, such cells of terrorists would have been almost impossible to create. Did this 'tectonic shift' harbour the portents of a third global conflict? Very probably. How would National Intelligence Agencies be able to adapt? Merely listing the incidents since we went online would suggest that the answer is – not very well.

Arguably, the thrust of Adolf Hitler, during the 1939-1945 world conflict, is a perfect example of nurturing potentially unseen futurism. We are now capable of observing the theatre of war, any war, from one's living room on a large screen TV. Buried somewhere in the confluence of this research was a lesson; one which seems to require re-learning with worrying frequency. Frontiers and pitfalls are implicit bedfellows. One is easy to recognise while the other lurks invitingly to those who see the world differently.

Printed in Great Britain
by Amazon.co.uk, Ltd.,
Marston Gate.